FREAKS

IMBRIFEX
BOOKS

Also by Brett Riley

The Subtle Dance of Impulse and Light

Comanche

Lord of Order

FREAKS

A NOVEL

BRETT RILEY

IMBRIFEX BOOKS

IMBRIFEX BOOKS
8275 S. Eastern Avenue, Suite 200
Las Vegas, NV 89123
Imbrifex.com

IMBRIFEX.
BOOKS

Freaks, a novel

Library of Congress Cataloging-in-Publication Data

Names: Riley, Brett, 1970- author.
Title: Freaks : a novel / Brett Riley.
Description: First edition. | Las Vegas, NV : Imbrifex Books, 2022. |
    Audience: Ages 14+. | Audience: Grades 10-12. | Summary: After accidentally opening a
    portal to another dimension, four bullied high school friends find themselves endowed
    with strange superpowers and they must team up with one of their tormentors to save their
    families and friends from the bloodthirsty creatures invading their small Arkansas town.
Identifiers: LCCN 2021017965 (print) | LCCN 2021017966 (ebook) | ISBN
    9781945501531 (Hardcover) | ISBN 9781945501548 (E-book) | ISBN 9781945501555
    (Audiobook)
Subjects: CYAC: Monsters--Fiction. | Bullies--Fiction. | Ability--Fiction.
    | Friendship--Fiction. | LCGFT: Novels.
Classification: LCC PZ7.1.R5475 Fr 2022 (print) | LCC PZ7.1.R5475 (ebook)
    | DDC [Fic]--dc23
LC record available at https://lccn.loc.gov/2021017965
LC ebook record available at https://lccn.loc.gov/2021017966

Jacket design: Jason Heuer
Book Design: Sue Campbell Book Design
Author photo: Benjamin Hager
Typeset in ITC Berkeley Oldstyle

Printed in the United States of America
Distributed by Publishers Group West
First Edition: March 2022

For Nova Rae and Luna Shae

CHAPTER ONE

When three sets of hands grabbed him from behind while he stood at the urinal, Micah Sterne cried out, but not because he was surprised. Honestly, he didn't know why it had taken so long; he'd been expecting something like this since school had started a month ago.

He struggled and fought for as long as he could, but as one against three, he barely lasted ten seconds. They dragged him into a stall. Two of them grabbed his ankles from behind and yanked. Micah stuck out his hands to break his fall, but he still landed on his face. Someone knotted a meaty fist in his shirt. His collar dug into his throat, the pressure making his temples and eyeballs feel like pus in a zit. He tugged the collar away just as they raised his legs and pushed his head into the bowl. Micah inhaled and squeezed his eyes shut. His face submerged, then his ears, then most of his head.

Please, God, let this water be clean.

He held his breath until he nearly blacked out. When they pulled him up, he hacked and choked and inhaled through his mouth. His nose felt clogged, as if someone had filled his sinuses with wet gauze. The toilet water was pinkish. A drop of blood the size of a nickel fell in, darkened the water, dissipated.

"Looks like you got a nosebleed, pussy," a voice said.

"Bite me," Micah croaked. Two more drops fell into the toilet. He felt little pain yet, but it would come.

"You heard him, boys," said another voice. "He wants some more."

Micah knew the voices. They had been saying shit like that to him for years. In fourth grade, one of the kids now holding Micah's legs had told the whole class that Micah's mom cooked babies and cats in her witch's cauldron, just because she was Wiccan. In sixth grade the same kid told everyone, his voice dripping with certainty, that Micah and Jamie Entmann were faggots, queer for each other and maybe any other guy. Last year, at an eighth-grade football game, Micah was walking underneath the bleachers toward the concession stand when one of them punched him in the back of the head. He had fallen on his face and blacked out for a minute, and as the kid who did it disappeared into the shadows, Micah heard that same slur again, drifting through the cheers and mutterings of the crowd overhead. The same old story, told week after week, sometimes more than once a day, and it always ended the same way—with Micah alone in his room, choking back tears of rage and humiliation.

And now this. They raised his legs again. A hand twisted Micah's shoulder-length straw-colored hair. His nose throbbed with each heartbeat.

One of them leaned in close. Despite his plugged nose, Micah winced at the bully's foul breath, like bologna and onions and stupidity. "Now, you might feel like you should grab the rim of that crapper and push. I wouldn't advise it. I'd hate to accidentally stomp on your fingers. You get me?"

Micah nodded. Speaking would just make things worse.

The toilet rushed toward him again. Just before the water covered his ears, a third voice said, "Look at it this way, geek boy. Maybe that cold water will feel good on your nose."

CHAPTER TWO

An hour later, Jamie Entmann sat in fourth-period study hall, writing his English essay and dodging spitballs. Mrs. Coopersmith wanted a thousand words on *Lord of the Flies* by Friday. But some joker in registration had stuck him in the same class with B3, as Jamie and his friends called Kenneth Del Ray, Brayden Sears, and Gavin Cloverleaf. The name had originated in fourth grade, though back then it had been the Double Bs, for Brainless Brothers. It had eventually morphed into Brainless Bastard Bros, or B3. Here in study hall, Gavin sat two rows to Jamie's left, Brayden two to the right, Kenneth two behind.

Today, a spitball had hit him in the ear as soon as he sat down. Another landed in his hair and stuck in his burst-fade Mohawk. He had picked both the spitballs off and dropped them, wiping his hands on his pants. Since then, several more wet, boogery gobs of paper had struck his head, his face, his shoulders and upper back—a barrage that would have done a medieval army proud.

Even these peckerheads gotta get bored sooner or later. Don't they?

Mrs. Murray, Jamie's study-hall teacher, saw nothing. Micah had once described her as a butternut squash with stringy red hair and thick, black-rimmed glasses. Like a lot of the shit that came out of Micah's mouth, that had sounded pretty harsh to Jamie, but he had to admit she wasn't much of a teacher. She spent most of her time reading magazines and scribbling on yellow legal pads. Jamie had no idea what kind of degree you needed to be a study-hall teacher, but he couldn't imagine how Mrs. Murray had passed.

Another splat against the back of Jamie's head. Mrs. Murray saw nothing, apparently. No help in this room. It was not the first time he

9

had looked to his teachers for help and found nothing. That would have been in third grade, when two white kids—Julian Cloverleaf, a cousin of Gavin's whose family had moved a year or so after the incident, and Jason Kopp, who eventually apologized and went all emo and now hardly ever spoke—tracked Jamie down on the playground, herded him away from his friends, and pinned him to the ground behind a tree. Jason sat on his chest while Jamie bucked and struggled and yelled for him to get off; Julian ran his hand through Jamie's hair. "I heard y'all don't like people touching your hair," Julian had said. "I can see why. Feels like wire or something." Jamie had heard the N-word all his life, but it had never been aimed directly at him before. Those kids had laughed and mussed his hair and used that word like punctuation while Jamie swore darkly and promised to get them back.

When they finally let him up and ran away, Jamie had stood up and brushed himself off, forcing himself not to cry, not even to sniffle, and when he had walked out from behind the tree, he had seen the teacher leaning against the fence, scrolling on her phone. Those bastards could have cut Jamie's throat and she would have missed the whole thing.

Now Mrs. Murray was writing a novel or a grocery list or whatever, and Jamie was once again at the mercy of assholes. Worse, the spitballers had trapped him in a kill box. A skinny kid with a hooked nose and pimples sat behind Jamie but provided little shelter. Kenneth tapped or kicked the kid's desk; the boy ducked or moved to the side. Then a spitball thwacked against Jamie's skull. Similar treaties seemed to have been signed in blood with the kids on Jamie's right and left. If there had been four dumb jocks in this study hall, they could have positioned someone right on Mrs. Murray's desk. She had well and truly checked out. Spitballs accumulated at Jamie's feet like tiny hailstones.

"Hey," Brayden whispered, craning around the girl to Jamie's right. "I wouldn't put up with this shit if I was you. Maybe you should meet us after school and do something about it."

"Yeah, right," Gavin said. "He's gonna run home like a bitch."

Jamie could feel their excitement washing over him like a breeze blowing off a landfill. It curled his lip and wrinkled his nose.

Think of the essay. Get back to the words, the ideas. They can't touch you there. They think you're Piggy, but you're really Ralph—the kid who keeps his head and stands against the idea that holding the biggest club or the sharpest spear makes you strong.

Jamie turned and glared at Gavin, who flipped him off. Jamie gritted his teeth. His dad would kill him if he slugged one of them, after school or not. And fighting had never really been his thing. Once, in sixth grade, he had swung on Kenneth. Seconds later, he was upside down in a trash can, something gross and wet in his hair. So now it seemed healthier to try to get back to his essay.

You're Ralph. They're Jack and Roger and the rest of those weak-ass punks. They can gang up and hunt you. They can set the jungle on fire. But they can't kill you. You'll outlast them, and in the end, they'll cry like babies on the beach.

"Nothing?" Kenneth said.

"That's what I thought," Gavin said, laughing.

Another spitball struck Jamie's left shoulder. The class giggled and whispered. Better you than us.

"It's like you can't miss him," Brayden said.

"It's that big ol' nappy head," Gavin said.

Jamie closed his eyes. *Don't do anything. Don't do anything. If you get expelled, Dad will kill you.*

The after-school challenge might have been tempting if he could have fought just one of them. Even if they pounded his face in, at least they'd know he would stand up. But they would never fight him one on one. They ran in a pack, like wild dogs, and Jamie was not suicidal. Much better to use his words. In a battle of wits, B3 always showed up unarmed.

Jamie turned around in his seat, ready to verbally slap Kenneth Del Ray upside his meatball-looking head, but when he opened his mouth, a thick, dripping spitball careened through the air and down his throat.

It stuck on his uvula. Jamie turned back toward the front of the classroom, hacking and coughing, tears dripping onto his shirt. He stood and staggered forward as B3 burst into laughter. Half the class joined them, pointing and whispering. Kids were taking videos and texting. And Mrs. Murray glared at Jamie as if *he* had done something wrong. Behind her lenses, her green eyes blazed. She frowned and set down her pen. Jamie was still hacking and coughing when she handed him a hall pass, her lips pressed into a thin line of disapproval.

"Be quiet, all of you!" she barked as Jamie stumbled into the hall.

But the laughter continued until the door closed behind him, shutting it off.

He ran to the nearest water fountain and gulped several mouthfuls until the spitball dislodged and slid down his throat. He shuddered and gagged and nearly threw up. Only the knowledge that more people would laugh kept his breakfast down.

Jamie shook his head and wiped his eyes. Surely this day had nowhere to go but up.

CHAPTER THREE

Near the end of her lunch period, Gabriella Davison—Gabby to her friends, who numbered exactly three—stood in the school courtyard, her wet T-shirt and jeans clinging to her skin. Her long dark hair was plastered to her face. Some hung over her eyes. Her drenched backpack lay at her feet, textbooks and spiral-bound notebooks absorbing water. Later, they would bloat and swell like dead bodies. What seemed like half the student body encircled her, pointing, laughing like the studio audience in a bad multicamera sitcom. And more kids showed up with every passing second.

Gabby had seldom been the center of attention, and when she had, it was always like this—humiliating and painful. The only good thing about being so wet? No one could tell she was crying.

Nearby, in the crowd, Tyrone Hecht leaned over to Marsha Dickens. "What happened?" he said. Why did he bother leaning close? Gabby heard every word.

Marsha looked at Gabby as if she were a zoo exhibit. "Water balloons. The moron just stood there and covered her face. They must have hit her with thirty or forty."

Tyrone laughed. "That's awesome, man. Who did it?"

"Kenneth Del Ray and them."

A rising breeze chilled Gabby. She hugged herself and shivered, even as her muscles tensed with anger. Most of it was directed at B3, but she reserved some for herself. She had let her guard down, had left her friends at their usual picnic table and walked alone, had not watched her own back as she should have. When the first balloon struck her between the shoulder blades, soaking her shirt and her ass, she had stupidly turned around instead of running for the door, and B3 had been standing here, holding backpacks loaded not with books but with their weapons of choice. And when all three boys had opened fire, she had stood there, hands raised to shoulder level, looking down at herself as every inch of her was splattered. The shredded remains of dozens of balloons lay around her like shed snake skins.

Her friends had come running, as if they might rescue her, but what could they do? B3 would only make their lives even more hellish if they interfered. Still, those three jackasses saw her fellow outcasts coming and, cackling, walked past Gabby as if nothing had happened and went inside.

The crowd broke up. Even as a spectacle, Gabby couldn't hold their attention for more than a couple of minutes.

Jamie, Micah, and Christian gathered around. Christian's face grew red. Her fists clenched and unclenched. Jamie and Micah just seemed embarrassed for Gabby.

"You good?" Jamie asked.

"It's just water," Gabby said. "It'll dry."

"Those shitheads," Christian said through clenched teeth.

"Yeah," Micah said, watching B3 and the other kids file inside. "Somebody ought to run 'em over with a dump truck or something."

The bell rang. Lunch was over. They had to go inside.

Gabby picked up her backpack. Water poured off and out of it in thin streams. It weighed a ton. Snot ran from her left nostril. She wiped it on the back of her shirt sleeve. But she couldn't go to class like this.

She said goodbye to her friends and walked to the principal's office. Mrs. Calvert, the administrative assistant, sat behind her desk. She was talking on the phone and twirling her curly black hair with one finger. She did not look at Gabby, who dripped on the carpet. In the blasting air-conditioning, Gabby's teeth chattered.

Mr. Hoon's door stayed closed.

When Mrs. Calvert hung up and turned to Gabby, her eyes widened, and her mouth dropped open. "Good gracious, child, what on earth happened to you?"

Gabby had to be careful here. If she told Mrs. Calvert what had happened, she would forever be branded a narc. *I guess they can add it to all the other stupid names they've called me my whole life.* Geek. Nerd. Half-breed. They had ostracized her for everything from being a band geek to her heritage. The kids in this school punished you for being good at anything that wasn't football, basketball, track, or cheerleading, and if you were different in any way, well, that was the cherry-shaped turd on the shit sundae they served you. Could she really afford to give the kids in Quapaw City any more ammunition?

Still, she had to tell Mrs. Calvert *something*. At least she had just returned from lunch, where anything could have happened. "There's a puddle out on the grounds, from the sprinklers," she said. "I was texting, and I tripped and fell right in it."

Mrs. Calvert stood and examined her clothes and shoes, which were stained by not even one speck of mud or blade of grass. Gabby looked at the floor. Mrs. Calvert sat back down, crossed her arms, and sighed. "Why don't you tell me what really happened?"

"That *is* what really happened."

Mrs. Calvert looked at the principal's closed door. "So you're not gonna tell me."

"I already did," said Gabby. "Twice."

Mrs. Calvert glared at her. "Don't get smart with me, young lady. Whatever happened to you, I didn't do it." She took out a pad and scribbled on it. She ripped off the sheet and handed it to Gabby. It was a permission slip to leave campus during school hours. "Do you live close enough to walk home and change?"

"Yes, ma'am."

"Don't dawdle. That pass isn't good for the rest of the day. If you don't come back, we'll call your parents."

Gabby took the slip and hurried out before Mr. Hoon could

materialize and start another interrogation. She lived a mile from school, and she didn't really feel like walking it, but she wasn't about to tell Mrs. Calvert that. Nor would she call either of her parents. Mom and Dad would not buy the puddle excuse. They knew her history with B3 much better than Mrs. Calvert did. But even they didn't know the extent of it. No one did, except her friends.

She walked out of the building and headed toward her house on Mississippi Street, thinking about that hot July day the summer before seventh grade when she had ridden her bike to the park. She had arrived at her favorite bench by the pond to find a little kid's birthday party in progress at one of the three pavilions on that side of the grounds. The kids chased each other around, played on the swings and the slide and the monkey bars. Gabby wondered if she had ever been that carefree.

After a while, all the noise and happiness drove her off her bench and down to the water's edge. She stood just out of the mud, hands tucked into her pockets, watching the sunlight sparkle on the water's surface while half a dozen black ducks paddled around. She let her mind go blank, wanting to forget the way some people at mass looked at her skeptically, as if she had come as part of some Jewish infiltration team that planned to tear down the confessionals and the crucifix hanging over the pulpit. Or how the kids at school sometimes called her "Sister Gabby" because she didn't show much interest in boys, as if she'd just as soon take her vows and disappear into a convent.

But she was thinking about the very stuff she had come here to forget. Better to think about the way the water glistened on the ducks' feathers—

"Aw, look at the little geek, playing with the ducks," said a sarcastic voice from behind her. "Where are your friends, geek? Oh, that's right. You ain't got many."

She turned. Gavin Cloverleaf stood there between her and the park, arms crossed. Even then, he had been a head taller than her and thick as a tree trunk. He was smiling, but not in a nice way.

He took two steps down the embankment toward her. She took a step back. Her feet slipped in the mud.

"Get away from me," she said. Behind them and practically on another planet, the birthday party went on, the kids now gathered on the pavilion, the parents encircling them. Why couldn't one of those grown-ups—just one—look this way?

Gavin took two more steps. Now he hooked his thumbs in his shorts pockets. "Nah," he said. "It's a free country. I think I'll stay right here."

"Fine," she said. "I'll leave."

But when she tried to move past him, he grabbed her with one arm and shoved her back toward the pond. She skidded in the mud again, pinwheeled her arms, nearly went over backward into the water.

"I got a question," Gavin said.

"Leave me alone," she hissed.

"The question," Gavin said, "is how you can live with yourself. I mean, your daddy's a Jew, right? Which makes you one, too. Y'all killed Jesus."

Gabby felt the blood rush to her face. She hated herself for it. Why should she care what this dumbass thought about her or her father? But it wasn't Gavin's opinion that made her feel embarrassed. It was the fear that everyone else in Quapaw City thought of her that way, too.

"You stupid asshole," she said, crying now. "I'm *leaving*."

He pushed her again, just enough to back her up another six inches. "Nah."

"Stop it!"

"Christ-killer," Gavin said, grinning.

Gabby slapped him.

Gavin stared at her for a moment. He touched his face, lightly, as if making sure it was still there.

"Bitch," he said, and then he shoved her, hard, with both hands.

Gabby fell into the pond, the water in the shallows warm and muddy. It squelched into her shoes, her pants, her shirt. She looked up at Gavin, who glared at her like he wanted to follow her in and drown her, and she burst into deep, hitching sobs.

Gavin watched her for a moment. Then he laughed, turned, and made his way up the bank.

After he was gone, Gabby struggled out of the pond. She stood there a moment, at the border between the land and water, like a fish that had crawled for the first time out of the muck.

When she passed them on the way to the bike rack, the partygoers finally noticed her, but all anyone did was stare.

That was more than two years ago, but today had brought every-thing back. Sometimes it seemed like her entire existence depended on the only three friends she had in the world. Without them, she belonged nowhere—a creature of the land who had been doused in water again, like B3 had baptized her into the only kind of life they would allow her to have. Half Jewish, half Latina Catholic, living in two worlds and truly belonging to neither. At home in her room, she stripped off her wet clothes. She would put them in the dryer before she left. When she got back home that afternoon, she would have time to put them away, as if nothing had ever happened.

All those balloons. All that water. All that pointing and laughing. People either pretended she didn't exist or they tortured her. There was no middle ground.

Gabby picked up a pillow, held it to her face, and screamed. A string of curses broke into ragged sobs. When it felt as if she could move or think without falling apart, Gabby went out back and laid her books on the concrete slab that served as their patio. Her notebooks were a lost cause. As she weighted down her warped textbooks with red bricks, she thought about B3. She hated jocks who picked on band geeks. She couldn't stand popular kids who would never be satisfied until the unpopular crowd had been destroyed. It was like living on the wrong side of the scorched-earth campaigns they had read about in history class, like she was the Confederacy and the jocks were a gang of General Shermans.

Nobody would stop Kenneth and his thug buddies. Not the other students, not the teachers, not Mr. Hoon, not the football coaches. Except for her three equally miserable friends, Gabby Davison was on her own, and so was every other student who lived on the margins. Even though they seemed to constitute the majority, they were alone.

CHAPTER FOUR

When the final bell rang that afternoon, Christian Allen thought the worst was over. She had spent the day trying not to feel stupid. Algebra I seemed like Latin, Spanish I like brain surgery, Earth Science like mortification, study hall like death. She hated her schedule, with the occasional exception of her Honors English class. Her teachers were boring and old. She could not wait to get home, and that was before three gorillas had pantsed her in front of the whole student body.

Once, B3 had been her friends. They had played baseball together, back in Little League, before your average Southerner's nineteenth-century conception of gender roles led to the other kids' parents protesting a girl playing for the boys' team. Learning so early how the world could break your heart had been bad enough, but once a bunch of adults' sexism gave them permission, B3 turned into jerks.

Christian had never stepped foot on a baseball field again and had sworn off sports in general. It didn't help that she hated all the usual girly-girl stuff—makeup and high heels and all that bullshit. She liked her sneakers and her baggy jeans and her rock-band T-shirts. She kept her hair short. Once, she even shaved her head, though when her usually cool mom burst into tears, Christian let it grow out some.

As far as Christian knew, she was the only lesbian at Quapaw City High, maybe the only one in town, though that could not be true. The rest just hadn't come out.

Or so she told herself.

Christian's father had left them years ago and was now living in Montana. He took his homophobia with him and had not spoken to Christian since she came out in sixth grade.

When B3 heard, Gavin called her a dyke, and Brayden made obscene gestures meant to represent what he thought lesbians did in private. It would have been funny if they hadn't seemed so pathetic. She had offered to fight them, but Mr. Myers had been standing in his yard nearby, so they had left her alone.

One day, though, they caught her alone and smacked her around. She gave as good as she got, but there were three of them. After that, as if stomping a girl had bothered their consciences just enough, they had limited their abuse to the verbal.

Until today, when they had come up behind her and yanked off her backpack. Then Kenneth Del Ray bearhugged her from behind while Gavin unbuttoned her pants and Brayden yanked them down.

At least they left her underpants alone.

Kenneth let go, and the three of them backed up ten feet or so, pointing and laughing and fist-bumping. Everybody turned to look. Some joined in the laughter. Others gathered around, waiting to see if the gender-nonconforming lesbo would swing on the boys.

Christian's face reddened. *This is sexual assault. I could get 'em expelled, maybe even arrested.* But she would not give those douches the satisfaction of knowing they bothered her. So she left her pants around her ankles and looked at the growing crowd and shrugged, as if to say, *What are you gonna do?* Then she wiggled her butt at the girls, some of whom giggled or squealed. Others made barfing noises.

Christian pulled up her jeans and refastened them. B3 weren't laughing anymore. She had taken the steam out of their joke. She retrieved her backpack and walked toward the bus lot. At the base of the semicircular driveway, the school's sign read, GO BUFFS BEAT THE BULLDOGS. Beyond it, Kentucky Boulevard was lined with small one-story houses and relatively neat yards. It looked like any street in any small town. The kind of place where a girl could have her pants yanked down in the schoolyard, the boys who did it not even trying to pretend they hadn't, and no one would do or say anything to help.

It should have stung her. It should have infuriated her. But she felt no surprise or anger or pain. It was just another Tuesday in America.

"Next time, we're stealing your pants and running 'em up the flag-pole," called Gavin.

Christian turned. "You sure do seem fascinated by my pants. But y'all ain't my type. Or is it a money thing? I guess if your family can't afford clothes, my mom could buy you a pair."

Gavin's face slackened. He stepped closer to Christian. "You just bought yourself an ass-kicking, dyke."

"You coming alone this time, or are you bringing your sisters with you again?"

They would have jumped her right there if a duty teacher hadn't come along. Christian retrieved her bike from the rack and waved to the three of them as they stood in the gravel, glaring. Kenneth gave her the finger. Christian returned it. She had gotten the best of them today, but it wouldn't always be like this. If she didn't get them off her back, the next four years would be a nightmare.

CHAPTER FIVE

Biking home to his shabby place on MacArthur Road, Micah watched the town pass by him and thought, as he did once or twice a day, how much he hated it. Quapaw City was hardly distinguishable from thousands of small towns dotting every state in the union—a little prettier than some, drabber and duller than others, but average in most ways. Unless you played sports or fished or enjoyed sitting in the freezing early mornings so you could shoot helpless animals, there was nothing to do. No wonder most kids who could drive already knew where you could buy bootlegged beer and park in a steamed-up car. Try to do anything more imaginative than that, and you got your head stuffed in a toilet.

When he got home, Micah walked into the living room, the air-conditioning washing over him. His mother wouldn't be home for a while, and his father was on another cross-country haul, so he had the cramped and cluttered house to himself, as he usually did in the afternoons. He headed for his bedroom. His homemade Keep Out sign had yellowed with age, but the duct tape he had used to affix it back in sixth grade still held. He tossed his backpack on the bed. On the tiny desk against one wall, his five-year-old computer—a desktop, for God's sake, like they were living in the Dark Ages or something—sat like a giant bullfrog on a tiny lily pad, the screensaver flashing pictures of his best friends. Christian Allen, Jamie Entmann, Gabby Davison. The four of them played video games and did homework together. He and Gabby used to LARP in a local Dungeon Wars group. Christian had taught him to throw a football and catch a baseball without breaking his fingers or his nose. And Jamie had been his best friend since first grade. But because they were all smart to some degree and into geek culture, the four of them were moving targets. Micah had heard about what happened to Gabby and Jamie. He couldn't live like this every day of his high-school life.

He sat in his folding chair and took out his battered phone with the cracked face that nearly shaved off his finger skin every time he used it.

He had a DM from Christian: Have you seen this?

Micah opened the message.

Christian had written, You're the only one who didn't get tagged, check Kenneth DR's feed. Micah did.

At the top of Kenneth's feed, three new videos had been posted. Micah watched them: Jamie staggering out of class, choking and wiping his watering eyes; Gabby standing near the school building, soaking wet and ankle deep in burst water balloons; and Christian shaking her ass at the camera, her pants around her ankles.

The likes and comments numbered in the dozens already.

Those shitheads.

I guess I should be grateful I got out before they could get me coming outta that stall looking like I fell in.

Micah's stomach gurgled and swirled. Things could have gone a lot worse in that bathroom. Everyone could be talking about him now, laughing at him, as they were undoubtedly laughing at his friends. But Micah would not puke. Not over anything B3 did. He would not let them win, not now or ever, not even here, where nobody else could see.

He dropped his phone and stomped out of his room and down the hall, through the kitchen, and out the back door. The grass needed mowing, but he had no intention of doing yardwork. He needed a break, an escape, and he could not face Christian or Gabby or Jamie. Not yet.

It would only bring the shame back to the surface and make him want to kill someone, and he knew his friends probably felt even worse.

Micah's mother was Wiccan, which, from what he could tell, was mostly about respecting nature. She would have said he should let it go. But ignoring Gavin Cloverleaf or Kenneth Del Ray would likely result in a busted nose.

Give me a baseball bat and ten minutes alone with one of y'all in a dark alley. Just ten minutes. But Micah weighed maybe a hundred and ten pounds soaking wet. Even an equalizer might not help.

God, those asshats made him feel so powerless.

He crossed the yard to the wooden storage building. Old and slowly disintegrating, it had been here when his mother and father bought the house. A strong wind might blow it over. They kept the lawnmower and gas in there, as well as the rakes and hoses and a small ladder. His father also stored a couple of old wooden trunks out there, the ones Micah's grandfather and great uncle had passed down. Micah had seen inside his grandfather's trunk a long time ago. It held his uniform from the Korean War and some pictures and other junk—things that made his father's eyes mist over and that bored Micah silly.

The other trunk, though, his great-uncle Baltar's—that one his father had shoved into the farthest corner. Then he had threatened to ground Micah for the rest of his life if he ever dug through it. Micah had asked why. "My uncle is a strange fella," his dad had said. "Maybe even dangerous. I don't want you anywhere near his shit. I'll knock a knot on your head if you so much as sit on it. You understand?"

One day, though, Micah *had* opened it and, risking whatever passed for his social life, looked through the contents. And then he understood that Baltar was into some genuinely nasty stuff—black magic, maybe even human sacrifice, Satanism, or some *-ism* as out of place in small-town Arkansas as a Viking horde.

Some old black hooded robes, the kind you pulled over your head, made of some heavy material that would probably help you drop twenty pounds of water weight on a summer day. Several crystals and bags of herbs—some sweet-smelling, some that nearly made Micah puke. A long, razor-sharp knife that looked like it might have belonged to the world's first serial killer. And over a dozen ancient, musty, heavy books, some written in something that sort of looked like English, some in Latin. There were pictures in these books—acts of violence, creatures grotesque enough to have stepped out of a maniac's nightmare. Using an online translator, Micah had read a few pages from each one. Some were histories of the supernatural. Some held spells and potions and rituals. At least one seemed to demonstrate how to summon demons. And the books looked *real*. Just touching them creeped him out. Who knew what they were made of? He had repacked everything and had promised himself he would never handle any of that stuff again.

But every time he felt the world conspiring to make him miserable, he came out here and flipped through the books. He held the knife and slashed the air, pretending to eviscerate his tormentors. He had even put on a robe a few times and skulked around the lawnmower like a wizard sneaking through a medieval forest, though if anybody had seen him, he probably would have died of embarrassment.

Now, his eyes burning with rage and shame, he entered the storage building and turned on the overhead light. The bare bulb spotlighted the lawnmower's rusty frame. In the corners, shadows pooled. Micah stepped into them and opened the trunk.

CHAPTER SIX

Christian climbed out of her mother's car, a red Chevy Malibu that needed a wash and a new left front tire, and walked up to Micah's door for their Friday night game session. She carried three pizzas from Johnny's: One cheese and two Sweep the Kitchens. It was Gabby's turn—well, her parents' turn, really—to provide the Cokes. Yesterday, Jamie told them he would bring his two new games, *Jungle Raider* and *Wizards vs. Romans*.

Micah opened the door and looked at the boxes in her arms. "Only three? What, is your mom broke?"

"Eat a bag of dicks," Christian said, pushing past him. She set the boxes on the Sterne family's kitchen counter as Micah closed the door. "Jamie here yet?"

"Yeah. Come on back."

An hour later, as they played *Jungle Raider* against a foursome from Australia, the pizza boxes lay open on the floor of Micah's room, three-quarters of the pies gone. Empty soda cans were stacked on every flat surface. Micah was leading their team through a temple level, firing head shot after head shot, dispatching the Australians before Gabby, Christian, and Jamie could do much more than aim. Christian wanted to punch him in the arm. Micah had always been good at shooters, but she wanted to play, too.

Micah took a drink of his Coke, leaving an opening for Jamie to frag an enemy with a grenade, while Gabby fricasseed another with her flamethrower and Christian hacked away with a machete. Gore flew everywhere. The tinny screams of dying characters filled Micah's room. The Australians' voices buzzed in Christian's headset, cursing and shouting instructions at each other. *Tough titty, boys. Never mess with a bad bitch.*

While Gabby set fire to the jungle, Micah cackled and sprayed the enemy with his machine gun. He almost sounded demented.

When the Australian team opted out of the game, Micah took off his headset, his face flushed. He grinned. "Man. That was fun. I wish we could do that to those asshats at school."

Jamie glanced at him. "You mean kick their butts at *Jungle Raider?* We could probably arrange that."

Micah looked pained. "No. I mean mess them up for *real.*"

Everyone stared at Micah, who ignored them and switched games. Gabby cleared her throat. Christian shook her head, frowning. Micah had always been intense, but things had gotten worse since B3 had stuffed his head in that toilet earlier in the week. Who knew how far he would go, if he had the chance?

"You're not serious, are you?" asked Gabby.

Micah sneered. "Hell yeah, I'm serious. They make our lives miserable every stinking day. They've done it since kindergarten. How long are we supposed to take their shit? Why wouldn't I want to get 'em back?"

He got up and left the room. Christian squirmed. No one seemed to know what to say.

Not that Christian didn't understand the sentiment. She knew Gabby sometimes daydreamed about scratching Kenneth Del Ray's face until he bled. Once, in Christian's hearing, Jamie had wished for the powers of flight and super strength so he could carry B3 to the top of Mount Everest, where he would leave them until just before hypoxemia set in. Christian had fought them once and had almost done it again several times over the years. She had never feared them; not much frightened her, especially not three big-mouthed knuckle-draggers she could probably outrun if she absolutely had to.

Still, none of them had ever considered really "messing up" anybody, as Micah had put it.

She would never have admitted it, but Micah scared her sometimes, much more than any bully. He reminded her of one of those geysers like Old Faithful, except he was more like Young Random. He could erupt at any time, and if you were too close, he would scald you.

Case in point: Just then, Micah walked into the room carrying his father's .30-06 rifle.

Christian leaped to her feet. Gabby's mouth fell open. Jamie sat on the floor, a forgotten controller dangling from one hand. Micah held the gun across his chest like a soldier drilling for a parade. He grinned, his teeth white and sharp-looking.

Christian gestured at the rifle. "What the hell?"

"Imagine what we could do to those dudes with this baby," Micah said.

Gabby stood. "This ain't funny, Micah. And I'm not gonna be part of it."

Micah pulled the rifle back to his chest, as if they had tried to take it from him. "I don't believe y'all. Those assholes beat us up and tear up our homework and throw our lunches in the mud. They roll our houses and chuck eggs at us. They spread lies about us online. They spend half their time dreaming up ways to torture us and the other half doing it, and you guys are looking at me like *I'm* the monster. Don't you wanna make 'em pay?"

Christian and Gabby said nothing. The three of them faced each other like gunfighters in an old Western movie, but only Micah was packing heat. Christian moved as if to take the gun from him, and Micah backed away.

"I'm with Gabby," Jamie said. "Not cool, man."

Micah lowered the gun. "So you're okay with bending over for the rest of our lives?"

Jamie stood. He wedged himself between Gabby and Christian, forming a human wall, shoulder to shoulder. "No. But a rifle? Bro, that's crazy. I won't be a part of it, either. Maybe you should hand it over."

He held out his hands. He and Micah looked each other in the eyes, not blinking. The moment stretched out, ready to break or snap back upon them.

Then Micah looked at the floor. He dropped the rifle in Jamie's hands and backed away, slumping against the wall. "Fine. I was just kidding anyway. The stupid thing's not even loaded."

Gabby exhaled. Christian relaxed. She realized she had clenched her fists just in case she'd had to deck Micah.

Jamie checked the chamber. "Yep. It's not loaded, y'all."

Micah brushed past them and sat down. He retrieved Jamie's discarded controller and started playing *Wizards vs. Romans* as if nothing had happened. After a while, Christian sat on the couch behind Micah, watching him. All the fun had drained out of the night. She felt like kicking Micah's ass up between his shoulder blades.

Jamie joined her on the couch. Gabby remained standing, as if wondering whether she should stay or go. Christian understood. They would need to be careful. If Micah had been pushed this far, God only knew what would happen the next time B3 decided to have a little fun.

They played in silence a while. When Micah's game ended, he handed the controller to Jamie, who later handed it to Gabby. Christian left the room and came back with more Cokes, plus a bag of pretzels the size of a suitcase. She took her turn after Gabby. Jamie told a joke that made them all laugh. After that, things almost got back to normal.

"I gotta go," Gabby said after her last turn. "It's getting late."

"Yeah," Christian said. "Mom will be here any minute. No sense starting a new turn."

Jamie jumped up. "Shit, I rode my bike," he said. "I'm gonna have to haul ass to make curfew."

Micah rubbed the back of his neck as he stared at the floor. *He wants to say something*, Christian thought. *Be careful, man. Don't ruin the illusion we're over what happened.*

They walked to the front door, Micah following them, clearing his throat. When Christian, Gabby, and Jamie stood on the front steps, looking back at Micah in the doorway, his body was silhouetted in the bright living room lights, his face in shadow.

"Look," he said. "I got an idea." Everyone must have looked angry or alarmed, because he held up his hands. "No, no. I just thought of a way we might let off some steam."

"Don't even ask us to do anything that'll get us kicked outta school or thrown in juvie," Christian said.

"Nothing like that. Just a little LARP."

Christian exhaled. Some of the tension drained out of her. Until this moment, she had not known how close she had been to punching Micah in the nose or running away as fast as she could. Earlier, something had come alive in his eyes, something beyond anger, maybe even beyond hate. But LARP—live-action role play—that was different. They used to do it at least once a week but had eased off a year or so back, when Gavin and Brayden had gotten wind of it. *Oooooo, wookit the wittle-bitty babies, pwaying in their wittle costumes. Ain't they cute?*

Gabby still went to Little Rock once a month for a Knights and Necropolis event, but the rest of them had pretty much forgotten about LARPing. Still, becoming someone else, an identity you created with abilities you dreamed up, your character wandering a world of imagination where they could stand up to any enemy—Christian missed it, and she suspected the others had, too. High school had turned out to be the worst kind of LARP. The roles were not of your design, the conflicts not of your own devising. It might be nice to get back to some kind of fantasy world for a night. Plus, it was better than punching her old friend in the face.

Christian clapped Micah on the shoulder. "I'm totally in. What did you have in mind?"

Micah smiled. It looked genuine, though the heat of that unnameable feeling coursing through him—the one that had seemed to be festering ever since Gavin Cloverleaf first gave him a wedgie in the recess yard back in elementary school—still danced in his eyes. Micah looked to Jamie and Gabby. "Y'all remember when I told you about my weird great-uncle? Well, we got a bunch of his stuff in the shed. And my mom's always got some funky herbs and shit laying around. I say we meet up here next weekend and make a Dark Wizard Society. Our world, our rules. And our first adventure will be casting a spell on B3. What do you think?"

Jamie and Gabby smiled. "I'm in," Gabby said.

Before she got home that night, Christian already knew what she would name her character. The only trouble would be doing her homework all week instead of spending hours on character design.

CHAPTER SEVEN

The next Friday morning, Gabby and Jamie stood in the hallway near the boys' bathroom. They had algebra next period. Jamie was good at math—well, he was good at everything related to school—but Gabby dreaded the hour-long lecture on the quadratic equation, plus all the subsequent in-class problems and homework that would follow. She liked English and did well in history and Earth science. No one but B3 had ever called her stupid, and to them, "stupid" just seemed to mean "different." But once Mr. Singh had introduced variables, everything on the page blurred. Even the other kids in class seemed to be speaking a dead language. Just another world Gabby lived in only halfway.

She dreaded math even more on this sunny morning because of the LARP. They had finished their character sketches, and though no one had found time to throw together a costume, they would make do, just this once.

Gabby and Jamie leaned against the wall, ignoring everyone who passed. Most of the other kids didn't talk to them much anyway.

"So. Tonight at five, Micah's place?" said Jamie.

"Yeah," said Gabby. "Think there's anything cool in that trunk Micah told us about?"

Jamie shrugged. "If not, we can always wrap it up in time for a movie or two. I'm thinking *Zombies from Venus IV*."

Gabby groaned. She couldn't understand what people saw in those *Zombies from Venus* movies. The first one was okay, though the screenwriter clearly stole the whole idea from a line in *Night of the Living Dead*. The rest of the series had been boring. She knew zombie and vampire movies—why *REC* was better than *Quarantine*, how many actors had

35

played Dracula, whether somebody she just met would be more of a *Shaun of the Dead* or a *Fido* person. *Zombies from Venus* didn't even make her top twenty. But she had no desire to argue about a movie they might not even watch, so she said, "Okay. But who's buying the food?"

"I think it's my turn. I'll holler at my moms at lunch. And hey, don't forget to look for some candles."

"Sure. I'm the candle wench. Because I'm a girl, I bet."

"No. Because we ain't got any at my place, and Micah's about as reliable as a zombie from Venus. Anyway, I gotta piss before class. See you later."

He ducked into the restroom. Gabby shook her head. "Thanks for sharing, dude." She turned and headed down the hall for Mr. Singh's classroom, where unsolvable riddles awaited.

✳✸✳

When Jamie walked into the restroom, the flickering fluorescent lights overhead somehow making the stained walls and graffiti-covered stalls seem even dingier than usual, he nearly ran into Kenneth Del Ray, who stood just out of the swinging door's range. Jamie froze. He and Kenneth regarded each other for an uncomfortable moment, Jamie tensing in case he needed to fight or run, Kenneth's mouth twitching like he wanted to grin but didn't want Jamie to see it.

"What?" Jamie asked.

Kenneth cleared his throat. "Why you talking to me in the bathroom? You like me like that?"

"Oh, for God's sake. What are you, six years old?" Jamie edged past Kenneth and into a stall. He unzipped and heard Kenneth giggling. The door creaked open and then clicked shut.

WTF? Jamie thought. *What was that idiot so happy about?*

CHAPTER EIGHT

Jamie's mother dropped him off in Micah's driveway just after five. When Micah let him in, Jamie handed him a wad of cash for the food. Johnny's delivered their pizza half an hour later. They played video games while they ate, Micah shouting at them to stop getting grease on his controllers, his mother popping in every so often to make sure no one had dumped the pies onto the carpet.

Mrs. Sterne kept turning off lights in the house. Every time she walked into Micah's room, she winced. She kept rubbing her temples, her forehead.

"Your mom's got a migraine again?" Jamie asked.

Micah glanced toward his doorway. "She said one's coming on. She'll go to bed soon."

"Sucks," Jamie said.

"She ever tried acupuncture?" Gabby asked as she grabbed another slice. "I read somewhere it could help."

Micah laughed. "Our insurance won't cover shit like that."

Gabby looked away. "Okay." She picked at the bedspread's seams.

It killed Jamie how Gabby seemed so damn sad most of the time, even more than the rest of them, even when nobody was giving her any shit. He was pretty sure Micah had been laughing at his own family's lack of funds, the way you do when the only other options are crying or screaming, but Gabby believed every laugh in her vicinity meant she was the joke.

We should all be nicer to her. We know what it's like.

They kept playing, eating, watching the clock, waiting for dark.

At eight fifteen, Micah turned off the game. "Mom, we're gonna go outside and hang, okay?"

"Okay, but don't bug the neighbors," she called, her voice barely audible. "I'm gonna take some Tylenol and lay down. Be inside by nine thirty, you hear?"

"Yes, ma'am," Micah said.

They would have roughly an hour, since the rest of them would need to leave no later than nine fifteen to make curfew, but it would do. Micah led them out. The world had dimmed; the sky had turned a deep blue-black, like a bad bruise.

In the shed, Micah turned on the overhead light and shoved the mower and rakes and Weed Eater and mildewed lawn chairs against the walls. Jamie and Christian helped, while Gabby set up the candles in a circle and lit some of Mrs. Sterne's incense. Near the back wall, flanked by three folded beach chairs with grains of sand still clinging to the fabric and some stacked boxes of God only knew what, Micah showed them an old-fashioned steamer trunk made of dark wood, its lid carved with ornate figures like moons, stars, and signs representing the elements—a flaming log of wood, a cresting wave, a tree bending as if in a strong wind, a tract of land plowed in long furrows. *That must have taken somebody a long time*, Jamie thought. *I bet you could sell that trunk for enough to buy a decent used car.* A thick padlock hung from the trunk's latch.

Micah grumbled. "Well, hell. I guess Dad locked it since I came out here last."

"You got a key?" Christian asked.

"No," Micah said. "Dad takes his key ring on the road."

Jamie shrugged. "Oh, well. We can make up our own spell."

Micah turned and brushed past Gabby, who was still lighting candles. He stopped beside the door and dug around in a tangle of hoses and old lifejackets left over from the bass boat his dad used to own. He pulled out a foot-long hatchet, its handle made of light wood, its black head streaked orange with rust. He carried it over to the trunk and regarded the lock.

Jamie and Christian looked at each other. Her eyes widened, but she said nothing.

"Hey, man," Jamie said. "Your momma's gonna kill us if you bust open that trunk. And if she don't, your dad will."

Micah didn't look at him. "This ain't for the trunk."

Before anyone could stop him, Micah struck at the lock. The blow glanced sideways into the wood, chipping off an inch-long piece. Jamie and Gabby groaned.

"Shit," Micah muttered.

Christian yanked the hatchet out of his hand. "Gimme that thing before you chop off your foot."

"We gotta get in there," Micah said. "Or this is gonna be really lame."

Jamie put his hand on Micah's shoulder. "Like I said. We can just make up a spell. No biggie."

Micah sneered. *"Lame."*

"Maybe try this instead," Gabby said. Having opened a toolbox hidden under a pile of old junk, she held a screwdriver. "Just unscrew the latch."

Christian shook her head and took the screwdriver.

"Well, how was I supposed to know we had screwdrivers out here?" Micah said.

"It's your shed," Jamie said. "You knew where to find a hatchet but not a toolbox? Dude."

"Look, I don't spend much time out here. Most of the time, it's because I've gotta do stupid yard work. It ain't exactly my happy place."

"Whatever."

Jamie stood over Christian and watched her work. It took her five minutes or so. The screws had rusted in the long, humid years. When she got them out, she handed them to Jamie. He put them in his pocket so they wouldn't get lost. Then she handed him the piece of latch she had removed.

Micah kneeled beside Christian and opened the trunk. They all looked inside.

"Wow," whispered Christian.

Micah pulled out a half-dozen long, flowing robes, all black or blood-red, festooned with the faces of snarling creatures the world had never seen outside its collective nightmares. "Throw one of these on," Micah said, tossing robes to Gabby and Jamie. The cloth felt coarse and thick. Christian selected a robe and pulled it over her head. Micah picked the most ornate one. The robes flowed past their feet.

The four of them looked each other over. Then Gabby burst into laughter. Jamie snickered, then cackled. Soon, they were all giggling.

They rifled through the rest of the contents. Jamie picked up one item at a time, examined it, put it aside. Some objects he recognized: a few crucifixes, crystals, gold and silver goblets decorated like the robes. Others he did not—vials of foul-looking fluids, dried roots, leaves sealed in plastic bags and jars. There were also several books. Micah pulled one out, oddments of all sorts avalanching off it. Something bounced on the floor with a metallic ping and skittered into the shadows. Jamie hoped it wasn't a priceless family heirloom or the One Ring or something.

They gathered in a circle and examined the book. Christian let out a long, low whistle. The blank cover was made of dark, cracked leather that looked as old as the Magna Carta. On the spine, two words in gold inlay: *Bēstiae Barathrī*. Micah opened the book and flipped through it. Its pages were filled with pictures of monsters—some humanoid, some animal-human hybrids; others appeared to be blobs with multiple mouths and limbs or thousands of eyes. Many of the creatures were pictured ripping humans apart; some projected menace in their postures and vicious, distorted faces. More Latin words were listed in small columns next to each picture. Underneath each column, even more Latin, though these words had been divided into stanzas like poems or song lyrics.

"What does that title mean?" Gabby asked, turning to Jamie. God, they *always* turned to him. Just because he made As in school didn't mean he was Google.

"I'd guess *Creatures of the Abyss*," said Jamie. He couldn't read Latin, if that was indeed the language, but the roots of the words seemed pretty clear.

"I know what this is," said Micah, looking at the pages as if he had found a compendium of downloadable content for all their favorite games. "It's a book of spells for summoning monsters. Look at this junk. I bet those columns are ingredients, and the poetry-looking stuff is what you have to chant." Micah's excitement baked off him like fever heat.

A tendril of unease sprouted in Jamie's stomach. "I don't think we should play around with summoning monsters."

"Come on, dude," said Micah, looking annoyed.

Gabby turned to Christian. "What do you think? I bet it would make the game seem real."

Christian shrugged. "I'm down." She checked her phone. "Besides, we ain't got time to write our own chant."

"I don't know," Jamie said. The tendril had twined about his guts. "My parents will kill me if they find out we've been messing around with demonic shit."

"It's. Just. Old. *Crap*," Micah said, as if Jamie were the dumbest guy he'd ever met. "Here's one that ain't even got ingredients. Let's try it."

"Come on, man," Christian said to Jamie as she and Gabby huddled up with Micah.

Jamie hung back for a moment. This felt wrong. He opened his mouth to protest again. But his friends were having fun. And monsters weren't real. What could happen, really?

He grinned and held out his hand. Micah nodded and gave him the book.

∗✳∗

Clouds passed over the moon, throwing the Arkansas landscape into deeper darkness. A northeast wind bent the treetops back and forth like the hair of dancing women. Beneath the rustling oaks between Micah's house and the neighbors', Kenneth Del Ray watched the storage shed. He'd been waiting around for hours before they came outside; he could have sworn he heard them say five o'clock. Now the geeks finally started to thump and bump inside, scraping junk back and forth on the floor, laughing, arguing—if he was honest, they sounded like him and Brayden and Gavin. In a different world, they all might have been buddies. But facts were facts, and in high school, jocks and geeks didn't mix, except when somebody needed tutoring. Kids like that would never be invited to the best parties. They were nobodies. They did nothing cool and had no popular friends. Sure, they were good at playing video games and stuff, but what was cooler, throwing a touchdown pass and knocking a home run or being really good at sitting on your ass and fake-shooting fake people?

Sometimes Kenneth felt bad about Christian. She had been his friend once. But if she chose to hang out with a bunch of losers, he couldn't help her. Besides, she was a lesbian. Even God didn't like queers. Quapaw City was no place for somebody like her. Were they *singing* in there now? No, not quite singing—chanting. Kenneth couldn't make out the words, but he could feel the rhythm, hear the repetition. Man, those kids just got weirder and weirder. They totally deserved what they were about to get—a good, old-fashioned smack upside their geek heads. Looking around to make sure no one was watching out their windows or walking on the street, Kenneth moved out of the trees' shadows and into the Sternes' backyard.

✸

Inside the shed, a consensus had formed: They couldn't memorize all that Latin. Well, none of them except Jamie, who could learn anything. Micah loved Jamie like a brother, but that shit got on his nerves. The rest of them gave up and gathered around Micah, who sat cross-legged on the floor and held the book in his lap.

"We can't stand in a circle if we can't remember the words," he said. "But we can chant 'em here and pretend we're dancing around a big fire, way out in some woods nobody else has ever seen."

"What if we got the columns wrong and we're reading off a list of ingredients?" Gabby said. "I'd feel pretty stupid if it turned out we was chanting 'Two gallons milk, one carton eggs.'"

"Well, there's no numbers. How could it be an ingredient list if the book don't tell you how much to use?"

"Besides," Jamie offered, "who cares? We're not *really* trying to cast a spell."

"I guess," Gabby muttered, though she still looked doubtful.

Man, Micah thought. *For a ninth grader, she sure can be an old lady.*

The others stood behind Micah, looking over his shoulders at the book. They took a couple of minutes to get into character—Jamie as a warlock called Kamizar; Micah as a demigod, Rickenracken; Gabby the warrior princess Xero; and Christian as a mighty swordswoman she named Squidward Agonistes. The names were silly, but they put on their role-playing game faces—serious, haughty expressions, narrowed eyes, set jaws.

Micah bowed his head for a moment. Then he looked to the heavens, or, more accurately, the cobwebbed shed ceiling. One of these days, Dad would need to come out here and get rid of that old dirt-dauber nest. Of course, he'd probably just make Micah do it. But anyway. "Oh, powers of darkness," Micah said, lowering his voice, "we disparate wanderers gather tonight to curse our tormentors. Give us the power to defend our realm. Let it begin."

The rest of them, still reading over Micah's shoulders, began to chant.

"Bēstiae obscūritātis profundissimae, vōs invocāmus. Patefacite vōs. Pūrgātē mundum. Dōnāte nōbīs potestātem vestram, ō magnae!"

At first, despite themselves, they giggled as their Southern tongues stumbled over the words. Micah shot them dark looks and told them to cut that shit out. This was supposed to be serious.

They kept trying.

In the fourth iteration, all the words sounded halfway decent. The others stopped laughing as they fell into the rhythm of the language. Together, the four of them chanted five times more, six, a dozen. Micah's body began to sway with the rhythm of the syllables. He could feel the others moving behind him. Soon, words sprang from their lips like water from a fountain, gushing with power and force. Some part of Micah realized he no longer needed to look at the words. He let the book fall into the circle of candles, where it lay open at the same page they had been reading. Now they danced around the book, still chanting, the flickering candles throwing their capering shadows on the walls. They moved faster and faster, chanting to the beat of their footsteps.

Once, when Mom had lain down with a headache and Dad had gone on an errand, leaving half a pot of coffee on, a seven-year-old Micah had drunk it all, filling about half his cup with sugar every time. When the caffeine and sugar took effect, his heartbeat had sped up, and he had felt as if he could run around the house forty or fifty times. Dad had come home to find him zipping through the house with his toys, eyes wide, panting. As their chants grew faster and faster, Micah felt that way again—full of an energy he had never even known existed, as if they were building to some great climax.

And just when Micah felt as if he might burst, a great ripping sound cut them off and drove them to their knees, as if someone had torn open the sky. The sound seemed to come from everywhere.

"What the hell?" Gabby said, her eyes as big as the full moon.

A thin beam of light shot from the book, its terminus at eye level. Micah cried out, stepped backward, and nearly tripped over some bit of junk. Gabby screamed. Jamie's hand went to his throat, as if he couldn't breathe. Even Christian looked stricken.

The beam expanded into a glowing ball that brightened with every passing second. The candles sputtered and went out, but the glowing ball lit the shed, a thousand-watt bulb sprung from an old book. The group shielded their eyes with their hands as they backed away, came together, huddled near the junk against one wall. Gabby gripped Christian's and Jamie's shoulders.

"What's happening?" Micah shouted to Jamie.

"How should I know?" Jamie snapped. "I got here when you did."

The glowing ball expanded, expanded, expanded.

Oh, shit. Oh, hell.

✳✳✳

Kenneth had just grasped the handles of the storage room doors when, from the crack between them, blinding light made him recoil. It was as if the geeks had turned on a set of sodium lamps in there. He stumbled backward and shielded his eyes. Then he looked back at the house. It would be just his luck for some interfering parent to rush out before he could bust up their little party. But no one came, so, squinting against the glare, Kenneth turned back and pulled open the doors just as the geeks began to scream, their angry, frightened voices rising above a weird ripping sound.

What the hell?

In the center of the room, surrounded by lawn-care junk and old boxes, a book lay on the floor, its pages open, and though a strong wind buffeted Kenneth, those pages did not turn. Above the open book, a ball of white light hovered. No, not just hovered—*expanded*. The geeks clung to each other, screaming. They wore goofy robes and shaded their eyes with their hands.

The light ball filled half the shed now.

Kenneth had no idea how they were making that light—some high-tech nerd project, no doubt—but it seemed to have gotten away from them. Typical. Too smart for their own good. Well, he was just the guy to rub their faces in it, hard. He stepped forward, leaving the doors open behind him.

＊✴＊

As Christian watched, her heart threatening to break through her sternum, the ball of light kept growing. She did not want that light to touch her. *Things* were moving in it, some more or less human, some just blobs that expanded and contracted, some shapes her mind struggled to comprehend at all. If she hadn't known better, she would have sworn their spell had worked, that it had created a portal to some other dimension where strange beings did God only knew what. That kind of thing happened in comic books and old horror movies, usually to dumb and careless people who messed with stuff they didn't understand. *People like us*, she realized.

Micah looked as scared as everyone else and had never shown the acting chops to fake it this well. Whatever was happening, it was no setup they would all laugh about when Micah said *Gotcha*.

The book seemed to be the key. Micah dropped it, and then that weird wind kicked up, but the pages weren't turning, as if they were glued down. If Christian could grab the book and shut it, maybe the light would go away.

Nobody else seemed ready to move. As with B3's bullshit pranks last week, she was the only one ready to fight. *It's like that old saying—it's a dirty job, but somebody's gotta do it.*

She tensed, took a deep breath.

When she stepped forward, Kenneth Del Ray tackled her.

They stumbled against some old boxes filled with heavy, solid objects, perhaps books. Christian tried to turn in Kenneth's grasp as they fell, the better to headbutt him in his dumb face, but the upper cartons rained on them. One hit Christian in the head. She turned just in time to keep her nose from being crushed, but the weight of the box wrenched her neck and sandwiched her head between the box and the floor. Pain exploded in the back of her skull. Her vision began to fade even as the ripping sound grew louder and louder.

Then other noises—growling, howling, more screaming.

Christian closed her eyes and let darkness swallow her.

✳✴✳

When Kenneth and Christian tumbled into the boxes, Jamie moved to help her, but Micah grabbed him and pointed to the glow-ball. It nearly touched the ceiling on one end, the book on the other, and moved outward, toward them. No heat emanated from it. It seemed to be all light, like a camera flash that had taken root in the air.

Jamie could not look at it for more than a second or two at a time, but he saw movement inside it, like people behind a movie screen. The shapes seemed to be struggling with each other—pushing, shoving, striking each other with fists and what might have been tentacles, pseudopods, talons.

God almighty, what did we do?

Micah was dragging him backward. They stumbled over the junk scattered around the shed as Gabby screamed, high-pitched like a police siren. Terror washed over Jamie, threatened to drown him, and he couldn't tell how much belonged to him and how much came from his friends.

Some of the shapes were spilling out of the glow-ball and onto the floor of the shed. The whole place shook as they landed.

One shape stood in front of the light, casting its long shadow onto Jamie and Micah, who grabbed each other and shouted, though Jamie had no idea what he was saying, babbling like a frightened child when the monster finally drags itself out from under the bed. The thing before them hunched over, its shoulders against the ceiling. It shifted, revealing four long, muscular arms, each ending in a four-fingered hand with sharp nails at the ends of its fingers. Its red eyes burned. Behind it, other things leaped from the glow-ball to the floor and dashed, flew, slithered past Jamie and out the open shed doors.

The hunched figure reached for Jamie and Micah.

"Get away from them!" Gabby yelled from somewhere beyond the light.

The thing turned its head toward her voice.

The glow-ball expanded again. It touched the ceiling and the book.

Then it exploded.

There was no sound, no heat, no shrapnel or discharge except light. The being looming over them emitted a deep and guttural cry like a lion clearing its throat as the force of the blast sent it flying over Jamie's and Micah's heads, driving them to the floor as it passed. It crashed through the wall and into the night.

Jamie was doused in the light. His head seemed to swell until he was sure it would burst. His lungs expanded. The light was burying him.

A voice in his mind spoke a language he had never heard and did not understand. It was a beast's voice, angry, *hungry*.

When the light and his own fear overwhelmed his senses, Jamie passed out.

✱

Gabby woke up on the floor of the shed, which was missing a wall. The doors lay in the darkened yard. Well, a bunch of pieces and powdery splinters did, anyway. The frame had been shattered; the once-rectangular opening now looked more like a badly drawn circle. Some of the junk from the floor lay scattered in the grass. Gabby got to her knees and crawled over to Micah. He and Jamie lay in each other's arms, but Micah had come to rest on top of Jamie, so she pulled him off and shook him. Nothing. She tried again with the same result.

Then she slapped him.

Micah's eyes fluttered then closed. She slapped him again. He roared and sat up, pushing her away. "What the *hell*?" he yelled.

She scooted backward. "I was trying to help, you asshole."

Jamie sat up and groaned. He rubbed his temples, his robe pooling around him.

Christian stood over the old book, watching it as if it might float off the floor and out the hole in the shed. She massaged the back of her neck and grimaced.

Gabby looked around. The overhead bulb must have shattered in the explosion, but even in the dark, she could tell that Kenneth had disappeared.

Micah struggled to his feet and joined Christian, whose face was inscrutable.

"Anybody see what happened to Kenneth?" Jamie said.

"Maybe he got disintegrated," said Gabby.

"That's not funny."

"Says who?" asked Micah. "He'd just as soon step on your throat as say hello. We got other things to worry about."

"He could be hurt bad," Jamie said.

"If we're lucky, he'll die and improve the gene pool."

"All of you shut up," Christian hissed. "What the hell just happened? We read that chant or whatever it was, and then we fell into an episode of *Doctor Who*."

The four of them gathered around the book. To Gabby, it looked ordinary, like someone had forgotten to return it to the library in 1920. Or like an old high-school yearbook. Its dust-coated cover showed their finger marks.

"Jesus," Micah said. "My parents talk about Baltar like he was a serial killer. I figured it was mostly bullshit."

Gabby shivered. "I don't know about him, but what just happened here—that seemed pretty real to me."

"Me too," Christian said.

"What do you guys think it was?" Micah said. "That glow? Those *things*?"

They looked at each other. Then they all turned to Jamie, as they always did whenever a tough problem presented itself.

He shrugged. "How am I supposed to know?"

Micah scowled. "Most times, we can't get you to shut up. *Now* you got nothing to say?"

Christian backhanded Micah on the shoulder. He glared at her, but Christian was looking at Jamie. "You're the biggest brain here," she said. "Give us a theory. Anything."

Jamie rubbed his temples again. Gabby wanted to go to him, to squeeze his shoulder, to tell him it was okay. They asked too much of him. But she couldn't make herself do it. What if, in his shock and pain and whatever else he might be feeling, he pushed her away, like everyone else? *I couldn't stand it if one of the people in this shed did that to me. I just couldn't.* And so she did nothing but watch.

"Look," Jamie finally said. "All I can do is guess. Everything I know about the occult, I learned from TV and comic books. Okay?"

They all nodded. "Yeah," Christian said. "We get it. You're no Niles Caulder."

"Here's the only thing I can think of," Jamie said. He looked both scared and defensive, as if they had already dismissed his idea. "You know how sometimes a superhero crosses over to another dimension? And sometimes, stuff from over there comes to Earth?"

"Yeah," said Gabby. "Like when the Annihilation Wave tried to destroy the Marvel Universe. Or when Cass and the Winchesters went to the Apocalypse World on *Supernatural*."

"Right. Maybe that's what happened. Like if Doctor Strange or Doctor Fate conjured up a portal. Only we didn't know how to control it. Didn't even know what we were doing. So it opened, and it kept growing until it touched something from this dimension, and then it snapped shut like a trap door."

Micah barked laughter. "Yeah, right. Whatever you're smoking, you need to pass it around."

"You got a better explanation, big mouth?" Christian said. "*You* saw what *we* saw. We didn't just open something. *We let stuff out.*"

They looked at each other, at the book, at the dead light socket. Gabby coughed and cleared her throat. "Y'all," she said. "What the hell do we do now?"

After a moment, Micah grinned and slapped Jamie on the back. "Maybe something will eat Kenneth," he said.

CHAPTER NINE

Kenneth Del Ray pedaled his bike into his driveway and leaped off while it was still rolling. It clattered to the ground, the front tire spinning. He walked up the three wooden steps onto the porch, through the front door, and into the living room, where his father sat watching a ball game. Kenneth muttered monosyllables in response to his father's usual "How was your day?" questions. His mother was cooking a late supper, the house filled with the smell of frying meat. He walked down the darkened hall to his bedroom. His door, the top half of it covered by a Gruesome poster, stood wide open. He flicked on his light and shut the door. The room lay in its usual state—bed unmade, PlayStation games and gear scattered in front of the TV, dresser drawers open with a sleeve or two hanging out. The walls were papered in posters from classic metal bands he loved, Megadeth and Slayer and Mastodon. Kenneth turned on his speaker and cranked up Godsmack, stopping just under the sonic level that would have brought one or both parents down the hall to bang on his door and hassle him.

He was still trying to make sense of what he had seen.

That weird light had shone from the storage building door, like somebody in there had turned on the sun. Unsure of what was happening, he had gone with his first instinct—to pound those four geeks into the ground and laugh. He tackled Christian first, figuring if he could make the fearless one pussy out or run, the rest would be easy pickings. He hadn't meant to knock over that box of bricks or gold bars or whatever it had been, and he certainly hadn't meant for them to fall on Christian's head. But once you started a four-on-one fight, you'd damn well better finish it, so he had turned to pick his next victim, and that was when he saw—well, there it was again. What *had* he seen? Shadows? The kinds of spots you got in your eyes if you accidentally looked at the sun? No, more like people, animals, shapes like you saw in a geometry book. Except these moved. But that was crazy, unless Micah Sterne was dumb enough to make shadow puppets while his friends got slapped around. Kenneth wouldn't put it past the little freak, but how could Micah make those shadow puppets run out the door? How did he make that glowing ball explode? And what the hell was that—that *thing*—with four arms?

Kenneth turned up the volume one more notch, skating on the edge of his father's wrath. Then he lay on the bed and clasped his hands behind his head. He closed his eyes. A short nap would do him good. Afterward, he would call Gavin and Brayden and tell them everything. They'd laugh their asses off at the image of Micah in a monk's robe, dancing like an idiot in a storage building. Kenneth smiled.

Then the cramps struck.

Pain ripped through him in sharp, fast waves, locking up his muscles and joints. His chest thrust toward the ceiling, his pelvis deeper into the bed. His jaw clenched hard enough to hurt his teeth. He could not scream, so he gurgled and moaned, though the music drowned him out. Veins stood out on his forehead and arms. Still clasped behind his head, his hands opened and closed in spasms. He felt something rip back there. His feet beat against the mattress. Someone had stuck an eggbeater in his guts. Every bone, every muscle throbbed and pounded. Worse, they were *moving*, growing, thickening, as if he were a blank space some clumsy artist was filling in with a dull pencil. Every internal organ, even his appendix, wrenched inside him, *changed*. He felt it, the same way you felt a muscle harden and bunch when you flexed.

Kenneth's whole body clenched, and he found himself facing his window. The curtains had parted a few inches, and though he could not be certain, given all the pain and the movement and how the bedroom light reflected off the glass, something appeared to be out there—something huge, a shape without real form. It blocked out the moon and the streetlights.

God, please let it be my imagination.

The shape seemed to move. Or was that an illusion, given how Kenneth's own head rattled and shook on his pillow? The spasms yanked him in the opposite direction and shook him off the bed. He fell to the carpet, feet still beating a staccato tattoo on the floor. One of his hands landed on the metal bedrail and gripped it. And just when it seemed the pain could get no worse, when he had resigned himself to being shaken apart from the inside, everything stopped. His hand fell to the carpet.

Where he had gripped the rail, it had broken in two. Deep indentions marked both sides of the break, indentions shaped exactly like his hand.

Huh, Kenneth thought as darkness closed in. *That's not right.*

And then he passed out.

✶✹✶

Micah finished cleaning up the mess in the shed not long after the others had left—well, as much as you *could* clean it up, considering the smashed doors and missing wall. Frankly, it was a miracle the little building hadn't fallen in. The parentals would ground him for forty-seven years when they saw this, even though they would likely have no theories as to how a few kids his size had done so much damage without heavy machinery.

He stepped outside the shed and thought about what else to do but had no idea what that might be. It wasn't like he could throw a tarp over a missing wall and expect his parents not to notice.

Screw it. I ain't a carpenter.

Micah turned toward the house. And then the pain hit.

It felt as if a mule had kicked him in the stomach, the cramps ripping through him with every heartbeat. He tried to scream, but his jaw locked. He collapsed, muscles spasming, brain on fire, and there he flopped, his hands clawing the ground. Who knew how long it lasted? It seemed like forever.

Oh God, make it stop. That, or let me die. Please.

Just when he could take no more, precisely when it occurred to him that physical pain could drive you insane, it tapered off, leaving him writhing on the ground, panting and moaning. And as his muscles relaxed, he fainted, embracing the darkness that enveloped him.

✶✹✶

Christian had almost made it home. She was pedaling her bike as fast as she could down the middle of the street, hoping to make curfew and slip into her room unobserved. She didn't want to answer the usual questions about what she and her friends had done, the kind of well-meaning chitchat parents loved and kids barely tolerated. She needed to think. She had seen something extraordinary, done something reckless, tapped into something inexplicable, and only time would tell whether—

Agony ripped through her body, locking her legs. Her feet jammed on the pedals. She flew over the handlebars, body contorting in the air, and hit the pavement on her boobs and chin, feet bent over her head. *I scorpioned, and nobody even filmed it.* Her shirt ripped, the asphalt digging into her skin as she somersaulted twice. When she came to rest on her back beside a parked car, the seizures had not abated. Her bike lay in the street. As her body jerked, the moon peeked through the gaps in the tree limbs above her. Somewhere nearby, a dog yapped in a high, shrill voice.

Shut up already, doggo.

But the mutt kept barking and barking, even as Christian closed her eyes and wondered if she were dying.

✳

A couple of miles east, on Mississippi Street, Gabby awoke in Jamie's arms. He was still out, breathing evenly, groaning deep in his throat. She disentangled herself and sat up. She had once heard Dad describing a hangover—like a whole street repair team jackhammering your skull from the inside, he had said. Her own head felt that way now.

Their bikes stood in her driveway near her parents' Honda Civic. She and Jamie lay in the front yard, hidden in the shadows of the oak Gabby's mother pretended to hate—the way it dropped branches on the roof after a storm, how its leaves piled up every fall—even though everyone knew Mom really loved it, and she knew they knew. One of Jamie's feet protruded in the lights from the street, and even that probably looked, at first glance, like a shoe someone had left in the yard.

Gabby shifted, and a fresh bolt of pain shot through her brain. Grunting, she held her head and tried to reconstruct what had happened.

They had been sitting under the oak and talking about the shed, about Kenneth, about Micah's scary intensity. After a while, they had fallen silent. Jamie changed positions, and his hand came down on hers. He left it there, just for a moment, and then pulled it away. Gabby thought that was weird, but her hand felt warmer somehow, tingly, and her stomach fluttered in a way she had never felt before. She cleared her throat. Even though it was dark under the tree, they both seemed to be trying not to look at each other.

What was happening? She had known Jamie all her life, had touched him a million times in a million friendly, innocent ways, and vice versa. Now a brief caress had left them both speechless, uncomfortable—and, in Gabby's case, confused. Gabby had never had a real boyfriend. Well, she'd kissed Micah once, in seventh grade on a Halloween hayride, but that didn't count.

That warmth, that tingling—was that what attraction felt like?

Did she like Jamie? As in *like him* like him? And was it even possible he might like her back—her, Gabriella Davison, who had never belonged anywhere or with anyone but her parents?

Then the agony, like lightning strikes. When their bodies spasmed, their heads banged together. She remembered nothing after that, but apparently they had clutched each other, her head coming to rest on Jamie's chest. They had probably looked like a couple who had fallen asleep in each other's embrace.

Gabby touched her forehead, from which pain still radiated, skull to neck to spine to limbs. She found a hematoma the size of a goose egg. *I hope we didn't crack each other's skulls.* She sat in the grass, every muscle sore, as if she had lifted weights for six hours. Even her nostrils hurt.

Something about her senses—a car passing by two streets away sounded like a tank, each revolution of its tires making a *whomp* sound that drove into her ears like a spike. She put her hands over her ears. *Stop it,* she thought. *Stop it! Go away!* After a moment, the sound faded, as if she had turned down a volume switch in her head. She opened her eyes. Despite the darkness, she could see Jamie perfectly well, including the bruise forming on his forehead.

His eyes fluttered open. He grimaced and sat up, covering his ears as Gabby had done. That was strange—as if they were suffering the same after-effects of whatever had happened. She touched him on the shoulder. He groaned and jerked away. After a moment, he turned to her, blinking.

"Jesus," he said. "I've never been knocked out in my life until tonight, and now it's happened twice. I don't like this movie."

"Right?" Gabby said, not sure how else to respond. All this was new to her, too.

"How come I can see you so good?" he whispered. "I mean, I know you're right next to me, but I can even see every eyelash. Like you're in HD."

"I dunno," she said. "When I woke up, it seemed like I could hear everything in the world until I thought about how much I wanted it to stop. Then it got quieter."

At each word, Jamie clenched his hands tighter over his ears. He squinted hard, grunted with effort. After a moment, his eyes slowly opened. He took his hands away from his ears and blinked.

"Wow," Jamie said. "That actually worked." He sniffed. "You smell that?"

She *could* smell something—many somethings, in fact. Fried chicken from inside her house. The garbage sitting in the Meddars' can on the curb across the street. Something foul emanating from Jamie himself. She wrinkled her nose. "Did you fart?"

"I might have, with all that straining," he said. "Sorry."

She closed her eyes, thinking, *Turn it down. Turn it down.* Sure enough, the odors grew duller, the feel of every grass blade under her butt and legs less acute. When she looked at Jamie again, he was mostly a shadow, the bruise invisible in the dark. "I did it," she said. "I thought about how I wanted the smells to go away and how I wanted to see like normal. About how I didn't wanna feel every speck of dirt though my jeans. And it all eased up."

He followed her lead, growing quiet. "Yeah," he said after a second. "It definitely works."

"Cool. Let me try something." Gabby concentrated again. This time, as she watched, Jamie coalesced, as clear as if they were sitting under the noonday sun. "You can turn it all back on, too."

"What happened to us? I felt like my insides were being ripped out with a fork, and then—"

"Then we cracked heads," she finished. "I know. It's gotta have something to do with what happened in the shed. You think we're dying? Did it give us radiation sickness?"

"I don't think radiation sickness works like this. But it sure did *something* to us. I wonder if Christian and Micah felt it, too."

"Maybe we should ask 'em," Gabby said. She took out her phone and texted them. Then she turned to her house. The front window was dark, but the TV flickered behind the curtains, probably her father watching a ball game or a late movie. "I don't think my parents would mind if you come in, if you wanna try—Jamie?"

He was gone. She had not heard him leave. Why would he just take off?

Well, why wouldn't *he?* said the voice that spoke in her mind whenever the latest crushing disappointment fell on her head like a meteor. *You didn't really think that little touch meant anything, did you? Puh-leeze. Remember how he jerked away. Nobody's ever gonna love you. There's no place for you in the world except that pathetic room in your parents' house, and there never will be.*

Shut up. I don't have to listen to you.

Now that she was alone, though, fear sank deep into her gut. Too much had happened. She shivered and stood, ready to dash inside.

Then Jamie crashed to the ground in front of her, as if he had hidden in the tree and fallen out.

Gabby squealed, and in that moment, when surprise mixed with fear, her hands started to tingle, to vibrate—to *burn*. She held them in front of her face. They glowed bright white, like the ball she and her friends had seen—had *summoned*—in the shed. They grew brighter with every passing second. Energy surged through every inch of her. She thrummed with power, her hands white-hot. She wanted to scream but could not catch her breath.

Jamie struggled to his feet. "Okay, *ow*. Man. You wouldn't believe what just happened. I—"

She held out her hands. He started to take them, his mouth falling open, his eyes widening.

The energy inside her ramped up, blood rushing in her ears. Her teeth clenched. *God Almighty, I'm gonna spontaneously combust. I'm gonna die in my front yard with Jamie's fart in my nose.* "Help me," she whispered.

Jamie grabbed her shoulders and turned her toward the street. "Point away from the house!" he cried. "Aim at your mailbox!"

Aim? Aim what? He gripped her shoulders, his chest pressed against her back. *Lord, if I explode, don't let me hurt him, or anybody else.* She held her hands out like a sleepwalker in a cheesy movie, sighting down her arms, focusing on the mailbox. The energy kicked up another notch, rattling her brain. Jamie's grip tightened. Pure force pulsed from her toes, her legs, her stomach, flowing into her arms. *Whatever happens, it's gonna blow my hands off. I'll soak the grass like a sprinkler.*

And then, from each hand, a burst of white light shot across the yard, striking the mailbox. It exploded, the bang loud enough to rattle windows six houses down, and flew off its wooden post. The metal clattered on asphalt, misshapen and gnarled like a Coke can someone had crumpled and discarded.

With all that tension and energy released, Gabby fell against Jamie, and they tumbled to the ground.

Porch lights winked on along the street. Curtains in picture windows were pushed aside, and adult faces pressed against glass like little children looking at reptiles in a zoo. In her own house, heavy footsteps thumped across the floor—probably Dad.

And then Gabby was zooming upward, the ground receding, tree limbs slapping her as she passed. She clamped a hand over her mouth to keep from yelling. Jamie's arms had snaked around her waist. Whatever this was, it was happening to him, too. That tingly heat returned everywhere he touched her. They rose until they were near the treetop, and then they settled on a branch and perched like a couple of owls, Jamie's arm around her waist. Gabby felt too stunned to say anything. She looked down.

Her father stomped out the door and into the yard. Neighbors poured out of their houses and gathered around the ruined mailbox, staring at it as if it were a dead body.

Mr. Davison spotted the bikes and looked around. "Gabriella!" he shouted. "Where you at?"

"What the hell happened out here?" someone cried from down the street.

The adults muttered among themselves, but their conversation did not interest Gabby. "How'd we get up here?" she whispered.

They adjusted positions until Jamie's mouth was near her ear, his breath stroking her skin like a feather. A chill ran through her. "I flew us. Wasn't sure it would work, considering how I landed the first time."

"You can *fly*?"

"Apparently. I mean, here we are. But I ain't very good at it. A minute ago, I kinda fell outta the tree."

"And you ain't hurt?"

"No," he said, giving himself a once-over. "I don't guess I am. Not even a scratch. Huh."

"What's happening to us?" she asked, knowing how scared she sounded, hating it. She would not be the weak, wilting-flower girl. She just wouldn't.

But Jamie's hands trembled too.

"I don't know," he said. "We gotta talk to Micah and Christian ASAP. What are you gonna tell your Dad if he asks where you were when the mailbox blew up?"

"No idea," she said.

✳

Christian dragged herself to her feet by bracing on the car fender. She touched her chest through her torn shirt. Her hand came away bloody. The bike still lay in the street. No one had come along and run over it or checked to see if she were still alive. *Feels like I just went five rounds with an MMA heavyweight. And I still gotta get home. Or to a hospital. Or a nuthouse.* She staggered back to the bike and picked it up and walked it down the street, wincing with every step. No one passed by or looked out their windows.

Man, you could get killed on this road, and nobody would notice. Or maybe somebody did look out, and when they saw it was me, they just let me lay there. Who cares, right? It's just the dyke.

She gave two or three houses the finger. Her back wheel squeaked. She had been meaning to oil it for two weeks now.

"I wonder if the others felt—whatever that was," she said to the bike, which answered in its shrill language.

She got on and pedaled, leaning low over the handlebars, trying to ignore the pain in her lower back and right shoulder. The squeaks increased in frequency and pitch, as if a hyperactive kid were jumping on an old bed. On the road far ahead, someone backed out of their driveway and then accelerated away from her, their taillights glowing. She pedaled faster, the car a marker of progress. She needed to get home. Who knew how long she had slept?

Her legs ached. Breath tore in and out of her lungs.

And then the pain coursing through her faded. She began to tingle, to *vibrate*, as if she were a tuning fork someone had struck. Everything sharpened into focus—the blades of grass in the yards, the leaves in the trees, the smell of the car's rubber tires and its carbon monoxide, the bike's wheel squeaking in time with her pedaling. She moved faster and faster and gripped the handlebars so tightly her fingers sank through the rubber handgrips and into the metal. *What the hell? Oh, shit. Oh, damn.* Houses and trees flew by in comic-book speed lines. She gained on the car, passed it, blew through stop signs and out of the residential areas, hit the highway, turned right. The bike slid out from under her. As it went over, she stepped off neatly, as if she had done it on purpose, and began to *run*.

Scenery flew by—houses on residential streets, trees along the rural roads, cars on the highways. She wove through traffic, tore down straightaways, hurdled potholes in great sailing leaps that felt a little like flying.

She circled town twice, three times, before she slowed and thought about where she was going.

Home. Run home.

She skidded to a stop in her front yard on Hickory Street. Her passing generated wind sufficient to bend small trees and shake leaves and acorns and hickory nuts out of larger ones. Her shoes and clothing seemed intact, except for what she had damaged in the bike wreck. She pulled her tattered shirt away from her body; the cuts and scrapes already seemed to be healing. They no longer hurt. Hell, she wasn't even tired. She had tapped something deep inside herself. Was this what the Flash felt, or Quicksilver? She had never thought running sounded like much of a superpower—lame when compared to flight, super-strength, walking on walls, traveling in outer space, or invulnerability. Now it felt like the best thing in the world.

It must have been the glow-ball. If comic books and sci-fi movies hadn't lied to her, she should have died, but her trauma had ignited powers instead. *Would* this kill her? For all she knew, she had been exposed to radiation that would turn her to a puddle of goo in days.

But before it did, she would *run.*

Still, the sensory overload was driving her to her knees—the feel of the imperfections in the soil under her shoes, how every speck of dirt on Mom's car stood out in sharp relief against the paint, the smells of food and earth and bird shit.

"Stop it," she whispered, squeezing her eyes shut. "Just stop. Ease up."

After a moment, she risked opening her eyes. The night looked normal, the sounds and smells and textures only so much background. Thank God.

Her phone beeped. If she walked inside right now, she would make curfew.

You don't really wanna go inside. You want to do all that again.

Yes. But then Mom would ground her. Christian forced herself to stop looking at the road, to stop thinking about how it could take her anywhere. The pull of it was almost physical. She wanted to zoom down it more than she had ever wanted anything in her life.

Instead, she walked up the driveway—slowly, so damn slowly—and went inside.

✳

Micah still sat outside the storage building, looking through the hole in the wall. The site of their LARP now lay deep in shadow. *Except we should have just called it Live Action, because that wasn't no damn Role Play. That book has power. Real power. And we saw what only one of its spells can do.* It had seemed like little more than a light show, sure, complete with scary-looking silhouettes, but still—it was only *one*. What might happen if he could talk the others into trying out the rest of the spells, or rituals, or whatever they were? Maybe they could summon an alien-demon thingy to roast Kenneth or Gavin.

And if the others wouldn't agree, he might just have to try by himself.

He stood. It was still warm, even with the wind, but fall would soon come to southeast Arkansas. Parents would rake leaves into piles that little kids would dive into, forcing the grown-ups to do the work all over again. The grass would turn yellow. Neanderthals in shoulder pads and helmets would chase a berth in the state playoffs, which, for them, would be the most important goal on earth. Neighbors would hang cheesy Halloween decorations. Then Thanksgiving, where people who could barely stand each other would pretend to be happy while eating dry turkey and those crummy casserole dishes full of sweet potatoes topped with marshmallows. Christmas would descend on America like an avalanche, with moms fist-fighting over the last Movie Star Barbie or whatever little girls played with these days. Then the truly cold weather would set in—not Siberia cold or even Minnesota cold, but too cold for Micah, who hated winter weather even worse than he hated Kenneth and his dumb-as-rocks friends.

Micah couldn't stop the weather, but maybe the book would help him with the Neanderthals—even if, at first, he had been pretty sure it would kill him. All that pain, the convulsions, the sickening feeling his insides were moving, like a xenomorph had hatched in his chest.

Once the pain had subsided enough for Micah to sit up, he had taken a few moments to gather his wits, catch his breath, and feel reasonably certain he wouldn't explode. He had wanted to go back and get the book. Kenneth might double back and steal it. After all, Del Ray had seen what it could do, and even if he wouldn't initially believe his own eyes, even a dumbass like him would grow curious. Micah had to hide it, along with anything else that looked halfway valuable, powerful, or just plain cool.

But every time he took a step toward the shed, his legs refused to go any further, no matter how much he mentally shouted at them. Perhaps they had more sense than the rest of him. The logic centers in his brain suggested that going back in there, touching that book and its creepy cover again, might be lunacy, at least without the others around to pull him out of any trouble.

And then there was what had happened to his senses. Micah had barely restrained himself from tasting the grass. The Earth moved beneath him, its rotation a tangibility he would not have believed in had he read it in a comic book. A blackbird took flight from a nearby tree. He could see each individual feather, hear them rustling, sense the bird's heart beating. If his mother had walked outside, she probably would have accused him of being high and grounded him for the rest of his life, because he couldn't stop staring, cocking his head to listen, sniffing like he had the worst cold ever.

He had figured out how to stop it, but now he wondered if he could also bring it back.

Micah braced his feet shoulder-width apart and balled his hands into fists. Then he closed his eyes and concentrated. And in a moment, the sheer power and variety of the world struck him again. He opened his eyes. Now the shapes of things in the shed, their textures and details, their minutiae—the flecks of rust on the lawn mower, the undulating cobwebs in the corners—seemed as clear as a summer day viewed through a clean window.

If he stared long and hard enough, could he see molecules?

Then, from somewhere near his waist, light emanated. He raised his hands to eye level.

His right hand glowed bright red.

He concentrated. Energy flowed into his clenched fist, which shone brighter and brighter. Wavy heat lines rose from it, as if he were a roaring fire. On a hunch, he reached down and grabbed a stick.

It burst into flame.

Micah pumped his other fist in the air. "Yes!"

Then he paused, staring at his left hand.

It glowed, too, but it had turned a deep blue. He grabbed another stick with that hand. Ice crystals raced up the wood until a thick frost covered it. And yet his hand felt normal.

Holy shit, *this is cool. Scary, but cool.*

One more thing to try. He dropped the sticks, letting the one burn and the other thaw. With his right hand, he gestured at a dead branch. Energy flowed into his arm, and he *pushed* it, flicking his wrist.

Fire flew from his hand and set the branch ablaze.

Micah whooped.

He flicked his left wrist at the branch. A rope of pure ice shot from his fingers, across the yard, and onto the flames, extinguishing them. The ice's back-trail fell and shattered. Smoke curled from the limb and dissipated into the night.

He could make fire and ice. With his *hands*.

Micah grinned. He laughed. Then he shivered. He had never felt so awesome, or so alone. Had anything happened to the others?

He would text them. They would talk. Maybe they would even help him figure out what to do about the shed.

But first, he strode into the shed and picked up the book.

✻✱✻

Kenneth awoke the next morning at six when his phone's alarm blared. *Hell*, he thought. *Didn't I set that for Monday through Friday? I bet Gavin changed it just to mess with me.*

When he touched his screen to silence the phone, his finger smashed through it, all the way to his last knuckle, and struck his side table so hard the top cracked down the middle.

Kenneth sat up, wide awake. He had barely tapped the button. If he had struck it any harder, he would have splintered the table into kindling.

First the bed, now the phone. What's next? I sit on the toilet and crash through to the floor? Mom's gonna kill me.

Someone pounded on the door. "Kenneth," his mother called. "What was that crash? Did you fall out of bed again?"

"No, Mom, *God*!"

His mother harrumphed, but her footsteps faded down the hall.

He yanked the phone off his finger and stuffed its remains under his mattress. Then he grabbed a dirty shirt from the floor and tossed it over the table. The shirt bunched up along the crack. *That looks horrible. Dammit. Maybe I can blame it on Gavin. Mom's caught him sitting on it a hundred times.*

Just yesterday, he had known every possibility inherent in his grip strength. Now it was like he had woken up with someone else's hands—maybe Superman's. Or what was the name of that guy in the superhero movie all the geeks loved—the one with the big-ass glove that could destroy the world?

I can't think of anybody but comic-book characters. Like I'm one of those freaks. If Gavin and Brayden knew, I'd never hear the end of it.

He sat back on his bed in a pool of morning light diluted through the white curtains his mother had hung last month. What was he supposed to do now?

CHAPTER TEN

At lunch on Monday, Jamie sat at one of the campus picnic tables, this one located under a walnut tree near the building's south end, well away from any others. Gabby sat beside him. Micah and Christian had taken the other side. The group had staked its claim to this table on the first day of school, and no one had seemed interested in challenging their squatters' rights yet. All four of them pulled out their sack lunches. Then they passed around ham sandwiches and chips and Ziploc bags full of cookies until everyone had what they wanted. They ate in silence until, suddenly, everyone spoke at once.

Christian stood and held up her hands. "Wait a minute. *Wait a minute!*" she yelled. Everyone quieted down. Then she gestured to Jamie.

"Okay, so we all know what happened on Friday night after everybody went home," he said as Christian took her seat again. They had texted all weekend. Even though Jamie had flown, and despite having seen what Gabby had done to her family's mailbox, he still couldn't believe Christian had super-speed or that Micah could create fire and ice from his hands. "Any ideas what we do now?"

"I say we meet up after school and test ourselves," Micah said as they threw their garbage in the green can nearby. "If we can lock down these powers, we could totally rule this town."

Gabby shook her head. "For all we know, they could be killing us from the inside. Shouldn't we, I don't know, tell our parents or something?"

Micah groaned and threw his hands up. "Our *parents*? Are you nuts? They're the last people we should tell."

"I think Micah's right, at least for now," Jamie said. "They'd freak out. We need to figure out what we can do before we show anybody else, if we ever do."

"But shouldn't we go to the doctor and make sure we won't, I don't know, grow a second set of heads?" Gabby asked. "Or get cancer or whatever?"

"It hurt when it first happened, but I've felt great ever since," said Christian. "I think we should wait on the whole doctor thing, too. If somebody gets sick or turns into a giant spider, then we can talk about a doctor."

"Fine," said Gabby, her tone and expression suggesting that nothing was anywhere close to fine. She crossed her arms and looked away.

Jamie squeezed Gabby's shoulder. Low-grade fear wafted off her; he could almost smell it. And he had begun to notice how often the others shot down her ideas. Sooner or later, they would need to address that.

"Four o'clock," Jamie said. "At that old pavilion on the back side of the park. Nobody goes back there but joggers, and there ain't many around except early in the morning or late afternoon. Be careful. We don't want people knowing we're there."

"Not much room back yonder," said Micah. "Just the sidewalk and a bunch of trees."

"Well, we can't do it at the football field," said Christian. "I think the team would notice."

Micah shrugged. "Okay. Whatever."

"Four o'clock," Jamie repeated. "And remember—be careful."

Everyone grew quiet. They sat there for a while longer, waiting on the bell that would signal the end of lunch. Jamie spotted Kenneth Del Ray as he walked past them into the building, apparently lost in his own thoughts. And it hit Jamie that Kenneth had been in the shed, too.

Kenneth wasn't listening as the teacher wrote notes on the board and lectured about some war that happened in a country a million miles away. Brayden and Gavin sat on opposite sides of him, but he had not so much as looked at either of them. He was thinking about the crushed furniture, the figures he had seen in the light, the pain. The broken rail, the busted phone, the cracked table. It all added up to a big pile of shit for Kenneth, yet those four geeks had walked into school today, chatting each other up like nothing had happened. Thinking about them drifting through their lives while his guts could be liquefying made him sick. He wanted to turn their faces into meat sauce.

The teacher droned on and on, his voice like a mosquito, handwriting like a drunk third grader's.

Gavin tossed a note onto Kenneth's desk. Kenneth took it, held it in his lap, and unfolded it. *I've been texting you. Where's your phone? What's up with you today?*

Kenneth refolded the note and tossed it on Gavin's desk without replying.

"Fine," Gavin whispered, palming the paper. "Be that way."

Let Gavin get mad. Kenneth had other things on his mind. If only he could tell someone about what had happened, but every time he thought about talking to Brayden or Gavin, his throat constricted. They would think he was crazy, or worse—that the geeks had infected him with their bullshit. If that happened, he had no doubt that Brayden and Gavin would turn on him. It made him want to punch *them*, too. But if he punched anybody, they might end up like his alarm clock, like his bedside table. And then he would go to jail.

Assuming the cops could hold him.

When the bell rang, he gathered his books and dashed out, well ahead of his friends. He felt like an outsider, an outcast.

A freak.

After school, as Kenneth lay on his bed and thought about his situation, someone knocked on the front door. He turned up Slipknot, in no mood for visitors. No one else would answer because his parents were at work. But the pounding continued. He could even hear it over the music. "Son of a bitch," he muttered, rolling off the bed. He stomped through the house, grumbling under his breath, and yanked the door open.

Brayden and Gavin stood there, grinning at him, but when they saw his expression, their smiles faded. They looked at each other.

"Hi," Gavin said.

"Hi?" Kenneth said. "I didn't answer because I'm busy. Can't you guys take a freaking hint?"

Brayden looked offended. "Hey, man. You're the one that told us to come over here."

Kenneth blinked. "What are you talking about? I barely said two words to you all day."

"Last *week*," Gavin said. "You told us to come over the first day both your parents were gone so we could map out some plans to mess with those geeks."

Kenneth stared at them. They stared back. Brayden grinned again, apparently unsure of what else to do.

"Sorry," Kenneth finally said. "I can't deal with this now. I got stuff on my mind."

"Okaaay," said Gavin. "Guess we'll head to my house and play some *Jungle Raider*."

"Whatever," Kenneth said, and he shut the door in their faces.

Brayden called him a dick. Gavin laughed. Kenneth pulled the curtains back just enough to show a slice of the road. A few seconds later, Gavin and Brayden pulled out of the driveway on their bikes. Gavin gave Kenneth's house the finger. Then they were gone.

Kenneth let the curtain fall back in place and went back to his room, where he lay on his bed. He stared at the ceiling, at his football picture from eighth grade hanging crooked over his dresser. His mother must have been drunk or half asleep when she drove the nail. The picture slanted at least twenty degrees to starboard.

He closed his eyes and thought about his life, how it had changed, what might happen next. He could not tell Gavin and Brayden about the shed, the pain, the bedrail. He could not tell his parents; they would lose their shit. He could not tell the guys on the football team. Besides, no one would believe him unless he showed them. And if he did that, he might as well join the circus, because he would well and truly be a freak. He could not even ask the geeks about it, because for two-thirds of his life, he had gone out of his way to make them miserable. They brought it on themselves, with their stupid comic books and role-playing games. What would people like that think "help" meant—calling the Justice League?

Kenneth found himself fighting back tears. He had not cried since the second grade when he skinned his knee on the sidewalk. But he knew why he felt so sad now. For the first time in his life, he was completely, totally alone.

CHAPTER ELEVEN

That afternoon, Jamie and the others met in the park by the old swing sets they had all played on when they were little. Cracked rubber seats hung from rusty chains. Gabby sat in one, swinging in a short arc, dragging her feet in the bare spots generations of little kid feet had worn in the ground. After a while, they all walked to the paved path that circled the park. They followed the walk until they reached the pavilion on the far side of the pond. Eight picnic tables sat in two rows on a concrete slab. Wood columns that had been sunk into the concrete braced up the gabled roof. Underneath, cobwebs and a bird's nest hung in exposed rafters. Birds had spattered the table underneath with splotches of white. Beyond the pavilion, in a clearing amid the park's trees, sat another old swing set, some rusting monkey bars, and a tall slide that had been buffed by years of weather and kids' asses. Three grills' metal bases were set in concrete that was buried in the ground. Weeds and briars partially obscured the path down to the water, where a couple of ducks and one white goose floated several yards offshore.

For a while, no one spoke. They stood next to the pavilion and looked at each other, unsure how to start.

"Who wants to go first?" Jamie asked. No one said anything. Micah shrugged. Jamie sighed. "Fine. One of these days, one of y'all needs to take charge of something."

He stepped away from them and concentrated. For a moment, nothing happened. Then, slowly, his feet rose off the ground. He hovered a foot or so above the sidewalk, grinning.

"Wow," said Christian.

"Big deal," said Micah. "You can make yourself a foot taller. What else you got?"

Jamie frowned. Anger flashed inside him, and, at that moment, he zoomed upward as if fired from a cannon. He yelled in surprise as he smashed through tree branches, frightening birds and squirrels, and careened past the canopy, arms and legs flapping as if he were having a seizure.

Oh shit oh shit

A blackbird flew past him. He soared up and up, shivering as the air grew colder, goose bumps breaking out on his arms. Below him, the park, the pavilion, his friends looked as small as toys.

I'm gonna keep going until the air gets too thin, and then I'm gonna pass out and fall and when I hit they'll have to pick me up with a sponge—oh shit.

The others were yelling and waving their arms. They were so small. Jamie could not make out the words. He couldn't tell which one was Gabby. He would never see her again. They had touched, and he had felt something loosen in his chest, and now he would never get to know what might happen between them, never get to touch her hand again, never get to hold her—

Stop it! You wanna see her again? Make it happen. Do it now.

He closed his eyes, took five deep breaths, and counted to ten, once on each inhale, once on the exhale. As he did so, he visualized the park. Then he was plunging downward, headed straight for the trees.

This ain't better, oh shit it's worse it's worse

A scream welled in his throat.

Stop it. Don't panic, or you'll smash into the ground like a meteorite.

He pictured a car braking. A boat sputtering up to a dock. A feather floating down on the breeze. And his descent slowed. He eased down through the trees and came to rest in almost the exact same spot he had left. Christian and Micah had paled. Gabby bit a fingernail and drummed one heel up and down. Trembling, Jamie tried to smile.

"Now *that* was cool," Micah said, starting to regain some color. "Can you go forward and backward?"

Still floating, Jamie crossed his arms and flew backward along the sidewalk until he rounded a bend. Then he flew back, much faster this time, stopping again in the same spot.

"I think I'm getting the hang of this," he said. "But I gotta get better at turning it on and off. Every time I get a little mad or scared or upset, I zoom away like a dadgum rocket." He wiped sweat from his forehead as he settled back to the ground. "Concentration's the key. And, like, feelings. Until we get used to this stuff, we gotta keep ourselves under control."

Christian laughed. "Sure. No problem. Mom's always telling me how us teenagers are full of hormones and weird moods, but I guess we can just chill, all the time."

Jamie ignored her. "I feel like I could eat a horse. Anybody got a candy bar or something?"

Nobody did. Jamie sighed.

Micah stepped forward. "I'll go next. That okay with y'all?"

Christian gestured for him to proceed.

Gabby shrugged. She still looked troubled.

Jamie went to her and nudged her. "I'm okay."

She turned to him and smiled, but she did not look convinced.

Micah picked up a pine cone. He held it up in his right hand. Then he knitted his brows and clenched his teeth. For a moment, nothing happened.

"What's he supposed to be doing?" Christian asked.

"He looks constipated," Gabby said.

Then the pine cone started to crackle. A wisp of smoke curled from the top. Then it burst into flame. Everyone cried out and stepped back. Micah held the cone aloft in his hand. "Ta-da!"

"Holy shit," Jamie said. He stepped forward and squinted against the heat and light, trying to get a good view of Micah's hand. It seemed to be unharmed.

"You look like the Statue of Liberty," said Christian.

"Or the Human Torch," Gabby said.

Then the flame shot down Micah's arm all the way to his shoulder. He yelped and dropped the pine cone. Christian leaped forward and stomped on it, likely worried about the fire spreading to the grass. Micah waved his arm back and forth. The fire went out. Oddly, his shirt hadn't even been singed.

"Oops," he said.

"Oops?" Gabby cried. "*Oops?*"

"Chill," Micah said, frowning at Gabby. "It didn't hurt. I was just surprised." He moved past Christian and picked up the pine cone again, this time in his left hand. His brow furrowed, and frost formed on the cone, sparkling in the afternoon light. As solid ice grew from the base of the cone, covering it, Micah grinned. He dropped it onto the sidewalk, where it shattered. Christian stared, open-mouthed. Micah slapped her on the back, laughing, but she roared in surprise and turned in circles, swatting at her back. Micah stepped away, looking bewildered, as Jamie and Gabby tried to grab Christian. They finally managed to make her keep still and found an icy handprint on her shirt. The cloth had frozen to her skin.

"Can you do anything about this?" Jamie asked Micah.

"Yeah, just give me a second," said Micah, holding out his right palm.

"No!" Christian yelled. "He's liable to burn me alive!"

"Just hold still, you big baby," Micah said, heat waves emanating from his hand. "I'm getting better."

"Get away from me!" shouted Christian.

She ran, Micah pursuing her with hands outstretched. They made it perhaps ten yards. Then Christian seemed to disappear, her passage marked by a loud whooshing sound and a rooster tail of dead leaves and pine straw.

Micah ran several more steps until he realized he had no one to chase. Then he turned back to Gabby and Jamie. "Well," he said, "I guess she wasn't kidding about what she can do."

That whooshing noise again, and Christian stood between Gabby and Jamie, grinning.

"Like I said: I'm fast," she said.

"Duh," Jamie said, and then the debris field from Christian's sprint caught up with her and splatted against their backs—more pine straw and leaves, trash and dead flower petals, one very confused squirrel. Everyone brushed detritus from their clothes. Jamie took Christian by the shoulders and turned her around. The frost handprint was gone. "Huh. Either you burned it away, or you healed."

"That leaves you, Gabby," Micah said.

"I don't know," she said, crossing her arms. "Last time I did this, I blew up our mailbox."

"You gotta show us," Christian said. "Or we can't help you get better. And it ain't like there's anybody back here to hurt."

"Yeah," said Micah. "Just do like I did. Pick a target."

Gabby looked at the ground.

Jamie laid a hand on her shoulder. "I believe in you," he said. "You can do this."

"I know I can do it," Gabby said. "We just can't *undo* it if I screw up."

"We got your back," Micah said. "Come on. Don't hold out on us."

Now Jamie hugged Gabby. She stiffened, probably surprised, but then she wrapped her arms around him. "I don't wanna hurt anybody."

He let her go and looked into her eyes. "You don't have to do anything you don't wanna do. But they're right. We got you."

Gabby considered this for a moment. Then she set her jaw, stepped forward, and pointed to a tree several yards away. "See that really long limb that sticks out over the sidewalk? Watch it." Jamie stood behind her and put his palms flat against the backs of her shoulders. The others backed away. Gabby clenched her fists and held them parallel to each other, perhaps six inches apart. At first, not much happened, but after a moment, a crackling sound, like static electricity. Some sort of force waves began to flutter between Gabby's fists. Then they hovered around her arms, wavering like heat from asphalt.

The waves pooled out from her fists and mixed, seemed to solidify, and ripped through the air. When the energy struck the limb, it exploded, raining wood fragments everywhere. Everyone whooped and pumped their fists.

"What happens if you try to blow up the whole tree?" Micah asked, grinning.

"I don't know," said Gabby. "I'll try to give it a little more oomph."

"I don't think that's such a good—" began Jamie, but Gabby fired another bolt, this time at the tree trunk. With an ear-splitting crash, the tree disintegrated. So did a long line of trees behind it. Wood and dust and leaves fell everywhere. The group covered their heads with their hands, Gabby staring at the long swath cut into the forest with wide and frightened eyes.

"Oh, *shit*," she cried.

Jamie ran for the trail Gabby had carved in the woods, the others close on his heels. A line of jagged stumps marked the beam's passing, the ground covered in shattered limbs, leaves, and wood dust a foot deep. Picking their way through this wreckage, they followed the path of destruction until they came to the road. Across it, in the parking lot of the Arkansas Scenic Hotel, a smoking, misshapen hulk sat in a parking space. From the sheer size, Jamie figured it had been somebody's SUV.

People poked their heads out of their doors and looked around the lot. Some trotted onto the walkway and talked among themselves, gesturing at the wreck.

"My car!" one man cried as he ran down a stairwell.

"Gabby, just how much 'oomph' did you try to give it that time?" asked Jamie.

"Not *that* much," she said. "It was like I went from pushing an empty shopping cart to pushing a full one. But it wasn't like trying to move a car or whatever."

"So you could have done more if you wanted," Jamie said. His stomach flip-flopped.

"Yeah," Gabby said. "A lot more."

"We gotta jet before somebody spots us," Christian said.

"No problem for you, Road Runner," said Micah.

"Shut up," Christian said. "Let's go, y'all."

They backed into the woods, turned, and trotted parallel to the path. Jamie wondered how the others would have answered the question he had asked Gabby. He hadn't put anywhere near full effort into his flight demonstration, either. What could Micah do if he really tried—set the whole park on fire? The whole town? The world? Could his ice generation help the Arctic? Could Christian run across the ocean, like the Flash used to do?

"Hey," he said. "Is anybody else, you know, stronger than before?"

The others stopped and looked at him. Everyone nodded. Jamie swallowed hard and felt as if someone had replaced his spine with an icicle.

✳✳✳

Micah grew closer and closer to owning a brand-new punch in the nose. Christian just wanted to eat her Quarter Pounder with Cheese and think, but Micah would. Not. Shut. *Up.*

"I'm telling y'all, now's our chance," he said, ignoring his McNuggets. "They've treated us like shit our whole lives, and we ain't done nothing about it. Christian was the only one who ever fought back, but she was always outnumbered. Not anymore. Now we got the power to stand up. I say we use it."

Christian shoveled more burger into her mouth, trying to keep her expression neutral. Several times over the years, she had suggested catching each of the Bros alone and jumping them. It might have done no good; it might have changed her life and those of her friends. But no one, including Micah, had been willing to step up. Now that he had a power—one he couldn't control all that well—he had found his guts. That wasn't bravery. But she could also understand the sentiment. If anybody deserved to get punked out, it was those three.

Gabby just slurped her shake. No surprise there. Gabby had always struck Christian as the least hot-headed person in town.

Jamie stared at his fries as if he had discovered a secret code in the patterns of salt. "I don't like this kind of talk," he muttered.

"Come *on*," Micah whined. "You wanna sit there and tell me you ain't thought about it? We could make those jerks wear their asses for hats!"

"Dude, what does that even *mean*?" Christian said. Micah had never thrown a punch in his life. Hell, he didn't even watch MMA.

"Ahhh," said Micah, sitting back in his chair, disgusted.

They ate in silence for a while. Half a dozen people approached the counter, got their orders, sat down. On the TV mounted above one of the corner tables, a cable news show played clips from the president's latest speech.

Finally, Gabby finished her shake and pushed the cup away. "I agree with Micah."

Christian almost dropped her cup. She would have been more surprised if Gabby had climbed on top of their table, stripped naked, and danced, but not *much* more.

Micah leaned forward, grinning.

"You do?" Jamie asked. "You wanna go after B3?"

"I don't wanna hurt nobody," she said. "I wanna be real clear about that. But you remember what they did to me with those water balloons. It's been like that forever. If we can get 'em back, just a little, I say we go for it."

Damn, Christian thought. *I never would have guessed.*

"That's what I'm talking about," said Micah, fist-bumping Gabby.

"We've dreamed about having powers our whole lives," said Jamie. His forehead was wrinkled, his brows furrowed. "But we always pictured ourselves as the heroes. Spider-Man and Superman, even Wolverine and the Punisher. But what you're talking about—it ain't justice or even revenge. It's just petty. Like leaving a bag of burning dog shit on an old man's porch."

"So?" Micah said.

"*So?*" Jamie said. "That's your argument?"

Christian slurped the last of her Coke. "I think it's about time we showed 'em how it feels."

Jamie looked pained. "Not you, too."

"Look," said Micah, stealing one of Jamie's few remaining fries and gesturing with it, "I just wanna scare 'em. Embarrass 'em. Give 'em something to think about next time they wanna harass some poor kid who likes anime. That's all."

Jamie turned to Christian. She shrugged. He shook his head. Then, after a moment, he said, "I'm not saying I'll do it. But what did you have in mind?"

Micah grinned.

Christian took the rest of Jamie's fries, keeping her face blank even as her heart pounded. Her blood sang. Finally, after all these years, the others were ready.

CHAPTER TWELVE

The dark figure stood under the trees. His name was Na'ul, and among his own kind, he was a prince. And he hungered.

He watched the dwelling across the stone thoroughfare, hoping to spot the young sack of guts he had followed the night he had fallen through the dimensional portal into this strange world. The youngling had smelled delicious—like the meat back home, but also exotic, as if cured in spices heretofore undiscovered. So far, the child had not ventured out after nightfall, but Na'ul could wait. This youngling, he believed, should be taken before the others present that night, because he was so much bigger, and so much darker inside—darker, at least, than all but one, who would taste even better. Prince Na'ul knew pain—the pleasure that could be taken in doling it out, the way it transformed the taste of blood from everyday staple to delicacy. He wanted to draw that pain out, deepen it, make it last. Having fasted for days, he could not afford to wait forever, but if the fates were kind, he would consume this boy soon. And Na'ul had always gotten what he wanted. He had never been the largest creature on his planet, nor the most powerful, but his lord father had always praised his resourcefulness, his patience, his intelligence. No one hunted like the prince. Sooner or later, the boy would die. And then Na'ul would eat the rest of this world's creatures, one by one.

But hunger had ever been an irresistible master, even to the royal family of the Go'kan. As the day wore on into night, Na'ul's appetite grew, raged. And so, when the door to another dwelling along this road opened and a different boy-child emerged, Na'ul pulled himself into the trees and clambered to the topmost branches, gripping the trunk and the limbs with all four hands, balancing his weight.

Below, the boy-child opened another aperture in his lodge—this one larger, revealing a cave filled with oddities—and brought forth a lean two-wheeled vehicle. He balanced himself on the seat and gripped two metal bars rising from the core and branching in opposite directions, and then he propelled the vehicle forward.

On Na'ul's world, wheels were carved from wood or polished bone. These seemed made of some pliable substance. Curious.

The boy drove onto the road. He would pass directly below.

Na'ul released the tree and plummeted to the ground, contorting around the branches as he fell. And as the boy-child passed near the tree, the prince landed, leaped, and crushed the youngling's shoulders under enormous cloven hooves.

The vehicle crumpled beneath them like paper. Sounds like tree branches snapping emanated from the boy-child's body. He screamed, but Na'ul shoved a huge clawed hand over his mouth. The sound that escaped would not have disturbed the birds nesting one tree over.

The prince rose to his full eight-foot height as he picked up the boy and held him at eye level. Then Na'ul's mouth yawned open. He closed it around the child's head and let him scream for half a second, then clamped down on the neck, severing major arteries with his many incisors. Vertebrae cracked and exploded. The boy's scream faded and the body went limp, and as blood flowed into Na'ul's gullet like wine, he skittered back up the tree, carrying his victim in one arm. He paused three-fourths of the way up and finished his meal.

The strange vehicle lay on the street, bent horribly, one wheel spinning.

CHAPTER THIRTEEN

Two days later, after school, Gabby, Micah, and Jamie stood in a copse, putting on their robes plus some cheap ski masks they had bought at Walmart. As superhero costumes went, the robes and masks weren't much, but they would do for now, assuming the three jocks were nearby.

Micah and Gabby had followed B3 to the pavilion, which sat thirty yards away—the same secluded one Gabby and her friends had used as a training base. She wasn't entirely sure why she had come. Maybe Micah picked her for the mission because she'd been the first to agree with him back in McDonald's, or maybe he just thought she was the least likely to get in his way. *And he'd be right, I guess. If the whole school uses the four of us for doormats, I'm the one that gets the muddiest. Why do people hate me so much?*

Under the pavilion, Brayden Sears burst into laughter, bringing Gabby out of her own head.

After B3 had settled on a table, Micah had texted Christian, who DMed Jamie. Christian's mom had slowed her down at home, so Jamie got there first, stowing his bike somewhere in the woods and floating over to Gabby and Micah. Ever since, Jamie had been whispering a list of the five million ways this could go wrong. Micah kept waving him off. Jamie looked to Gabby for support, but she pretended to watch B3 closely. If anyone was going to chicken out today, it would not be her. She had spent her whole life holding back, following rules, being nice. Today, she would try something new.

A stiff breeze, a smattering of leaves, and Christian stood beside them, holding her robe and mask. Micah slipped his costume on. Gabby leaned against a tree, trying to adjust her mask. Her hair kept sticking out of the eye holes. Jamie helped her fix it. She smiled. "We look stupid. Like bank robbers who just came from a Harry Potter convention."

Jamie laughed and turned away. Gabby's smile disappeared. Jamie was fretting like somebody's dad. Usually that was her job. It felt good to let go for once. At the same time, watching Jamie undergo a low-key freak-out made her feel like shit. Maybe that was just life; no feeling could ever just be itself because it was inextricably tied to a dozen others.

Micah bounced up and down on the balls of his feet. "Come *on*. Hurry up. They might leave any time."

"Fine," Jamie said. "Let's go make fools of ourselves."

Micah grinned, but with the mask, he looked demented.

He turned and led the others toward the pavilion, skirting from tree to tree. As usual, this part of the park was deserted except for the four of them and—hopefully appearing for today only!—B3. They crept toward the clearing until Micah signaled them to stop in the trees near the pond. Everyone spread out and watched Gavin and Brayden scarf pizza. Kenneth sat farther away, silent. What was wrong with him?

"Okay. Everybody remember my plan?" Micah whispered.

"Yeah, yeah," muttered Christian. "Gabby freaks 'em out. You and Jamie corral 'em. I do the rest."

"That's right," said Micah.

Gabby did not like the wild look in his eyes. *Maybe I should stop this after all, before something bad happens.*

Then Micah nudged her past the trees.

B3 looked up. Gavin put down his slice of pizza. Brayden stared at her, mouth open. He looked even dumber than usual.

Oh, screw it.

Gabby ran to the swing set and raised her hands. "Hey, y'all."

The three boys seemed puzzled.

Micah burst from the woods and broke toward the slide as Kenneth,

Gavin, and Brayden stepped out from under the pavilion. They were six or seven yards from Gabby, who gestured at them like a crossing guard, demanding they stop. She wanted to turn and run, hide, slink back home like she always had whenever B3 had come after her.

But this time, she and the others had started this. She couldn't run, even though a voice inside her head kept insisting. *Get out before they punch you! Are you crazy?*

"What are you supposed to be?" Brayden sneered.

That's a good question, Gabby thought. Then she lowered her voice. "Your worst nightmare," she said, and winced, realizing how cheesy she sounded.

"Come on," Gavin said to his friends. "Let's go pull that mask off."

Kenneth hung back, but Brayden and Gavin stepped toward Gabby. Gavin led the way, cracking his knuckles. Brayden trailed a couple of steps behind, half smiling, like it was all a game. But the look on Gavin's face suggested that if he reached Gabby, he might do a lot more than take off her mask.

Don't let him get that close. Do something.

But what if she hurt them? What if she killed them? Or what if she pointed at them and nothing happened at all? What if—

Gavin was five feet away.

Do something!

Gabby clenched her fists and fired a force burst at their feet. The shock dug up the ground, spattering Gavin and Brayden with dirt clods, dust, hidden pebbles. Gavin stumbled into Brayden, and they fell in a heap. Then they scrambled to their feet, eyes bugging.

"What was *that?*" Brayden cried, his voice shaking.

Holy shit. He's afraid.

Gabby smiled.

She fired another burst, this one at the ground to their left. Dirt rained everywhere. Gavin and Brayden ran toward the monkey bars in the center of the clearing, which seemed about right, considering they were as dumb as a hunk of metal, and the bars would provide no real cover. *That's right, you turds. Run. Run like you've made us run all these years.* Gabby kept firing just behind them until, looking at her instead of where he was going, Gavin ran full speed into the monkey bars' ladder. Something crunched. He bounced off and skittered to the ground, where he lay prone, moaning. He was bleeding from somewhere—his forehead? His nose?

Gabby stopped and put one hand over her mouth.

Brayden skidded to a halt and turned to Gavin. Micah had not moved from his spot, but now he was doubled over, laughing. Jamie and Christian hadn't come out of the woods.

Up near the pavilion, Kenneth kept silent. He seemed to be scrutinizing Gabby. If he hadn't already figured out who they were, he was probably putting it together now. He finally stepped off the concrete and trotted to his friends.

Micah climbed to the top of the slide and stood there, arms raised like an orchestra conductor.

Is he seriously going ahead with this? "Don't—" Gabby began.

But as Brayden helped Gavin to his feet, Micah gestured toward them. Fire leaped from his right hand and shot to the ground. He made a circular motion, drawing a fiery ring around B3.

"What the—?" Gavin muttered.

"How are you *doing* that, you freak?" shouted Brayden.

Micah laughed at him. Gavin's nose had been mashed sideways. It looked like a *C*. Blood poured from it, soaking his shirt. If Micah noticed, he apparently did not care. "That's right, you idiot," he said. "We're freaks. And we're gonna be the last thing you ever see."

"Screw you!" yelled Brayden. He raised his middle finger, even though he looked terrified.

Micah gestured. The fire crept inward a foot or so. The three boys pressed against each other as Micah made a "come forward" gesture with his free hand.

Jamie burst out of the treetops and circled overhead. Gavin stared at him with dull eyes. Brayden backed up a couple of steps and almost stepped in the fire. He yelped and scooted back to the center of the ring. Jamie zoomed down and over them. They ducked, covering their heads and shouting each time he passed. Then he circled back to the forest.

"Where'd he go?" Brayden yelled, eyes bugging out. "Where'd he go?"

"Chill," Kenneth said, glaring at Gabby.

Jamie flew back out, carrying the box they had brought. It was filled with four dozen eggs. He hovered above Gavin, Brayden, and Kenneth, hurling the eggs at them, striking their heads, their faces, their abdomens. He hit Brayden in the crotch. Kenneth just watched, taking each egg to the face or chest with stoicism. What was up with him, anyway? Gavin, who must have gotten a concussion, looked up with his mouth hanging open, like one of your less intelligent cows.

Micah cawed like a crow and pumped his fist. He gestured at the fire. It vanished, leaving a black, smoking ring around the Bros. Brayden tried to run, but he took only two steps before Christian whooshed by, knocking him back toward Kenneth and Gavin. Brayden looked around wildly. Kenneth grimaced and walked toward the grills. Christian sped by him, only the breeze in her wake marking her passage, and Kenneth stumbled backward.

He regained his balance and moved forward again.

"Forget him!" Micah said, reaching under his robe and taking his phone out of his pocket. "Just get the other two!"

A blur circled Brayden and Gavin. Then it disappeared, leaving the two of them with their pants around their ankles. Gavin wore a pair of bright yellow boxer shorts. Brayden's once-white briefs were stained and full of holes.

"Ewww," Gabby said.

Micah snapped pictures and hooted. "Just wait till everybody in school sees this!"

Then one of the grills from the other side of the clearing, its base covered in concrete that was blackened with soil, sailed by Micah's head and crashed into a tree. He almost dropped his phone and hiked up his robe to jam it into his pocket.

"What the hell?" Gabby said.

Brayden's eyes grew even wider, as if they might pop right out of his skull.

Kenneth ripped a second grill out of the ground, concrete base and all. Metal groaned. He turned to them, pausing, as if undecided about who might look best wearing it on their heads. He threw it at Micah again. Micah dove aside as the grill smashed to the ground where he had been standing. He came up firing, a long ice rope flying across the clearing right at Kenneth, who dodged. The ice rope hit a tree and froze the whole trunk solid, the ice radiating to the limbs, all of which began falling with cracks like rifle blasts.

"Take it easy!" Jamie shouted at Micah.

"I know you, Sterne!" Kenneth called. "I know *all* y'all!"

He picked up a frozen limb and threw it at Gabby. It whirled through the air like a javelin, heading right for her. Something zipped in front of Gabby—Christian again. The limb was gone.

"Kenneth! What—?" said Brayden. But Kenneth had reached the third grill. He uprooted it, metal bending and screaming in his hands. He raised it over his head, but a bolt of fire flashed across the clearing and struck it. The metal instantly turned bright red. Kenneth dropped it, but it seemed more out of instinct than actual pain. He looked at his hands curiously. They weren't burned.

"There, you dick," said Micah.

Kenneth smiled, flexing his hands. "I'm coming for you first, Sterne."

"Bring it, you douche," Micah hissed.

Then someone screamed, high-pitched, like a train whistle.

Somehow, Gavin's hair had caught on fire.

He danced in and out of the charred circle, smacking himself on the head with open palms, howling. Brayden took off his shirt and tried to throw it over Gavin's head.

Jamie flew over and picked Gavin up. Gavin kicked and screamed. The smell of burned hair and eggs made Gabby's eyes water as she watched Jamie carry Gavin fifteen feet out over the pond and drop him. Gavin went under with a sizzling sound and came up sputtering and thrashing. Jamie flew back to shore as the others ran to the water's edge.

Brayden looked like he might be in shock. Kenneth glared at them all, as if wondering how it might feel to mash them like empty aluminum cans. After a moment, he stepped into the pond and went to Gavin. They met in waist-deep water. Together, they waded to shore, Kenneth's arm around Gavin.

Kenneth turned back to those he called freaks. "I know *all* y'all," he repeated through clenched teeth. A vein stood out on his forehead. It looked like he could barely stop himself from bashing everyone in sight.

"Is he okay?" Christian asked Brayden. Gavin's head looked scorched and pinkish.

"What do you *think*?" Brayden snarled, going to Gavin and putting a hand on his back. They walked toward the pavilion. Brayden glanced over his shoulder, as if afraid they would set him on fire, too.

Kenneth stared a hole in Micah for several moments. Gabby sighed and tensed, waiting for the fight to start again. Who would win, with Kenneth this close?

Then Kenneth spat near Micah's feet and walked away. He caught up to his friends and tried to take Gavin by the arm.

Brayden shoved him away. "Get away from him! *You're as big a freak as they are!*"

Kenneth stepped backward, mouth hanging open. He stood there, halfway between Jamie's group and his retreating friends. Brayden and Gavin slowly made their way past the pavilion and out of sight.

"Look," said Jamie, turning to Kenneth. "We didn't mean for it to go this far. All we wanted to do was prank y'all."

"Speak for yourself," said Micah. "The stupid redneck got what he deserved."

"Shut up," hissed Gabby. God, Micah could be a tool.

"We didn't mean to set him on fire, or even break his nose," Jamie said. "We just wanted to pants him."

Kenneth said nothing. His gaze lingered on Micah, who took off the mask and glared right back, defiant and unapologetic.

Kenneth's fists clenched.

Micah's hand started to glow red.

Christian punched Micah in the shoulder. "Enough," she said.

Micah shook his head and muttered something. The glow faded.

"We mean it," said Gabby. "This was messed up. If we had known—"

"Messed up," Kenneth said.

"Look," Christian said. "Those grills you threw—something happened to you, too."

"And I saw your hands," Gabby said. "That red-hot metal didn't hurt you."

"Maybe we should talk," Christian said.

Kenneth snorted. "Yeah, right. You freaks just cost me my best friends. You really think I wanna talk to you?"

"If we're freaks," Micah said with a sneer, "then so are you."

"That's right," said Kenneth. "And now Gavin and Brayden know it."

He walked away. They watched him go. No one knew what to say, except for Micah, who seemed positively cheerful. "I could totally go for a Big Mac. Who's coming?"

CHAPTER FOURTEEN

Kenneth lay on his bed after dark, scrolling on his new phone—and man, had Mom and Dad given him a lot of shit about breaking the old one—when the sirens swelled, louder and louder, until the radio cars' flashing lights strobed through his curtains and the sirens cut off. He scooted over to the window and pushed aside the curtains. Sure enough, what looked like most of the town's police cars had blocked off Royal Del Ray Street. One cop strung yellow crime-scene tape from tree to tree and across the road. *What now?* Kenneth thought. He got up, put on his shoes, and headed outside.

His parents had already joined the growing crowd at the waist-high line of tape. "That the police chief?" he asked.

His father started. "I didn't know you were out here."

"Well, I am. Is that the chief?"

"Yeah. Mark O'Brien. Most of his deputies, too."

Kenneth grunted. The cops stood in a circle around a heaped human form. Had there been a hit and run? Kenneth hadn't heard any kind of thump or squalling tires or a scream, but then, he had dived pretty far inside his own head tonight.

The residents of Royal Del Ray milled and gossiped. Like most neighborhoods in town, Royal Del Ray was sleepy and edging toward poor—asphalt studded with potholes, single-story houses with old aluminum siding or plain white paint, cracked driveways and carports bearing ten-year-old cars or trucks. Everyone here clipped coupons and shopped at Walmart with their circulars in hand and watched Fox News or CNN. Mostly, nothing interesting happened on this street. Mostly.

"You think it's the Hoeper boy?" someone said. Jake Hoeper had been missing for two days, ever since he had left home but failed to show up at his girlfriend's house. Word around the campfire claimed he had probably just bought some bootlegged booze secondhand and then headed out to the woods, though Kenneth had heard that the Hoepers were worried sick.

One of O'Brien's men walked over with a tarp and covered the body. On the very spot where they'd found Jake's bike.

Sergeant Lyman Heck, who had once chased Kenneth and Gavin through the dark streets after he'd spotted them rolling the mayor's house, dashed over to the Joneses' yard and vomited. Then he wiped his mouth on his shirtsleeve and walked back over to O'Brien. "My God," Heck said, loud enough for the crowd to hear. "What could have done this?"

"Done what?" Mr. Jones shouted. "What's going on here?"

O'Brien glanced at Mr. Jones and then looked back at the tarp. The other cops on duty—four of them, not counting Heck or O'Brien, out of the town's eight officers—walked the perimeter, making sure no looky-loos tried to slip under the tape. Meanwhile, the residents of Royal Del Ray gawked. One cop or another wandered over at different times, telling the crowd to scatter—*go on home, folks, nothing to see here*—but the neighbors had only drifted and coalesced and come back.

"Let me through! Let me through! I wanna see him! I wanna know if that's my boy!"

Kenneth turned. Another cop—Kenneth was pretty sure his name was Gillen—struggled to hold back an unshaven, heavyset man with corkscrew salt-and-pepper hair. The man's bathrobe was open, revealing a T-shirt and a ratty pair of boxers over thick and hairy legs. Joe Hoeper, Jake's father. According to Kenneth's mom, Mr. Hoeper had called the police as soon as he found his son's bike.

The cops had given interviews with the *Quapaw City Reporter*, the papers from Parkview and Pinedale, and the *Democrat-Gazette*, in which O'Brien or another representative had explained what they knew and what they had done. After taking statements and concluding the kid had probably not simply run off for an underage drinking spree with his buddies, who were all present and accounted for, the department had put out an Amber Alert, had interviewed people, had searched the woods around town. They had not yet dragged the nearby ponds or the Quapaw River, but Kenneth's dad had expected it to happen in a day or two.

Now O'Brien approached the struggling men and laid a hand on Joe Hoeper's shoulder. He said something that Kenneth could not make out over the rustling of the crowd.

Hoeper stopped fighting Gillen and looked at O'Brien with red, swollen, haunted eyes. "Is it him?" he asked. "Is it my Jacob?"

O'Brien squeezed his shoulder and nodded.

Hoeper's eyes filled with tears. He took a deep breath. And then he shoved O'Brien and Gillen aside and dashed for the body. The cops gave chase and shouted for him to stop, but Hoeper ignored them. Some of the other deputies turned and tried to brace for impact, but he plowed through them like a bowling ball and yanked the tarp aside.

Kenneth looked at the body. And he understood why that cop had blown his chunks all over the Joneses' yard.

The corpse might have been dropped from an airplane—the head canting to one side, the skin as pale as if Jake had lived in a cave for most of his life, the limbs jutting at unnatural angles. Huge puncture wounds ran in a rough circle along the neck. They looked like teeth marks from some kind of large animal. But *what* kind? Nothing in Arkansas could bite like that, unless great white sharks had learned to live on land and found their way here.

Except that ain't true, Kenneth thought. *Whatever did that, I don't think it's from Arkansas, but it's sure enough here. And with what I saw in Sterne's shed that night, those freaks brought it. They called it, and it came. This shit's on them.*

Joe Hoeper stood over his son's broken body, holding the tarp in his meaty hands, breathing deeply as if he had just run a quarter-mile sprint. O'Brien and Gillen reached him, Gillen trying to pull the tarp out of his hands, gently, as if too much force might shatter him like glass.

"You can't be here," O'Brien said, not unkindly. "You're gonna contaminate the crime scene." He nudged Hoeper backward.

Mr. Hoeper seemed to be in shock. He moved like a man who had just woken up from a deep sleep. "My son," he said. "My beautiful boy."

O'Brien handed him off to Gillen, who herded him toward his house, where he would have to tell Mrs. Hoeper that Jake would not be coming home.

Kenneth's mother put a hand on his shoulder. "Get back in the house. You've seen enough."

At most other times, Kenneth would have argued. He hated it when anybody treated him like a kid. But now, having seen what was left of a boy he had known all his life, he agreed with Mom. There was nothing else he wanted to see on Royal Del Ray Street.

CHAPTER FIFTEEN

The next afternoon, Micah and the others stood on the Main Street sidewalk, watching the flurry of activity with growing unease. They had biked up to Pizza of Mind, a rock-'n'-roll-themed restaurant on upper Main, for an afternoon snack and strategy session, but Sergeant Lyman Heck met them in the parking lot. "There's a curfew in effect, kids," he said, wiping sweat from his forehead. His dark brown hair looked like he had stepped out of an old picture from the times when men dumped styling gunk on their heads every day—grease or crude oil or whatever it was. "Anybody under eighteen's gotta be inside no later than eight p.m." Jamie elbowed Micah before he could complain.

With a new sense of urgency, they spent only half an hour in Pizza of Mind. Police cars cruised by every fifteen minutes, which was about how long it took to traverse the town's two main roads on a circuit, assuming you drove the legal limit of thirty-five miles per hour. Store owners were hanging signs in their windows announcing earlier closing hours due to the curfew. Some vehicles were crammed with groceries and practical supplies like batteries and toilet paper.

"God," said Micah. "What do they think, a hurricane's coming? They ain't confined to quarters like we are."

"They're scared," said Jamie. "See, they can't shoot fire outta their hands."

Micah scowled. Jamie could be so damn condescending sometimes. To Micah, at least. He'd never noticed Jamie taking that same sarcastic, superior tone with Gabby or Christian.

"We could help," said Christian.

Everyone looked at her. She was eating one of four slices of pepperoni and black olive pizza she had taken to go. Even more than the rest of them, she seemed to eat all the time now that she had powers.

"What are you talking about?" asked Gabby.

Micah grinned. "She means we could get our robes and masks and hunt down Jake's killer." His blood pumped harder at the thought. What good were superpowers if you didn't have a good villain to fight?

Jamie blinked. "You're saying we should dress up and fight crime. Like we're the Teen Titans."

Christian shook her head. "Naw, man. What would we do in Quapaw City? Beat up litterbugs and folks that drive too fast in a school zone? But in a case like this—well, it seems like we ought to do something."

"Like what?" Jamie seemed both repulsed and intrigued.

"Like Micah said. Look for the killer."

"But we aren't detectives," Gabby said. She looked like she usually did when anybody suggested they do something other than read comics or play Xbox—unsure and about five miles down the road to terrified. Big shock. Micah loved her like a sister—sometimes thought he loved her in other ways—but she was so mousy that she really should have had a little pink tail.

"So?" Christian said.

"We don't know how to look for clues or track people," Gabby said, her forehead still wrinkled. "Wouldn't we pretty much have to trip over the guy before we could do anything?"

"I'm just saying we should try," said Christian. "I mean, let's face it. This could be our fault."

Everyone looked at their shoes or developed a sudden interest in the cars parked a block away. Micah might have argued the point, but if it got the others moving, well, he could accept a little blame.

From down the street, a woman hurried toward them. She wore blue jeans and a T-shirt with the logo of the City Café printed on it. Micah had seen her working there from time to time, bussing tables and taking orders and running the register. She was old, probably around thirty. As she got closer, he noticed her name tag read *Meg*. She approached them and put one hand in her jeans front pocket. Her eyes were red, as if she had recently cried.

"Did y'all know that boy that got killed?" she asked.

"Yes, ma'am," said Christian.

She pulled out a wad of bills and thrust them at Christian, who shifted her three remaining slices to one hand and wiped the other one on her pants. She took the cash, looking at Meg with open curiosity.

"What's this, ma'am?" Jamie asked.

"His family eats at the café about once a week."

"Okay."

"I don't know 'em, but it feels like I do. I heard your school's taking up a collection. Can you donate this for me? Don't worry about giving my name."

"Be glad to," Jamie said as Christian pocketed the bills.

The woman nodded, wringing her hands. Then she turned and walked away, her shoulders shaking. She wiped away a tear. When she reached the City Café, she walked inside.

"That was weird," said Micah.

Jamie turned on him. "Why? She wants to do something nice for a dead kid's family. That makes a hell of a lot more sense than putting on our half-assed costumes and skulking around, hoping we find some footprints or whatever."

"Jesus," Micah said. "It wasn't even my idea."

Gabby sniffled. "That lady probably never knew anybody who got murdered."

"Well, neither did we," said Micah. "Anybody wanna go practice our powers? If we're gonna use 'em, we gotta get better. Especially if we're hunting a killer."

Jamie sighed. Then he shrugged, seemingly resigned. "Fine. I guess we need to do that anyway. But this conversation ain't over. I don't know that we're anywhere near ready for playing Batman with a murderer, or something even worse."

Micah didn't care why Jamie agreed as long as they got to practice, like a real-life X-Force. The better they got at using their powers, the more likely the others would be *willing* to use them. B3 would finally get what they had earned.

✳

Kenneth stood at the window in his darkened room, the curtains draped around him. In stressful times, he had found that watching the quiet street calmed him down. He enjoyed seeing lights come on in some windows and go out in others, dogs trotting from yard to yard, cats climbing trees and lounging on roofs. On cloudy nights, the deeper darkness seemed comforting, but when the moon and stars were out, the ordinary street took on the qualities of something dreamed.

Tonight, though, these sights brought him no comfort. The day had been cloudless, but if the stars were shining now, he could not see them. The neighborhood seemed on fire with headlights. Police cars passed at least every ten minutes. Everyone's porch lights were on, their doors surely locked against whatever had killed Jake Hoeper.

Kenneth pulled his phone out of his pocket. He texted Brayden and waited, and waited, and waited. Nothing. Neither Gavin nor Brayden had texted, called, DMed, or emailed him since that scene in the park. Kenneth checked his social media feeds. Nothing from his friends. He looked up their profiles. They had unfollowed him.

You don't get rid of me that easy, assholes.

He dialed Gavin's number. It broke the usual protocols, but that was how people once used their phones anyway. Might as well go old school.

Gavin answered on the second ring. "What?"

"Hey," Kenneth said. "How's your head?"

"Fine." Gavin sounded both curt and toneless. "What do you want?"

"I just wanna talk to one of my two best friends," said Kenneth, sounding testier than he intended. "Since when is that a crime?"

"I got homework."

"Look—" Kenneth began, but Gavin hung up.

Kenneth tossed the phone onto the bed. He looked out the window again. A cop drove by for the five millionth time that night. Kenneth felt cut off from the whole world, even though he had not been grounded. He had his phone and computer, his bike. In another year or so, he would get his license, and then he could drive wherever he wanted.

But he had never had to live a life without friends. It was lonely and, if he was honest with himself, scary. Even those four freaks had each other. If Gavin and Brayden abandoned him, who would *he* have? What would he do on weekends—drive around town by himself, patrolling empty streets like the cops, who at least got paid for it?

With nothing else to do, Kenneth kept watching the neighborhood, but nothing changed. It seemed like one of those TV shows you followed when you were a kid that, as you grew up, just seemed stupid. But he could not change the channel of his life, so he stood there a while longer until it was time to go to bed.

✳

In a tree across the street, Na'ul sat in the lower branches and watched his prey standing in his dwelling's window. Time and despair had seasoned the blood. Na'ul could smell it. In his father's kingdom, a violent land where his own kind fought a never-ending war against beings not unlike the ones in this world, bipeds with a strong grasp of simple tools and nascent industrial technology, the Go'kan ruled with teeth and violence, ripping life from the lessers whenever it suited them, keeping some in fenced herds, breeding them, allowing them to form their own hierarchies, slaughtering a few each day for food. But the bulk of these sorry beings lived in the wild, in what they imagined to be freedom, pathetically trying to resist the fate to which they had been born. Na'ul's father allowed them their illusions because it kept their spirits high and encouraged them to perpetuate their race, thereby providing more food for the Go'kan. Food, and the pleasure of the hunt.

This world, though—here, the lessers ruled, even though the species had almost no physical defense mechanisms. Their alien blood sufficed, but they presented no challenge. Na'ul wanted more.

If the Go'kan entered this realm, they could eat for centuries.

Na'ul had been standing in a dark field in his own world, fires from a village burning around him, two dead adults at his feet, a youngling cowering between the bodies. Then came a bright light, as agonizing as the accursed daystar, and an interdimensional hole had opened underneath him and swallowed him. He floated in that light, screaming until his throat ached, until the luminous ether coalesced, contracted, and cast him out on the shores of this place, jostled by beings of diverse shape and ravening desires. He had no idea how he would get back to his world, or even if it were possible. Perhaps the five who had witnessed his crossing would know. Perhaps the book he had spotted at their feet held answers, if he could read its language. He would find out at his leisure. The largest youngling, the one he had stalked since that first moment, was undoubtedly their leader. Na'ul would slaughter him, feed on his life and his energy, and then he would take the others, one by one.

He had been the heir to his father's kingdom since killing his older sister in battle. But here was a world he could rule *now*. It had its drawbacks—the bothersome skystar, for instance, so much closer and brighter than anything in his world. He had watched it rise that first morning, amazed and rapt, but its rays seared his skin. Who knew why? He had been forced to seek shelter in the thick trees outside this city before he burst into flame. He could move about, hunt, feed only so long at a time. But with will and cunning, any obstacle could be overcome.

He settled against the tree trunk and bided his time.

CHAPTER SIXTEEN

On Monday, Kenneth slouched toward school, his eyes red and watery. He had not slept well all weekend. Gavin and Brayden sat on the front steps. Whatever they were talking about, it seemed intense. Kenneth took a deep breath and approached. The other groups of kids on or near the steps were engaged in their own conversations, the odd straggler wandering among them and texting or listening to earbuds. No one paid any attention to Gavin and Brayden, which was good. If they rejected Kenneth again, maybe no one would notice.

What would be safe to talk about? What tied the three of them together? Gavin liked hip-hop. Brayden preferred eighties hair metal like Judas Priest and Ozzy Osbourne. Brayden's favorite movie of all time was *300*. Gavin's was *The Goonies*, though he had promised to beat the shit out of anyone who revealed that secret. None of them read much beyond what their classes required, but when they were younger, Gavin had loved the Harry Potter series, and Brayden worshipped Terry Pratchett. As far as TV, Gavin liked reality shows, while Brayden really got into procedurals like *NCIS: Broken Bow, Oklahoma* or whatever. They hunted deer and squirrel and duck with their relatives and had never met a fishing boat they didn't like.

All these other kids Kenneth had seen nearly every day of his life since kindergarten, the ones who surrounded him now—what did *they* like? What did *they* do after school? Where did they go, and with whom? How many of them would be friends with him if Gavin and Brayden kept shutting him out?

Kenneth knew the answer to that. Zero. Exactly none of them would reach out. Why would they? Every time they had ever tried, he had frogged their shoulders or something. No one understood him or wanted to try. He needed his old friends.

On the steps, he paused near them and shrugged off his backpack, letting it drop next to his feet.

They looked up at him and stopped talking.

He stepped in closer, dragging the backpack with his right foot. "Hey," he said.

"Hey," Brayden said.

Gavin backhanded Brayden in the chest.

"So it's still like that, huh?" Kenneth asked.

"Yeah," said Gavin. "It's like that."

"We've been friends our whole lives, and you're flushing me down the toilet like a turd," Kenneth sneered. Anger simmered inside him. He had done nothing to these guys. Nothing at all.

Conversations around them quieted. Everyone turned to watch.

"What'd you expect?" Gavin asked, laughing without humor. He got up and stood a foot away from Kenneth, lowering his voice but flexing like a cage fighter. "You're a bigger freak than them geeks. You acted like you was something else our whole lives, but now we know. The only reason we ain't told everybody about you is they wouldn't believe it. But you ain't our friend no more."

"You wanna get outta my face," Kenneth snarled, "unless you wanna find out how big a freak I really am."

Gavin glared at him, his upper lip curling, and for a moment, Kenneth believed he was going to throw a punch. If that happened, Kenneth would beat Gavin to paste. He knew himself well enough to be honest about that.

But Brayden tugged on Gavin's sleeve until he backed away. "Stay away from us," Gavin said. Then he turned, picked up his book bag, and walked up the steps. Brayden followed, looking over his shoulder, his expression a mixture of fear and regret.

Kenneth watched them go, working hard to stay expressionless. They walked through the front doors, even though the bell hadn't rung yet.

Once they were gone, Kenneth looked around and found, as he expected, that he was standing at the center of a crowd, concentric circles of kids bunched up shoulder to shoulder. They had been waiting to see if a fight would break out, and now they still waited, as if he might punch himself in the face just to entertain them.

"What are y'all looking at?" he barked.

Everyone moved away, muttering to each other.

Soon, the bell rang. Kenneth made his way up the steps, wondering what it would have felt like to toss Gavin over the building.

All those faces in the crowd, so familiar and yet so foreign. Even hemmed in by a couple hundred kids trying to get to their lockers before the tardy bell, he was now well and truly alone.

And it was all those freaks' fault. Jamie's and Gabby's and Christian's, but especially Micah's. He had been the ringleader of that attack in the park. He had the smartest mouth. Kenneth wanted to find him and make him wish he'd never been born. And after all, with no real friends, Kenneth had nothing better to do. But the freaks ran in a pack. If he fought one, he would have to fight them all.

✳

That afternoon, near the pavilion where Gavin had nearly died, Christian zoomed around the playground, dodging blasts from her friends. Hunger ached deep within her, but that same sense of freedom and joy she had felt on the night they got their powers overwhelmed any other feeling. Once, in middle school, their PE teacher had asked Christian if she had ever thought about running track when she got older. Christian had laughed. Who wanted to run for fun? With this kind of speed, though, running had become more than an action or a chore or a hobby. It was like taking a breath of fresh air after walking through a smoke-filled room. Like life.

And this session proved they were already controlling their powers better. It was all about focus.

"Soon," Jamie had said, "it'll be like walking. We won't need to think. It'll happen when we want it to."

That made sense to Christian, but it also scared her a little, mostly because of Micah. She had suggested they try to find Jake Hoeper's killer to protect the town, but ever since they had arrived in the park, Micah had refused to shut up about pranking B3 again. Sure, they had hurt Gavin, Micah said, but the big turd was basically okay. Besides, the Bros had never lost much sleep over how *they* hurt people. Micah had wanted to pay them back for years, and now that he had the means, he acted like a ten-year-old who had found his daddy's truck keys and couldn't wait to take it for a drive, even though he couldn't reach the pedals or see over the dash.

They had to watch Micah, all of them.

Now Jamie flew around the pavilion. He wanted to turn at right angles without losing speed, but he kept drifting and nearly smashing into trees. None of it had hurt him, though. When Micah had asked him to describe what it felt like, Jamie had said, "It's like clicking your teeth together after the dentist gives you the novocaine. You don't really feel it in your teeth, but there's an impact in your head. You hear the noise. It's like you understand what you're supposed to feel but something keeps you from actually feeling it. You know?" Christian thought about Kenneth's dropping the grill and crying out when the metal turned red, even though Gabby had reported seeing no burn on his hands, no pain in his expression, only surprise.

Gabby fired those force bolts of hers at Jamie, trying to keep her beam tight enough to hit him and nothing else. They couldn't afford to keep destroying whole sections of forest, she had argued. Plus, what would happen if she had to use her power in somebody's neighborhood?

She could do more damage than a tornado. And really, she shouldn't be shooting at Jamie, either, and so forth. Good old Gabby, afraid of her own shadow and too nervous to take a step in any direction. So far, she had hit Jamie three times with enough force to knock him off course but not injure him, so both her aim and her control were improving. Yet every time she spoke, she still sounded like she might burst into tears at any moment. Christian had run around the four-mile circumference of the park twenty times, each revolution taking less than a minute. She stopped only long enough to fill up on junk food she had swiped from the Korner Mart, and man, would Mom kill her if *that* ever came out.

Christian believed she could go much faster if necessary, but not on the park's walkway, and not with people around. What if a jogger got sucked up in her wake?

Micah had spent most of his time sitting by the one remaining grill. The rest lay scattered where Kenneth had thrown them. Micah piled his fourteenth mound of sticks and leaves inside the grill and then, only halfway paying attention, set them on fire. Smoke rose in thickening curls. Jamie flew through it several times, not even coughing. Plus, there was their newfound strength. Each of them could lift the picnic tables off the pavilion floor without straining, though none of them seemed anywhere near as strong as Kenneth.

And then there were the facts of Kenneth's hands, of Jamie's crashes. While they were using their powers, they were less susceptible to harm. Jamie theorized that some kind of invisible aura, like the Flash's, protected them. That would explain why Christian's clothes didn't disintegrate when she ran so fast and why Gabby's force bolts or the falls hadn't hurt Jamie. But, beyond Jamie using himself as a crash-test dummy up in the treetops, no one had wanted to test the limits of those auras just yet. Deflecting a little smoke or force was one thing. Keeping them safe from, say, a train wreck would be decidedly another. Still, they would have to experiment sooner or later. Knowing what they could withstand might mean the difference between life and death.

Jamie passed overhead again. Gabby's bolts shot by with a bacon-in-a-skillet sound. Micah flicked his other wrist at the grill, covering the fire, and only the fire, with ice. And Christian kept running, whipping up dust and pine straw in cool little spirals. Then she stopped at the pavilion and chug-a-lugged a two-liter Coke. She needed the energy, something to reduce the volume on her hunger. But God, did using her speed feel *good*. To tell the truth, she had found it hard to concentrate on anything else lately—school, video games, online shit. Everything moved so damn *slow*.

Micah walked over and sat next to her. They watched Jamie and Gabby do their dance, tree limbs crashing to the ground every time Gabby missed. Occasionally, Jamie zoomed right at her, at which point she would dive aside and roll and come up firing. The black circle of burned ground blighted the landscape.

"I still think we ought to find Kenneth and them and hang 'em from a flagpole or something," Micah said. Unless Christian concentrated on what he was saying, he sounded like he was talking in slow motion, every syllable drawn out. So she focused. *Run when you can run. When you can't, live in the here and now. Live at their speed. Otherwise, you'll be alone.*

Christian took another swig of Coke and shook her head. "Didn't you have enough last time, when we nearly knocked Gavin's brains out, set him on fire, and almost drowned him?"

Micah scoffed. "*Hell* no. And what about Brayden and Kenneth? They got away clean."

"You seen Kenneth lately? Those other two won't even talk to him. He might as well be us, for all the social life he's got. No, I think he got plenty that day. Maybe more than anybody else."

"Whatever. I still say that don't make up for everything they've put us through. Come on. Let's dump Kenneth naked in the middle of Main Street. Or burn all Brayden's textbooks. Let's do *something*."

Christian swigged Coke. Over half the bottle was gone. "If they come after us, that's one thing. But us going after them, over and over—that don't make us any better than them."

"Ahhh," Micah said, waving her off.

Jamie landed beside Gabby, and the two of them trotted over, smiling and sweaty and out of breath.

"You see that?" Jamie said, beaming. "We're getting *good*."

"Micah wants to mess with Kenneth and them some more," Christian said.

Jamie and Gabby stopped smiling. They looked at Micah with a mixture of trepidation and anger. Gabby moved closer to Jamie. Were they hooking up? Christian frowned. That might screw up their group dynamic. But still, no one knew better than she did that you couldn't choose who you loved.

"Nothing serious," Micah was saying. "Not like last time. Just some pranks."

"I had enough of that," Jamie said. "I don't wanna get anybody killed. If we haven't already."

"Quit it," Micah said. "We didn't kill Jake Hoeper. We don't know who or what did. And even if it's something we saw that night in my shed, it ain't our fault he's dead."

"I don't know if that's true," Gabby said. Her voice wavered, as it usually did when she tried to be assertive. "If we're going after anybody, I think Christian's right. We should find the killer. Leave Kenneth and them alone. They're mean and hateful, but they ain't murderers."

Micah moaned and walked away.

Jamie and Gabby sat next to Christian. The three of them brainstormed ways to find Jake's murderer while Micah kept pointing out that, for all they knew, a garbage truck had run over the kid. Or his dad got pissed when he didn't take out the trash. If some monster from another dimension ganked him, well, that was *his* hard luck. Micah had no problem with tracking down the killer as soon as somebody came up with a halfway decent plan, he claimed. But in the meantime, he had every intention of setting Kenneth Del Ray's feet on fire or showing Brayden Sears what frostbite on the butt felt like. If nobody wanted to back his play, he would simply do it alone.

Christian and the others tried to ignore him, keep things positive, but it was hard when the kid refused to shut up. And how could they really stop him? They couldn't watch him all the time, and there were plenty of ways to humiliate someone in front of the whole school. Kenneth and Brayden themselves had taught Micah that. No matter what Jamie said, Christian knew that Micah would thank them for the lesson, sooner rather than later.

Yeah, she thought, *but when can I run again?*

✳✳✳

Kenneth rode his bike home just after dark. He had spent the afternoon pedaling around Quapaw City's residential streets, maneuvering past the kids whose footballs and toy cars kept rolling into the road. Their mothers and shift-worker fathers sat in lawn chairs, sweating and keeping a close eye on their brats. Kenneth avoided the commercial sections of town, having no desire to see the curfew signs in the windows, the frightened faces of the people on the sidewalks. He already had too much to deal with, including Jake Hoeper, dead and mangled on the street named after Kenneth's own grandfather.

With his newfound strength—the power to crush cars and drive away his best friends—Kenneth had to watch himself at all times. If he let his concentration lapse too much, bad things happened. If he got too upset, he would crush the bike's handlebars right there on the street, in front of everybody. And then the whole town would know he had turned into a freak.

Caught in the web of these thoughts, he had stayed out too late, realizing while he was still three miles from home that dark would catch him. He had pedaled like mad, trying to make it home, but the sun had

set while he was still on Violet Street. He had always hated that name.
It sounded like the kind of street Micah Sterne should live on, a street
for girls and wimps. Even with what had happened, he preferred Royal
Del Ray—a sanctuary of sorts, his home turf. No one would call him a
freak there, even if they knew.

Would they?

As he turned onto Royal Del Ray, headlights splashed him, then
the reds and blues of a police car.

"Oh, *shit!*" he cried. Another stupid cop. His parents were going to
kill him.

The cops waited as Kenneth pedaled toward them. He braked beside
the patrol car, which had stopped across from his house, underneath
the Joneses' dogwood tree. The cop on the driver's side rolled down
his window. He was overweight, probably in his forties. A second cop
rode in the passenger seat. He was younger, early twenties, blond, short-
cropped hair. He seemed anxious. Kenneth did not know either man.
A shotgun was wedged between them.

"You're out after curfew, son," the older cop said.

"Yes, sir," Kenneth replied. "I was riding bikes, and the time just
got away from me."

"Uh-huh," said the cop, bored. "Where do you live?"

Kenneth nodded at his house. "Right there," he said.

"Your name?" the other cop asked.

"Kenneth Del Ray." He saw no point in lying.

The cops looked at each other. The driver turned off the lights.
"Wait right there. We'll need to talk with your parents."

"Yes, sir."

The driver pulled over to the curb and killed the engine. Both cops
got out and walked over to Kenneth. The older one gestured. "Lead the
way."

Kenneth got off his bike and walked it toward his yard. The cops
followed.

A loud thump behind them made Kenneth turn. His mouth fell open. He tried to speak.

A blue-skinned, four-armed giant had dropped out of the dogwood tree and now towered over the cops, who wheeled around. The thing from the trees was nearly as wide as both of them put together.

"Sweet Jesus," the older cop said. "What the f—"

The younger cop screamed and drew his gun.

"Run!" Kenneth cried.

Moving faster than should have been possible for something that size, the monster used his lower arms to grab the cops and fling them away, the younger flying twenty feet and skittering down the street like a motorcycle wreck victim, the older sailing parallel to the ground like Superman before crashing onto his chest and rolling along the asphalt. They shrieked, the sounds high and strained and so brief Kenneth wondered if the men were dead.

He faced down the thing alone.

It had to be eight feet tall, probably more, and was dressed in skins of some kind, the trousers and open vest tanned and cured and flexible. Long jet-black hair flowed past its shoulders. Every part of it was thickly muscled. Its four arms had four-fingered hands studded with three-inch talons. The skin looked blue, and there were small horns on its head. Its red eyes seemed to pulse. The thing, which looked very much like one of those shapes that had come out of the light ball in Micah's shed, grinned. Its hideous expression revealed what looked to be hundreds of long, razor-sharp teeth. The mouth looked deep and wide enough to easily shove a whole person in there.

Kenneth staggered backward and tried to scream, but his voice deserted him, as if his throat had sealed itself off.

The monster reached for Kenneth. The tips of those talons brushed the boy's shoulders.

Then the young cop tried to tackle the giant, ramming a shoulder into its hip and driving it sideways. Kenneth staggered back and tripped over his own feet, tumbling hard on the asphalt, his spine jarring as if someone had hit him in the tailbone with a sledgehammer. The older cop grabbed the thing from the other side. They tried to wrestle it to the ground as Kenneth scooted toward his house, mouth open in a silent scream.

The thing from the trees flung the older officer away again. The cop crashed against his cruiser, cracking the back windshield, and fell to the ground. As he struggled to rise, the giant grabbed the younger cop, brought him to eye level, and head-butted him, the sound like a .22 rifle discharging. The young cop went limp.

The monster opened its enormous maw.

This time, Kenneth managed to scream.

Porch lights flashed on. Mr. Hoeper walked out his front door and looked toward the noise, shielding his eyes with one hand.

"Get back in your house!" Kenneth shouted.

Mr. Hoeper kept staring. Other people opened their front doors, lingered on porches, stepped into their yards. Some shouted in confusion. Others seemed terrified. As they should have been.

The four-armed creature shoved the young cop's head in its gaping mouth and bit down with a wet crunch. The cop's body stiffened, then jerked, the feet flopping about, the hands clenching and unclenching. A sickening slurping sound filled the air. Kenneth sat there, petrified. *It's eating him. Oh Lord. It's eating him.* Over the cop's crawfishing body, those red eyes burned into Kenneth, pulsing brighter red with every slurp.

Kenneth turned away and vomited.

The tree-thing dropped the body like a piece of trash just as the older cop stood, drew his weapon, and unloaded. The bullets hit the monster's right arms and torso and drove him sideways a few steps, though he did not fall. His eyes never left Kenneth's. When the cop's weapon began to dry-fire, the tree-thing turned, and the older officer swore darkly. From the Hoepers' house, someone else cursed in a strangled voice. A door slammed. *Well, at least Mr. Hoeper went back inside.*

The monster turned and moved toward the cop, who shouted, "Get away from me!" and threw the gun at it. The thing batted it aside and kept coming. The cop crouched against his car, fumbling with his nightstick. As if that would do any good. It was too small for that monster to pick his teeth with. The man was going to die unless someone did something. Where was everybody? Why didn't anybody try to help him?

What about you, dummy? said Brayden's voice in Kenneth's head. *You're pretty strong now. Maybe get off your ass, huh?*

"Easy for you to say," Kenneth muttered. "You don't have to go get killed."

Still, the voice was right. What good was his newfound strength if he sat on the ground like a baby who couldn't even crawl?

He shook his arms out and clenched his fists.

He took two steps toward the thing from the trees.

It leaped upon the older cop and took the man's head into his mouth.

From inside those unimaginable jaws, the cop screamed.

No, thought Kenneth. He stopped walking.

That all you got? Brayden's voice said. *Two steps and you pussy out?*

Another crunch.

More horrible slurping sounds.

"No," Kenneth said. He trembled, feeling tears on his face. His traitor feet would not move, even though that man was dying right in front of him.

From inside the monster's mouth, a long, low moan.

The cop's fists and feet thumped against the monster's body, weakening with every passing second.

And something inside Kenneth broke. Fear washed over him in a great wave.

He turned and ran for his front door, faster and harder than he had ever run before, screaming *No* over and over, unable to stop, looking back over his shoulder.

On the street, that thing stood, the cop's limp corpse dangling from its mouth. It grasped the lower legs, opened its mouth, and raised the body over its head. Then it smashed the carcass into the cruiser. Kenneth put his hands over his ears, still screaming. He burst through his front door, splintering it into kindling, ignoring the startled roars of his mother and father, who had been watching a ball game with the volume cranked. Kenneth dashed down the hall and into his room. He slammed the door and dove under his bed, where he had not hidden since he was a four-year-old afraid of the dark.

✳✳✳

Na'ul used the corpse like a cudgel, crushing the vehicle's roof, its lights, the frame, until the cop's body fell apart. Then he leaped up onto the metal wagon and stomped it, pounded it with all four fists, flattening it. A horn sounded, blatted, sputtered, and died. He bashed and bashed and bashed, ignoring the faces pressed to windows in the houses all around him.

Eventually, he turned back to Kenneth's house, raised two fists, and roared.

✳✳✳

The noises outside ceased. Kenneth forced himself to crawl out from under the bed and stood on trembling legs. He took several deep breaths. In the distance, sirens wailed. Cops, ambulances, probably even the fire department. It was about time, not that all the backup in the world would do those two officers any good.

Kenneth's parents banged on his door and demanded to be let in.

When his heart stopped trip-hammering, he willed himself toward his bedroom window. He stared at the curtains for several moments before he could bring himself to reach out and part them. But he had to see what that thing had done. It had obviously been after him. Those cops had just been in the way, and they had died for it. For *him*. The least he could do was look at them, or what was left of them.

He grasped the curtains with both hands, took another deep breath, and pulled them apart.

The hulking blue-skinned figure blocked out the landscape. The creature was squatting, so they were almost at eye level. Blood-red eyes bored into Kenneth. That shark's mouth opened. Blood dribbled out like water from an overflowing pan. The creature pushed the hedges back with its four hands. Kenneth cried out.

Then it spoke, and Kenneth heard a strange language of clicks and growls and grunts. But in his mind, all that noise somehow became English: *You are the strongest of your tribe, so you shall die first. Come out, boy. Come and face me like a warrior. Your blood shall replenish me, and then I will slaughter your friends.*

The creature seemed to smile.

Kenneth screamed again.

From behind him, the sounds of footfalls on carpet, at least one of his parents rushing down the hall, probably to the kitchen phone. *I hate to tell y'all, but the cops are already here.* He turned around. He had to make sure neither his mom nor his dad went outside to see what had happened.

His father slammed through the door, splintering the lock. His face was red, his eyes as wide as moons. "What's wrong? You sound like somebody's trying to kill you. What did you do to our front door?" He looked past Kenneth, at the open window. "And what the hell happened out there? Did the cops drive into a tree?"

Kenneth looked back. Nothing was there. In the darkness under the Joneses' dogwood tree, the ruined car sat like a monument to the bodies scattered around it.

Every cop in Quapaw City and half the Branson County Sheriff's personnel crawled over Royal Del Ray Street all night. Ambulances and paramedics, the county coroner—the whole street swirled in color and the sharp beams of flashlights. Four different people questioned Kenneth about what he had seen. He spent every session lying like a rug, describing the perpetrator as a six-and-a-half-foot-tall, three-hundred-pound, dark-skinned male of indeterminate race. *Black? Hispanic?* the cops asked. *I don't think either,* he said, and this part was true. *He just looked dark.* What had happened to the dead officers? Kenneth claimed that they had ordered him to run, and he had not looked back.

Coward, whispered Brayden's voice. *Chicken. Sad little boy.*

Someone asked if there was anything else he could remember about the perp, anything at all, but he couldn't tell them to look for a blue four-armed demon. It would probably have landed him in a Little Rock psych ward.

Mr. Hoeper didn't help. He had told the cops that, yes, without a doubt, Kenneth Del Ray had still been on the street when the officers opened fire. He had not been able to shed much light on the killer, other than to say the guy looked even bigger than Kenneth claimed. Soon after they sent Mr. Hoeper away, the cops had turned their attention to Mr. and Mrs. Del Ray and their front door, which, given its obliteration, seemed suspicious. Had the killer maybe followed Kenneth, maybe invaded their home and threatened to come back if they talked? No, said Mom and Dad. They hadn't seen anyone, either on the street or in their house. Sergeant Heck seemed convinced that Kenneth knew more about the killer than he was telling, that the killer must have come to the neighborhood looking specifically for the kid, that it was therefore Kenneth's fault two cops were dead. Officer Gillen eyed Kenneth with obvious malice and contempt. Neither suggested Kenneth had destroyed the door. Perhaps sensing danger, Kenneth's parents had not enlightened them.

The cops concluded the interviews by telling the Del Rays to keep Kenneth available for further questioning. Back in the house, Kenneth's parents gripped him in a dual bear hug that, under normal circumstances, might have cracked his ribs and spine. As it was, he barely felt it. Then his father chewed him out for twenty straight minutes—for missing curfew; for finding himself anywhere near a crime scene, as if Kenneth had sought out a double murder to witness; and for wrecking the front door, the repairs for which, according to his mother, would come out of his allowance. They said nothing about how he had struck the door so hard it had pretty much disintegrated. Maybe they hadn't processed it yet. He listened to them in silence, nodding at appropriate moments, trying to look disappointed or indignant when they mentioned his punishments. In truth, he couldn't have cared less, not even when his father said, "And by the way, you ain't leaving this house after dark until they catch this guy. You'll stay in public places all the time when you're not here. You break them rules and I'll tan your hide."

Aaron Del Ray was a big man—six foot two in his socks, two hundred and thirty pounds or so, well-muscled from his work in the lumberyard. Kenneth had always enjoyed the outdoors at night, even by himself. So normally, his dad's pronouncements would have angered and frightened and dismayed him all at once. Now, given everything, his father no longer scared him, but if Dad tried to spank him like he was an eight-year-old, he would probably let it happen. He loved his father and had no desire to hurt him. As for being yelled at and grounded after dark, he could take the one and ignore the other. He had no intention of braving the night.

Dad found some heavy plastic in the attic and duct-taped it to the door frame. Just to be safe, he slept that night in a chair, a shotgun across his lap. Not that Kenneth believed it would do any good against that four-armed abomination. He slept fitfully, the activity outside bothering him much less than the sight of that thing had. There was no doubt that it was after him. What had happened to those cops, the way it had crushed the car but stopped outside the window as if it were bad manners to come in without being invited, all those teeth—as crazy, as *stupid* as it sounded, Kenneth believed it was some kind of vampire. The bloodsucker had come out of the light show in Sterne's shed and had focused on Kenneth instead of the freaks. Just something else he owed Micah. And he intended to repay that kid, with interest.

How come you could run right through that heavy door without a scratch? he thought, but he finally drifted off to sleep before he could ponder the question.

CHAPTER SEVENTEEN

The next morning, Kenneth was leaving for school when his mother grabbed his arm. "Where do you think you're going?" she cried.

"To school," he said.

"Not by yourself, you're not." She grabbed her car keys from a hook beside the door. "You saw that killer's face. We know it. You know it. And he knows it, too."

"Awww, Mom," Kenneth groaned.

They went outside and got in the car. Much of the street was still blocked off with yellow crime scene tape. The ruined police car had been hauled away, as had the bodies, but fragments of taillight and glass were scattered about. Dark stains covered part of the road. A police car sat in front of their house, a uniformed cop inside it. Kenneth's mom pulled out and detoured around the crime scene, and the cop car followed them. When Kenneth entered the school, the cop was still out there, watching him.

A different cruiser was posted outside Kenneth's house that afternoon as he lay on his bed, staring at the ceiling and listening to music without really paying attention. He had barely heard a word anyone said in school. He missed an English pop quiz because by the time he realized one was happening, the teacher was already collecting them. Kenneth had eaten lunch alone and then sat on the front steps until the fifth-period bell rang. Gavin had refused to look at him. Brayden had glanced his way a couple of times and had even smiled once, but they had not spoken. Now the afternoon light was fading. Shadows grew longer. That thing would probably be out there, waiting for Kenneth to step outside—or, if he was right about its being a vampire of some kind, for someone to invite it in. Like *that* would ever happen.

A car pulled into the driveway, but he didn't bother to look out the window. It was probably just another cop relieving the one who had followed him around since he left school. The car pulled away a couple of minutes later. Kenneth closed his eyes and wondered if he could get some sleep. He had gotten very little the night before, what with that thing lurking around the house.

Someone knocked on the new front door that had been installed while he was at school. He heard two voices, his mother and someone else, low and mumbling. The visitor sounded young. Kenneth turned to his own door and waited. A moment later, someone knocked.

"Come in," he said.

The door opened. Gavin's face was red and sour. One hand rested on the doorknob. The other was thrust knuckles-deep into his pants pocket. Brayden stood behind him. He waved. Kenneth nodded.

"You gonna let us in or what?" Gavin asked, his voice toneless.

"Ain't no anchor tied to your ass," Kenneth said.

Gavin scowled and entered. Brayden came in and pushed the door shut. Kenneth tried to appear relaxed, though his heart pounded hard. His best friends. They had stayed away for a while, and sure, they looked nervous, but they were here now.

"What's up?" Brayden asked.

"Not a lot since my two best friends dumped me like an ugly girl on prom night," Kenneth said, looking at Gavin.

"What'd you expect?" Gavin sneered. "If one of us could lift a Chevrolet over our head and throw it like a football, you would have kicked us to the curb, too."

"That's bullshit," Kenneth said. "I would have thought it was cool."

"Like you think them other freaks are cool? Yeah, you seem real comfy with 'em these days. I reckon you should have been hanging out with *them* all these years."

Kenneth clenched his fists at his sides. "Why'd you come over here?"

"Momma nagged me half to death," Gavin said. "And when that didn't work, she threatened to ground me till I was outta college. It was easier to pretend like I can stand the sight of you."

Kenneth laughed. "Like any college would take you."

"Come on, y'all," Brayden whined.

"Shut up," Gavin said without looking at Brayden. "You wanna hang out with freaks? That's on you. Me, I'd rather be alone. Or dead."

Kenneth ground his teeth and forced himself to unclench his fists. *I was glad to see 'em for maybe ten seconds. Then we all opened our mouths.* But he could not fight Gavin. It would be murder.

"Bro," Brayden said, though it was unclear whom he meant. "Let's talk about this like friends."

"I got nothing to say," said Gavin. "Not to this freak. You'll be reading Archie comics with Sterne and Entmann by the end of the year. And I'll be kicking all y'all's butts, no matter how strong you are."

"You better pack a lunch," Kenneth said. "It'll take you all day just to tear up my picture."

Gavin snorted and shook his head. Then he slid down the wall and sat on the carpet, knees drawn up, forearms resting on them. He looked at Kenneth. "In the meantime, I plan to sit right here and say nothing until I can go home." He leaned his head against the wall and closed his eyes.

"Whatever," Kenneth said. He went back to the bed and lay down, lacing his hands behind his head. He stared at the ceiling and said nothing else. Brayden stood in the middle of the room, looking from one of them to the other, as speechless as his two best friends, who had somehow become each other's bitter enemies.

✳

Two hours later, Gavin, who had not moved from his corner, checked his watch. Outside, a car pulled into the drive, and then a horn honked. Gavin stood and put his hand on the doorknob. He turned back to Kenneth. "You ask me, them freaks killed Jake Hoeper and the cops. Ain't nothing else I ever seen got the power to do all that, unless there's a renegade rock-crusher driving around by itself."

"Naw," Kenneth said, without sitting up. "I seen what did it. It wanted to kill me, and the cops got in its way. It stood right outside my window."

Gavin scoffed. "So did this big, bad killer talk to you?"

"Told me I'm a dead man walkin'."

Gavin guffawed. "Yeah, right."

"I knew you wouldn't believe me."

"Maybe it wasn't just them freaks. Maybe you were in on it."

Kenneth sat up. Brayden flinched, though Gavin did not move. Kenneth glared at Gavin, who looked away this time. "I didn't kill nobody, and neither did they. Just because I know that don't mean I'm friends with 'em."

Gavin stared at the floor another second or two. Then he looked at Kenneth, a bit less defiantly than before. "You gonna take a shot at me? Your new friends had their chance. You might as well get a lick in, right?"

Kenneth's hands clenched and unclenched. He wanted to slug Gavin so much his arms shook. But if he did, Gavin might land in Mississippi. So he did nothing, said nothing.

Gavin turned, opened the door, and walked through it.

Brayden grinned sheepishly. "Sorry about that, man. *I* don't really think you're a freak."

"Watch your back," Kenneth said. "If you see something that looks bigger than a bear and meaner than Godzilla, run."

Brayden's grin faltered. He hesitated, probably wondering if Kenneth had lost his mind. Then he cleared his throat and followed Gavin down the hall and out of the house.

Kenneth went back to the window and watched them climb into Gavin's dad's truck. They backed out, narrowly missing the police tape, and drove away. Nothing else moved on the street, in anyone's yard, or in the trees. So Kenneth closed the curtains and headed for the kitchen to see what was for supper.

✶✹✶

Na'ul hunched in the underground tunnels where the lessers of this world sent their bodily wastes, the top of his head and his horns scraping the stone above, the stinking air and foul waters worse than any field of slaughter he had ever walked. He watched the youngling's dwelling through the grate, ignoring the wheeled conveyance sitting nearby. He had had no trouble with the last one or the beings within it, though their projectile weapons had annoyed him with their noise and stinging pellets. These would-be protectors could not keep Na'ul from his prey. Still, several vehicles had swarmed the area since he had killed two of their number, so perhaps it was time to draw them someplace else. Why fight a herd if an easier choice existed?

Two other younglings exited Na'ul's target's dwelling and got into a taller sort of wagon. Na'ul smiled—an opportunity. He pressed his face to the opening in the thoroughfare and breathed deeply, filtering and sorting scents until he recognized the meat—similar to the boy he hunted, but blander, dull. Every lesser had its own scent. Now he could follow these two anywhere. He would rise from this reeking pit when the skystar's horrid glow extinguished itself.

At night, this world had begun to remind him of home—he and his people prowling the darkness, the lessers screaming and fleeing and praying to their gods, the pathways and forests deserted so that Na'ul would have to depend on all his senses as he flushed them from their pathetic hideaways. He would catch one and rip open its neck, letting the lifeblood flow down his throat. They were safe in their dwellings only because sacred custom dictated he could not follow there, the Go'Kan's sacrifice to the gods of civility and homespace.

Still, when the hunger became unbearable, the Go'kan set fire to the dwellings and waited. If he were forced to drive out this youngling in such a manner, he would. For now, though, he enjoyed seasoning his meals with the spice of deep, abiding fear.

The world fell deeper into shadow. Soon, it would be dark enough for Na'ul to emerge.

After following the fetid caverns until he found the entrance he had used hours earlier—a stone circle faced with a metal grate he had ripped off—Na'ul tracked the younglings who had visited his target, dashing from the woods to the shadowed areas between dwellings and onto roofs and into the cover of trees. The strange wagon the children had gotten into was parked on an artificial walkway next to a second, similar conveyance. This one was red, like fire.

This dwelling looked smaller and shabbier than the one Na'ul had stalked these last several nights. He scrambled into a tall, stout tree lush with thin, sharp leaves. Once he had climbed high enough to conceal himself, he settled in the branches and watched.

After a while, the boys left the dwelling and approached another of the thin, two-wheeled vehicles his first victim in this world had ridden. Those contraptions left their riders fully exposed. What kind of stupid, complacent beings would drive such? Had nothing ever hunted them before? Was that why they died so easily?

"Gavin, seriously. I wish you'd cut Kenneth some slack," said one of the younglings.

The other one, bigger and dimmer, with a sloping forehead and thick lips, scowled. "God, Brayden, you just don't quit. You were there when them freaks nearly killed me, right? What, I should forget that?"

"I'm not gonna argue," said the first one. "Just sleep on it."

"Whatever," said the bigger boy, the one called Gavin. He climbed onto the fragile vehicle and guided it toward the thoroughfare.

Which boy made the better target—the one who lived here, or the one riding away?

After being underground all day, Na'ul wanted to stretch, to feel the wind in his hair and the thrill of the hunt.

The smaller youngling returned to his dwelling. Having marked his scent, Na'ul could find him at leisure. *Another night, child. Thank whatever gods you worship.*

Na'ul dropped from the tree and pursued the bigger boy, the one called Gavin. More prey, more mess. This world's sad protectors would have no choice but to turn their attention that way.

Then Na'ul would return to his true hunt.

CHAPTER EIGHTEEN

Before the first-period bell rang the next morning, Gabby, Jamie, and Christian walked toward Kenneth, who was leaning against a tree. When he saw them coming, he groaned. "God. That's all I need."

"We gotta talk," said Jamie. Gabby and Christian flanked him, forming a semicircle around Kenneth, cutting off his avenues of escape.

"Don't you know I can throw you over the school if I want to?" Kenneth said. "I could pull the arms off one of you and beat the other two half to death with 'em."

"We know," said Gabby. "Just listen, okay?" She managed to keep her voice from shaking, but Kenneth was right. If he could grab one of them, he could kill them before they could use their powers. Gabby was so sick of being afraid. It felt like she spent half her time waiting for something awful to happen. *What is wrong with me? I could probably knock the whole school down with my force beams, but I can barely stand in front of a kid my age.*

"Where's Sterne?" Kenneth asked. When none of them said anything, he laughed. "He don't know you're here."

"No," said Christian. "But we still need to talk."

"No, we don't," said Kenneth. "Especially not here. I got enough problems without everybody thinking I'm a freak like y'all."

"You *are* a freak like us," Gabby said, startling even herself. "You said it yourself. And we saw what you did with those grills."

Kenneth turned to Gabby. When he spoke, his voice was cold. "Call me that again, and I'm liable to forget you're a girl."

"Look," said Jamie. "Three people died on your street, and the cops ain't got a clue. From what I've heard, they can't even decide if it was

133

a person who did it or some kind of animal." He looked around, and though no one seemed to be paying the four of them much attention, he lowered his voice to a whisper. "We think it's something the five of us brought through that night. And we got the power to stop it."

"I didn't bring *shit* through," Kenneth said, still glaring at Gabby. She took a step backward and hated herself for it. "That's on y'all."

Gabby cleared her throat. She had to show him she wasn't afraid. Maybe he would even believe it. "If you hadn't busted in, we might have stopped the ceremony. You're in this as much as we are."

Kenneth shifted. Gabby took another step back. *Damn it, cut that out. Don't let him see how much he scares you.*

"You don't know that," he said.

"No," she said. "But you don't know you're innocent, either. Don't act like you do."

Kenneth scowled. Several times, he started to say something, but the words died. Finally, he shook his head. "I can't talk about this here," he said.

"Fine," said Jamie. "Where, then?"

"I'll let you know," Kenneth said. He stepped forward. None of them moved. He raised one eyebrow, as if to say, *What now?*

Jamie sighed and stepped aside. Kenneth brushed past them and walked toward the front steps. A moment later, the bell rang, and everyone filed inside. He did not look back.

Well, Gabby thought, *that could have gone better. But at least we didn't fight. And you didn't let him shut you up. Maybe that's progress.*

As the four of them stood under the tree and talked like old friends, Micah watched from the corner of the building. His only three friends in the world, chatting with that moron Del Ray like *he* had been their

Dungeon Master, like *he* had let them play video games at his house when their own parents were too cheap to buy them anything decent, even though Micah's family was poorer than the rest of them. No one had even tried to slug Kenneth, after all he had done to them over the years. They should all be pointing at him and laughing, enjoying the way the dumb jock's even dumber jock buddies had abandoned him. Instead, Christian, Jamie, and Gabby seemed intent on making Kenneth feel *better.*

That would not stand. Not if Micah had anything to say about it.

He turned on his heel and, as the first-period bell rang, marched off campus on foot.

✳✺✳

That afternoon, Micah hung back fifty yards or so as Kenneth walked the quarter mile from school to the football team's field house. The big douchebag would spend the next three or four hours running into the rest of the ninth-grade team on their half of Quapaw City High School's shitty practice field. Micah had seen a few practices in eighth grade, when Kenneth and his teammates spent every fall afternoon on a field full of molehills and cigarette butts from the weekend's delinquents. Last year, the team's star quarterback, Steve Whitehead, had stepped in a hole and broken his ankle on a routine option play, after which the team lost every one of its games. Unfortunately, B3 made it through the season with nothing more than bruises and scrapes.

That would change today. The Bros and any other dumb-jock-popular-kid-brainless-idiot would suffer a lot more than a broken ankle.

Lost in what he would probably, and inaccurately, call his thoughts, Kenneth never even noticed he was being tailed. Dumbass. Micah carried a duffel bag over his shoulder. It would take him only a minute or so to get ready. He planned to let the jocks take the field and spread out in symmetrical patterns for warm-ups. They would be caught in the open, defenseless. Micah would show them what it felt like to be picked on, to feel helpless, to be humiliated in front of all your friends.

❋

Jamie and Gabby had biked to school, but Christian's mom had dropped her off, since she had lost her bike on the night they got their powers; when she ran those same roads to look for it, it had vanished. Some kid out that way had probably hidden it in the woods or something, so they could ride it when their parents weren't around. And, to be fair, Christian had had a lot on her mind that night. The bike had been the least of it. Since Christian had no ride, Gabby had suggested they all just walk to the Quapaw City Bowl-o-Rama next to the practice field, where they could wait for Kenneth. They had not actually discussed this decision, but they seemed to have made it anyway. As they walked, they kept silent.

Jamie had no idea what the others were thinking, but he spent most of the time wondering how to separate Kenneth from the other football players; if he refused to talk to them by a tree at school because of what people might think, there was no way he would do it in front of the team. But how could they signal him without everyone seeing? Maybe Christian could zoom in, whisper something in his ear, and zoom back out before anyone noticed? Was she that fast?

Ahead lay the lush green game field, the track that circled it, the small bandstands on either side. Behind all this sat the field house, and across the street from that, the practice field, bordered on one side by Main Street and on the other by the Bowl-o-Rama. Despite their nonexistent social lives, Jamie and his friends would go unnoticed there. It was a popular after-school hangout with pool tables and video games and a snack bar with crushed ice, like you could get at Sonic.

They approached the parking lot. "How are we doing this?" Gabby asked.

"We'll signal him to meet us in the alley back yonder," Jamie said, having decided now would be a bad time to test Christian's powers. "And if he don't show up, we'll talk to him at school again. And we'll keep on doing it till he gives in."

"Or beats the crap out of us," said Gabby. She kept walking at the same speed, did not suggest they abort, even though Jamie would have bet his Xbox that she wanted to. Some days, Jamie could barely stand next to her and all that nervous energy. And if it was like that for him, he couldn't imagine how it must have been for her.

"We got more say in folks picking on us than we used to," Jamie said. "Especially you. You could probably knock him into orbit with those beams of yours."

Gabby smiled. Jamie's heart leaped. Reaching out to her always felt good.

"Wait," Christian said. "Y'all hear that?"

Everyone shut up. Jamie concentrated and turned up the world's volume, as they had all learned to do. And, sure enough, he heard it.

People were screaming. It was coming from the practice field. They all looked at each other.

"Micah," Jamie said. "Christian, go!"

But she was already gone. Jamie and Gabby ran after her, but he knew that by the time they reached the field, it would be too late to stop whatever they were hearing.

Damn it, Micah. Damn it to hell.

✶✹✶

Around the time his friends exited the school, Micah was watching the ninth-grade team take one end of the field, helmets in hand, jerseys bulging with shoulder pads and rib braces. Then he ducked into the Bowl-o-Rama, which was practically empty and would stay that way until the kids walked or biked or drove down—another ten minutes, tops. The attendant swept down a lane, and back in the arcade, some truant was playing one of those stupid dancing games. Neither noticed Micah slipping into the bathroom, where he checked the stalls to make sure he was alone. Then he donned his robe and ski mask. He thought he looked pretty cool. Grinning, he zipped up the duffel and walked out. The truant's game had ended. He waited at the snack bar. When he saw Micah, he raised one eyebrow. Micah held his shoulders back, his head high, and walked out of the building.

He traversed the parking lot and the alley between the Bowl-o-Rama and the field. As he stepped onto the grass, the varsity team ran plays on the far side of the field while coaches barked at them. On the near side, the ninth graders ran similar plays while similar coaches yelled similar platitudes, made similar demands. The players danced like puppets. It made Micah want to puke.

These were his tormentors and had been since grade school, the kids who called him names and made fun of his hobbies and pranked him—everything from wedgies and swirlies to borderline-violent acts like frogging your shoulder and purple nurples. Over the last few years, they had graduated to cyberbullying and, in the cases of B3, physical assaults Micah had hidden from his parents and the other kids. Every bruise had shamed him. Every DM asking why he didn't just kill himself burned in his memory like brands. These kids never invited him to their parties, never came to his, and questioned his place in school and why he might even exist. The ones who'd never beaten him up or talked to him like he was garbage still hung out with the ones who did. They had done nothing to stop his misery, and they had had *years* to step up.

Now, as he walked across the patchy grass, as the football players stopped what they were doing to gape at the Halloween reject daring to sully their precious field, as the coaches yelled at him for being there and at the players for paying him any attention, as traffic passed on Main Street like it had every day of his life, Micah said, "All you jocks get ready for some payback."

He dropped his voice an octave, trying to sound older than he was, but even so, Kenneth silently mouthed his name as he approached. For the first time, Kenneth was the helpless one—powerful enough to fight back but handcuffed by his own pathetic need to fit in. Gavin and Brayden looked at each other, fear in their eyes.

That's right, you shitheads. Be afraid. I'm coming.

Micah raised his hands, flipped both middle fingers, and opened fire.

A streak of ice shot to the left, flame to the right. The ninth-grade players cried out and scattered. Some formed clusters of meatheads he could have picked off in his sleep. Good thing for them he didn't want them dead. Instead, he ceased fire after one burst struck the field, the ice freezing over a three-square-foot area, the fire consuming dry grass. It would spread quickly. From the field's far end, the varsity players and coaches shouted. Some scaled the fence and fled up Main Street. Others bolted toward the bowling alley. Some ran around in panic. Micah couldn't have cared less. He concentrated on the jocks his own age, most of whom were booking for the field house. Idiots. Like he couldn't burn down the building.

Laughing, Micah gestured, and a wall of ice blocked their way, ten feet high and growing lengthwise. He would trap them between the spreading fire and the ice. Many of them turned back and ran toward the fire, maybe hoping they could still jump it and get to safety. Micah gestured again. Ice encased the feet of a half dozen padded, jersey-wearing boneheads. They sprawled on their faces.

Most of the varsity had made it over the fence without falling into traffic or trampling each other, though a couple of kids needed assistance. The fire had spread, already covering perhaps ten square yards, the smoke rising higher and obscuring Micah's view of that end of the field. *Better contain the fire before somebody down there gets hurt.* Micah wanted them to feel what he had felt his whole life, but he did not need a murder charge. He waved with his right hand, and the flames vanished, the blackened grass still smoking.

As for the ninth-grade jocks, a passel of them dashed for the Main Street fence, leaving their moaning, sometimes screaming friends behind.

"My feet!" some kid yelled. "Somebody get it off! It burns!"

Huh. I forgot ice can burn, too.

Still, he wasn't through with them. A rising breeze blew away much of the smoke, clearing Micah's view. He gestured at the fence. Ice began to cover it from the ground up. The vanguard reached it and started climbing like mad, their limbs moving with almost cartoon speed. Most of them reached the top and dropped on the Main Street side. But one kid, slower than the others, found both hands and both feet stuck to the fence. He was pinned there like a bug in amber. He screamed.

Part of Micah recoiled. He had not meant to do it. But another part of him cackled with glee. Being frozen to a fence seemed worse than the humiliation of getting slapped around, than all the stupid pranks. Maybe that screaming kid would think before he picked on the next nerd. Maybe they all would. Maybe every jock in the world needed to learn that lesson.

The two dozen or so players who had not escaped started running back toward Micah, leaving the screaming kid to his fate.

Chickens.

Micah gestured. The ice splintered, cracked, and fell apart, the stuck kid falling to the ground with it. Those with their feet encased found themselves free and tried to stand on their numb limbs. The rest of the herd headed straight for him. They had to go somewhere, he supposed, but a frontal assault? Puh-leeze.

Steve Whitehead led them. Of course. Mr. Quarterback. What was that old phrase—big man on campus? Over the summer, Steve had grown to nearly six feet tall. His arms were well-muscled, his blond hair even blonder. As he ran toward Micah, he still carried a football, and now he cocked his arm and threw, a perfect spiral that arced toward Micah, landed two feet to the left, bounced away. A football? Really? Micah wouldn't have even needed his handy new aura. Another old saying occurred to him—bringing a knife to a gunfight. He had always understood it to mean that you were picking a fight you couldn't possibly win. Superpowers versus an inaccurate forward pass seemed to apply. Micah cackled and set the football on fire. Steve Whitehead skidded to a halt, the other players stampeding around him. Then he turned and ran for the fence.

Micah fired bursts of ice at their feet, not trying to hit them, just turn the herd back. B3 ran in the middle of the pack, Kenneth hunching between Gavin and Brayden, all of them behind what seemed like most of the defensive line. Micah took careful aim, sighting down his arm, wondering if he could hit one of them on the run, if he could play a literal game of freeze tag and see how they liked it.

Then he felt himself being lifted, and the scenery rushed by like a cartoon background, herd and ice wall and street. He had just enough time to mark the feeling of strong arms bear-hugging him from behind, the sensation of his robe being pulled over his head, and then he was standing in the alley beside the Bowl-o-Rama, his costume stuffed in the duffel bag he had left against the building, his friends standing between him and the dozens of kids who were running everywhere, shouting and pointing and hugging each other.

"What—" he began.

"Shut your stupid ass up," Christian said. She and Jamie and Gabby faced the parking lot in a line. Micah couldn't see what was happening, but yells and curses still filled the smoke-scented air.

"What's going on?" Jamie yelled at the retreating football team. No one answered. Big shock, the jocks ignoring the geeks, never even considering that whoever assaulted the field might be willing to roast a couple of unpopular kids, too.

A minute or two later, Jamie turned. The look on his face made Micah recoil—disgust and anger, maybe even rage.

"Don't look at me like that," Micah said.

"Eat me," Jamie said.

He brushed past Micah. Gabby and Christian followed. Micah watched them go. After a moment, he went with them.

They circled the Bowl-o-Rama, slipped through the skinny trees and scrub bushes behind the building, and emerged onto Tenth Avenue. Jamie set a fast pace. Micah, hungry and tired now that the rush was wearing off, huffed and puffed as he tried to keep up. "Where we going?" he panted.

"We're gonna circle the block and try to get back to school. If anybody sees us, maybe they'll think we never left. In fact—Christian, you feel like taking this dumbass now?"

"Hang on—" Micah said, but then those arms grabbed him again. The scenery flew by, and he shut his mouth.

✳✳✳

Christian and Micah were sitting on their picnic table when Jamie and Gabby reached campus. Micah sat with his hands hanging between his knees, trying hard not to look at Christian. Probably a good idea, since she had been struggling with the urge to strangle him.

She stood. "A bunch of people saw us after we got back. I don't know if they were paying much attention, though. They just wanted to get down to the field and see what was up before it all ended."

"Great," Jamie said. Christian knew what he meant. With their luck, nobody would remember seeing Micah. So much for an alibi.

"Who cares?" Micah said, not looking at them. "Nobody saw me at the field, either. They just saw somebody in a robe."

"Dude," Gabby said. "Kenneth and them know. Besides, you attacked a bunch of students. The cops won't let that go."

Micah shrugged. Christian slapped him in the back of the head. He scowled at her but said nothing else.

"Let's go to the park," Jamie said.

✳

The wind had picked up. It tossed around the thick cobwebs in the rafters of the pavilion. Micah hunched on a table beside Christian, radiating impatience. Jamie and Gabby took their seats across from them. He brushed the dust off the bench for her. So sweet. Not for the first time since all the weirdness began, Gabby wondered why she had never seen him that way before. Her face felt hot. She was probably blushing. The others gave no sign they had noticed. Did they know she had never been kissed, except that one time with Micah, which had been so quick and clumsy it might not even count? Did they care?

She shook her head. Forget that. They were in deep trouble, and it was all Micah's fault. Everyone looked at him. Jamie crossed his arms.

"Look," Micah said. "I didn't do nothing you haven't wanted to do your whole lives."

Christian shook her head. "I can't believe you're gonna sit there and act like that was no big deal," she said. "You *hurt* people, man."

"And you pretty much ruined our only disguise," Jamie said. "How are we supposed to find Jake's killer now? If we use our powers, we have to wear the robes, but now, if we show ourselves in costume, the cops will shoot first and ask questions later. And it ain't like we can make new costumes. None of us can sew."

Micah had the audacity to grin. "It was worth it, man. You should've seen Kenneth and Gavin running like bitches. And I thought Brayden was gonna pee his pants."

Gabby winced. Every time someone gave Micah a chance to apologize or at least admit he screwed up, he made things worse.

Jamie sneered. "You just don't get it, do you? You terrorized a bunch of kids. On Main Street. We'll be lucky if Homeland Security don't set up office at City Hall. And what happens now if whatever got Jake comes after us? You gonna fight it in your street clothes and show everybody what you are?"

Micah stood and headed for the swing set. They looked at each other for a moment. Then they followed him.

"Answer us," Gabby said. Anger bloomed in her chest like fire.

They reached the swings, but instead of sitting in one, Micah turned on them. *"God,"* he spat. "It ain't like I knocked down a church!"

Before Jamie or Christian could do anything, Gabby stepped forward and squeezed Micah's arm and looked him in the eye. He smiled. She smiled back. Then she said, "You're being an ass. Jamie's right about everything."

Micah's mouth fell open. He yanked away from her so hard she stumbled backward. He glared, eyes blazing. The air around them rippled with heat. "Of *course* you'd take his side," he snarled. "I get it. You picked him. Big freaking deal."

She backed away, alarmed. "Picked? What are you talking about?"

Jamie pulled her away. "Forget it. We're getting off track."

Micah walked off, fists still clenched. He punched one of the swing's metal support beams, which shook and buckled. The top part bopped Micah on the head. Dirt and cobwebs rained into his hair.

"Ow," he said. Gabby figured that helped prove Jamie's theory about the auras. Micah hadn't been using his powers, so he wasn't protected.

She walked over to Micah but did not touch him this time. Could he possibly mean what she thought he had? Sure, they had kissed once, but that was two years ago, and he had never said anything about it, never made a single move. She had assumed he regretted it, or that she had been a terrible kisser, or that it had just been an experiment, something they had done only because they had never done it before. Now she was already starting to think back on every interaction, every word, wondering what she had missed, how it was all her fault.

But even if any of that was true, they all had bigger problems right now.

"I'm sorry," she said. "I didn't know you had—feelings, or whatever. You never said anything, so I don't understand why you're mad at Jamie or me. That ain't fair. But as for what you just did at the football field— we can't be like *them*. Remember how we tried it once, right here, and nearly killed somebody? And now we're all in trouble."

"Like the cops can stop us, or even find us." Micah turned to Jamie. "If we have to fight somebody, I'll wear the robe and mask, just like I did today. If the cops can't see I'm one of the good guys, that's their problem."

"Dude," Christian said. "After everything that's happened in this country, you really think they'll see you as the good guy? You or any-body dressed like you? When somebody attacks schoolkids, nobody stops to ask why. And they shouldn't have to."

Micah's expression softened. He seemed weary. "If it comes to that, I'll turn myself in."

"And say what?" Gabby asked, not unkindly. It felt good to speak up and not apologize for it. Confrontation wasn't in her nature, but she was starting to realize that silence could make other people see you as a doormat. "Kenneth and Brayden and Gavin know about us. If the cops throw you in juvie or run you outta town, or if the government shows up and carts you off to some black site, you think those guys will let the rest of us just go home?"

All the defiance drained out of Micah's face. He stared at the ground for a bit, eyes wide open. Like he was really, honestly, feeling the weight of what he had done now that they had pointed it out. After several moments, he hung his head. "Sorry."

"Say that to Kenneth," Jamie said. "He's like us now. We need him."

Micah reddened. His lips pressed into a thin line. His eyes were chips of ice. "No way. I'll do just about anything else, but I won't do that. Not ever."

Christian shook her head and walked away. Jamie sighed.

Gabby watched her friends turn from each other and lapse into silence. They were splintering. Micah had come back to them for about three seconds. Now, if there had ever been a chance, it seemed impossible that he would accept Kenneth, would ever apologize or make friends. And what could the three of them really do about it? They could threaten and cajole and plead and beg. They could gang up and beat the hell out of Micah. But they could never make him reach out to B3. Gabby would have bet a year's allowance Micah would die first.

"Well, what do we do now?" she said. "We could still use Kenneth. He's a lot stronger than any of us. But it won't help us if we lose Micah at the same time."

Micah snorted. Christian shot him a death glare.

"After today, Kenneth might try to kill us himself," Jamie said

They looked at Micah again. He held their gazes and did not back down. They stood there like that, unsure of what to say, for a long time.

CHAPTER NINETEEN

The next morning, a Thursday, when Christian's mother dropped her off at school, the campus was overrun with police and school officials. Cop cars took up most of the visitors' parking spaces. Uniformed officers and people in dark suits and darker sunglasses scurried about. Some had been posted at the various doors. Despite the moderate temperature, Christian shivered.

She saw Jamie pedaling onto the grounds and up to the bike rack. As he chained his ride, Mr. Hoon conversed with two men in coats and ties. Christian trotted over to Jamie while the adults at the doors checked bags and purses, dumping books and gym clothes and phones on the ground while furious teenagers picked everything back up.

"Look at all this shit," Christian said.

Jamie seemed strained, his jaw set, his brow furrowed. "Yeah. My dad heard the FBI's here. To assess the terrorist threat." He made air quotes around the last two words.

Christian's mouth went dry. *Of course. Just what we needed. Thanks, Micah, you jackass.* She had not expected things to happen this quickly. Quapaw City hardly seemed like a terrorist target.

"Shit," she muttered.

"Yeah," Jamie said. "Micah stepped in a big pile of it. And he's tracking it all over our lives."

They walked toward the building. A tall, skinny cop stood in the doorway, his gun prominent on his hip. Was it true some cops could read guilt on your face? Could they really tell when you lied to them, like on TV? As Christian and Jamie approached, the cop gestured at their bags. They handed them over. The cop set Christian's down and

147

unzipped Jamie's and pawed through his school stuff. Finding nothing suspicious, the officer searched hers next. He didn't dump out everything like some of his colleagues had done, so Jamie and Christian kept their mouths shut as he violated their privacy. Once he gave them back their property and moved aside, they entered the building.

"Well, that was fun," Christian said. "Maybe next they can strip-search us. Full body-cavity probe."

"They're just trying to keep us safe," Jamie said. "Nobody wants another school shooting." But he didn't sound like he really believed that.

"Micah used fire and ice, not bullets," she said. Jamie could try to see every perspective if he wanted to, but Christian focused her worry on herself and her friends. Nobody else would.

They turned down the hall where the freshmen lockers were stacked two high and sealed with combination locks. The tile floors had been waxed and reflected the glow from the double fluorescent lights overhead. Jamie and Christian passed an English classroom bearing posters of Shakespeare and James Baldwin; Mr. Singh's math class door and its little whiteboard with the problem of the day scribbled on it; Mrs. Kather's room, its door bare. From the ceiling hung a drooping banner reading, "Go Buffaloes! Beat Star City!"

Christian stopped at her locker. Jamie paused before heading on to his. "Speaking of which," he said, "you hear anything about how they're explaining away the ice and burned spots on the practice field?"

Christian transferred books and notebooks between her backpack and locker. "No. I got here when you did."

Marla Schott was passing by, typing away on her phone and bumping people, who grumbled and kept typing on their own devices. She heard this exchange and paused. "I heard those cops out front say they think the terrorist was using a flamethrower and liquid nitrogen."

Jamie laughed. "Geez. Do they think he drove a couple of fuel tanks onto the field without anybody noticing?"

Marla shrugged and went back to her phone, walking away on her designer flats that probably cost more than any four of Christian's outfits. *That was the longest conversation I've had with her since, like, fourth grade. And she didn't even say anything directly to me.* With her little almond-colored pixie cut and trim body, Marla had always reminded Christian of Emma Watson. Too bad she played for the wrong team. Even sadder that she was a stuck-up bitch who usually looked at Christian and the others like she wouldn't bother scraping them off her fancy shoes. The mere fact that Marla had bothered to speak to Christian and Jamie just proved how weird everything had gotten.

Christian shut and secured her locker, and they walked down to Jamie's. He opened it and got what he needed as Gabby and Micah walked up from the other end of the hall and huddled beside them.

"Y'all hear anything?" Christian asked.

"I listened to KQPC this morning, in case they covered it," Micah said. "They interviewed the chief of police. He said they don't see a connection between yesterday and Jake's murder."

Jamie blinked. "Dang, I was so worried about them thinking you were a terrorist, I didn't even think they might connect you to Jake."

"What Micah did wasn't near that bad," Gabby said. "The only connection is it all happened to ninth graders."

"*We* know that," Christian said. "The problem is that nobody got a clear look at Jake's killer. Everybody saw Micah just fine."

"And they say two events equal a coincidence, but three? That's a pattern," Jamie said. "If whatever's out there kills again, the heat's gonna make today look like Christmas."

Micah scowled. "How many times you want me to say it? I'm sorry. I was wrong. I'm not perfect. I won't do anything else. I'll be a good little dork, just like I've always been, and Kenneth and them can run right over me. Happy?"

He stalked away. The others exchanged glances. Christian couldn't speak for Jamie or Gabby, but she didn't feel happy. Not at all.

The bell rang. As she floated along on the current of students flowing down the right side of the hall, Christian wondered for the first time
if they really, truly, no-shit might not get out of all this alive and free.
She shivered and hugged her books to her chest. Up ahead, where the
hall took a turn to the left, a policeman stood with his hands on his
hips, his service weapon bulging against his hip like a tumor.

✳

Gabby arrived in class two minutes late and muttered an apology
as she passed the teacher's desk and took her seat. Her face felt flushed,
her back sweaty, and her heart thudded rapidly against her rib cage. She
trembled from the adrenaline dumping into her system and the fear that
had gripped her by the throat. Damn Gavin Cloverleaf.

She had rounded a corner just before the tardy bell and nearly
crashed right into his broad gorilla back as he leaned one shoulder
against the wall. Brayden Sears stood beside him, and as they watched,
Micah followed Marla Schott into a classroom. Gabby hung back around
the corner and turned up her hearing, focusing on the Bros' voices; if
they were watching Micah, she wanted to know what they were up to.

"Look at that punk-ass geek," Gavin said, voice dripping with contempt. "Now that he's a real freak, he thinks he's safe."

"Well, he knows all we can do is punch him," Brayden said. "He
could burn us to death before we could even get near him."

Gavin snorted. "That ain't the only way to skin a cat."

"Huh?"

"Nothing," Gavin said.

"Didn't sound like nothing."

"Well, it's not like I'd actually *do* it," Gavin said. He sounded con-
templative, almost like he had a working brain in his thick head.

"Do what?"

"I mean, we could turn him in," Gavin said.

Brayden was silent for a moment. Then he cleared his throat. "Dude."

"I know. We hate rats even more than we hate geeks. Like I said, I wouldn't do it."

"But you've thought about it."

"Hell, yeah, I've thought about it. Kid tried to freaking kill me."

"I'm not down with that, bro."

"For the last time. I wouldn't actually do it. It's fun to think about, though. Can you imagine what the government would do to that kid if they knew what he was?" Gavin laughed, and it was the darkest, coldest sound Gabby had ever heard outside of a horror movie.

A second later, some teacher came along and shooed the Bros to class. Gabby counted to five and then scurried to homeroom.

Now, as kids dug out their notebooks, she concealed her phone in her lap and shot a text to Jamie and Christian. If Gavin was even joking about going to the authorities, they needed to know.

✳✳✳

Between bells, Micah walked alone. Kids milled around him, talking and laughing. Even if they had known, none of them could understand the first thing about what he was going through. B3 had driven him crazy for years. Now he could pay them back with compounded interest, but his friends demanded that he bend over, take his ass-whooping, and ask for more with a smile. And the worst part? He hadn't even been caught. Nobody suspected him but Kenneth, Gavin, and Brayden, and they couldn't rat, not with Kenneth throwing grills around the park. Micah was living in the perfect storm of opportunity, and the others were ruining it.

Still, the possibility that the cops might try to blame him for Jake's terrible death wounded Micah. He could never do anything like that. Sure, he might set some jerk's feet on fire or encase them in a block of ice, but he had always intended to put out those fires and melt that ice before anybody got hurt too badly. He just wanted them to feel as scared and small and humiliated as he had always felt. What was so wrong with that?

But Jake was dead. He had been brutalized, and so had two cops.

Micah walked into Coach Graves's civics classroom and took his seat. Jamie wasn't there yet. Probably still out in the hall with Gabby hanging all over him. Well, let them have their little romance. Her loss.

Marla Schott sat in the row next to him, scrolling through her phone. He leaned back and pretended to pop his neck. She was reading something, but the font was too small for him to see. Micah closed his eyes and concentrated. When he opened them again, every object had grown sharper, more detailed, more *there*. Now he could see enough of the text. She was reading about the attack on the field, but she scrolled too fast for him to get a good sense of the meaning. He closed his eyes again, concentrated, went back to normal-vision mode.

Maybe two minutes till the tardy bell. No time to look up the article himself. God. He would have to talk to Marla Schott.

He cleared his throat and turned to her, smiling. He felt like a fake. "Uh, hey, Marla. Heard anything new about all this?"

She looked at him and frowned. They had been classmates all their lives, but they had exchanged maybe ten words over the last few years. He could tell she had no idea why he was talking to her now. "Yeah," she said. "My mom sent me this article."

"Mom slides into your DMs," Micah said, laughing. "Parents. Right?"

She raised her eyebrows and frowned. "I guess."

"Um." His face burned. Would she notice? "Does it say anything about whether that guy at the field yesterday had anything to do with Jake Hoeper?"

She scrolled and read. "'Local police refused to comment on the ongoing investigation other than to say they have no proof of a connection between the attack on the field and the death of high-school freshman Jake Hoeper or the brutal murders of Officers Thielan and Reiff.'"

"Cool, thanks," Micah said. He turned away and started arranging his books and pens on his desk before she could say something mean, like everyone did sooner or later.

She shrugged. "Whatever."

God, what a bitch.

Still, "have no proof" sounded like the cops were still looking for some. Not good. Maybe whatever killed Jake would lie low until they could find it, kill it, and hide their robes and masks for a year or so. After that, he could revisit the idea of burning the clothes right off Gavin Cloverleaf's body, preferably in front of a girls' PE class.

Micah glanced out the window, which faced Kentucky Boulevard. A black SUV pulled up to the curb. Two men climbed out, looking like they just stepped off the set of a TV show about some federal branch of law enforcement. They wore black coats and black ties and black pants and white shirts and mirrored sunglasses. The driver's brown hair was parted to the left and recently trimmed. The passenger's red mane was cropped close, inviting the sun to beam down on his pale skull.

More badges, Micah thought. *Great.*

✷✻✷

Sitting behind Micah, who had kept quiet since his hissy fit at the lockers, Jamie listened to the morning announcements squawking over the intercom above Coach Graves's head. Mr. Hoon's voice, already high—according to Gavin, anyway, who seemed to think all guys should sound like the lowest note on a bass guitar—sounded tinny and sharp. It cut into Jamie's head like an ice pick. He had taken a couple of aspirin before he left for school, but now, with all the stress from the cops showing up, the pain had intensified. It seemed his head pounded with every heartbeat.

"Don't be alarmed at the police presence," Mr. Hoon was saying. "They're here for our protection. They will also want to interview some of you. Members of the football teams will be exempt from interviews during practice times."

Micah turned toward Jamie, pretending to stretch his back, his go-to move when he wanted to say something in class. Jamie figured the teachers knew exactly what he was doing. Micah had never been as slick as he seemed to believe. "Figures," he whispered. "Can't make any trouble for our precious athletes, even though they suck."

Still wishing he could slap Micah upside the head but trying to keep the peace, Jamie grinned and nodded, one eye on Coach Graves, who flipped through his notes—the same ones, allegedly, that he had used since his first semester on the job.

"Your parents and guardians are being contacted now," Mr. Hoon said. "They will be present when you're questioned unless they give the police permission to proceed without them. In any event, I'd like to repeat this: don't be afraid."

"Unless you're a geek," Micah whispered. "Then you should definitely be scared, because nobody's gonna help you."

When the announcements ended, Coach Graves began his lecture on the Bill of Rights, reading straight from his notes, copying the bulk of it onto the board. Kids passed notes and texted and chewed gum and made obscene gestures at each other. When the Coach turned to face them, the class moved as one, ceasing all illegal activity, sitting up straight, scribbling in their notebooks as if they had never heard anything more important than the verbatim text of the Seventh Amendment. Micah believed most of their classmates were idiots. In a lot of cases, Jamie thought, he was right, but Coach Graves was not the kind of teacher who instilled a desire to learn. He obviously didn't want to be there himself. For today, at least, even Jamie paid him little mind.

Instead, he thought about Jake, about Kenneth, about the dead cops.

Jamie's phone buzzed. He checked his messages. Gabby had sent one to him and Christian:

Heard Gavin say he was thinking of turning Micah in
Said he wouldnt do it but who knows

Jamie's stomach crawled into his throat. Damn Gavin to hell. That was all they needed, more bullshit to worry about.

The rest of the day passed quickly. Jamie supposed time flew when you were terrified of what might happen next.

That afternoon, Jamie walked into the principal's office, which he had never done before. He had never even gotten detention. His dad was sitting in a chair in front of Mr. Hoon's desk. He craned his neck around when Jamie entered but did not speak.

Mr. Hoon and Chief Mark O'Brien sat in office chairs behind Hoon's desk. Two guys Jamie had never seen before flanked the desk, hands clasped at their waists. They were straight out of the movies—dark suits, faces as cold and serious as statues, eyes that looked right through you and into your browser history. Mr. Hoon smiled, but it seemed pale and weak under the clenched jaws of the strangers. Chief O'Brien kept a better poker face than any of them. He might have been waiting for a bus. As Jamie took the chair beside his dad, the redheaded man in a suit half turned and peeked through the cracked blinds, as if hoping the killer might have set up a booth in the parking lot. Jamie's dad's face matched the chief's, but his right leg bounced up and down. It was almost imperceptible, but if Jamie had spotted it, these guys had, too.

"Jamie, Thom, you know Chief O'Brien? And these men represent the federal government." Mr. Hoon forced his smile wider. "So. We all know why we're here." He probably meant to be reassuring, but he really looked as if he had just taken some bad medicine that Jamie would also be required to ingest, an *It's not so bad* expression no kid would trust.

"We're trying to figure out who might be involved with what happened at the field."

Dad kept patting Jamie on the forearm. Jamie wished he would quit it.

"My son's got nothing to do with it," Dad said. "This look like the kind of kid who could kill cops?"

"I don't know," said the dark-haired fed. "What does a cop killer look like to you?"

Dad jabbed a finger toward the man. "I don't know, but I bet I know what one looks like to y'all. Anybody that ain't white." Jamie glanced at Dad, whose muscles, honed from working as a spinner in the light-fixture plant outside of Pinedale, strained the seams of his button-down shirt and sport coat. From the set of his jaw, Jamie could tell he wanted to wrap his strong, calloused hands around someone's throat. *Chill, Dad. We know what happens when a black man and the cops get into it. Those bulges under their coats ain't their wallets.*

As if Jamie had said it out loud, the dark-haired suit hooked his thumb in his trousers pocket, pushing back his coat to reveal the butt of a service weapon. "For the father of an innocent kid, you sure do sound confrontational," the man said. "I wonder why."

"I'll tell you why," Dad said. "Tamir Rice. Sandra Bland. Philando Castile. George Floyd. Should I go on?"

"Be cool, Dad," Jamie said.

"I'd listen to your son if I were you," said the redhead.

"Now wait just a minute," Mr. Hoon said. "Agent Mossman, I think the people of Quapaw City have been through enough without all … this. And you *are* just upset, right, Thom? You have no intention of provoking these gentlemen."

Dad gritted his teeth. He probably wanted to go around the desk and show the feds what happened when he provoked someone, but he was the one who'd taught Jamie what happened when you fought the cops—and sometimes even when you didn't.

"Come on," Jamie whispered, leaning over to his father. "Cool out."

Dad sat back in his chair, but he gripped the armrests as if he wanted to break them. Maybe he did.

The feds still stood in that way only cops and soldiers seemed to know—relaxed on the surface, ready to go at the first sign of trouble. Jamie's heart pounded. His palms had grown sweaty.

Dad looked at Jamie, swallowed hard, nodded. "I'm good," he said. "But look now. My son ain't a murderer. He's a straight-A student on the college prep track. He's never even been in a fight, for God's sake. Besides, look at him. He look strong enough to you, considering what happened to the Hoeper boy?"

The feds said nothing.

"We've got no evidence putting Jamie near the Del Ray house when the Hoeper boy disappeared or when my officers were killed," Chief O'Brien said. "Not even any hearsay. We just need to know where Jamie was during the attack at the field."

Dad looked at Jamie and nodded.

Jamie turned to the chief. "I was walking down the road to the field house with my friends. We were gonna stop by the bowling alley and play some video games. I saw everybody running off the field. I saw smoke. But I never saw anybody in a robe or whatever."

The chief turned to the two suits and raised his eyebrows. The taller one shrugged.

"Who was with you?" Mr. Hoon asked.

"Christian Allen. Gabby Davison. And, uh, Micah Sterne." He had not planned to include Micah if they asked him that question. Micah had not walked with them, and someone might have noticed that. But what was Jamie supposed to do? If they caught Micah and found out what he could do, they would be very close to finding out about Jamie and the others. Soon they'd wind up in some government lab, being dissected like a frog in tenth-grade biology. Besides, it wasn't really a lie.

Micah *had* been with them when the players ran off the practice field.
Part of the time, anyway.

"All right, son, you can go back to class," the chief said.

Jamie and his dad stood up. The dark-haired suit stepped forward.
"Would you mind sticking around a moment, Mr. Entmann?"

Dad scowled, but his face softened when he looked at Jamie. "I'll
see you this evening," he said to his son.

"Okay," Jamie said. He shouldered his backpack and left.

In the hall, he walked quickly, glancing over his shoulder to make
sure no one had followed him. What were those feds even doing here?
The idea of terrorists in Quapaw City seemed even more insane than
what had actually happened. What were terrorists going to do here,
fly a plane into Larry's Grocery or suicide-bomb the Walmart, which
wasn't even a Supercenter?

After rounding a corner and finding himself alone in the hall, Jamie
leaned against the lockers and breathed deeply, trying to slow down
his heart rate. First B3, then whatever happened in Micah's shed, then
superpowers, and now this—local and federal authorities investigating
them. What could be next? How could things get worse?

But he had little time to worry about it now. He had to warn the
others.

He took out his phone and started texting.

✳

Micah's mom had taken the afternoon off from her job as manager
of the Huddle House. As she sat beside Micah in Hoon's office, she
played with the crystal she wore on a chain around her neck. Micah
rolled his eyes and scowled every time he saw her doing it. She had
probably spent half the night burning incense and spreading flower
petals all over her room, or whatever she did to invoke the Goddess.
Even before Jake, before the football field, before she noticed her shed

had somehow lost one wall and both doors, she had been watching him when she didn't think he was paying attention. He'd felt her standing in the doorway of his room, staring at his back while he played video games. She hovered nearby while he texted, glancing at his screen. Several times, he had come home from school and found his drawers a bit more disheveled than he had left them, or, even more telling, far neater. He had no idea whether she were looking for drugs or weapons or what, nor did he care that much. As long as she stayed out of his way, she could hunt and theorize to her heart's content.

At least his father was still long-hauling God-knew-what in his semi somewhere up in Washington State. One less meddler for Micah to worry about.

Micah hated Hoon's office. The walls were bare, except for the diplomas at eye level to the principal's right. Stained carpet the color of pea soup had worn nearly to threads in a path from the door to Hoon's chair. No one had dusted the venetian blinds in maybe five hundred years. Some of the slats were bent, a few broken. It always felt ten degrees too cool in there, as if Hoon was a reptile. Now, Mom sat beside him in the cruddy, squeaky chairs that might have been black once and now looked darkish gray.

The two suits he'd seen getting out of their car stood on either side of Hoon. They did not know they were looking for Micah. Even if they had known, they had nothing on him.

Hoon had been blathering on and on ever since they sat down— "we're not here to accuse anybody" this, "we fully support all our students and their families" that. Where had he and all the other principals been while Gavin and Brayden and Kenneth had tortured Micah for years on end? Where had all the teachers been? Or the parents? Micah had nothing to say to these dickweeds.

"So I'll just turn this over to Chief O'Brien," said Hoon, smiling like a politician in an election year.

Be cool, bro, Micah thought. *Nobody's looking to fire you.*

"Thanks," said O'Brien, sitting there in his stupid blue uniform with the hat in his lap. How long had he been sitting like that? How many times had he thanked Hoon for making him do all the work? "Mrs. Sterne, Micah, we've just got a couple of questions for now, so answer truthfully and we'll be out of your hair."

Bite me, thought Micah. "Sure," he said.

"Where were you when the football team was attacked yesterday?" O'Brien asked.

"Walking the roads like the ramblin' man I am," Micah said.

Mr. Hoon looked taken aback. He frowned. The suits' expressions didn't change. Micah winked at them.

"Don't get smart," his mother snapped. "Just answer the question."

He glanced at her and sighed. She was always butting in. "Fine. I was walking down the service road with my friends. Jamie Entmann, Christian Allen, and Gabby Davison."

Hoon nodded. As if on cue, all four men took out little notepads and scribbled in them. Micah grinned again, enjoying the pantomime.

"You four must be awful close," O'Brien said. "You're telling the exact same story in almost the exact same words."

"Of course we're close," Micah said. "We've had to be. When four kids get picked on practically from the day they're born, they're gonna gravitate toward each other. Doesn't take a degree in psychology to see that."

Mom smacked his arm with the back of her hand. Hoon frowned again. The suits seemed to stiffen. Maybe he had ruffled their feathers. But O'Brien just watched him, like Micah had a booger hanging out of his nose.

"These people who bullied you," O'Brien said. "Any of 'em athletes?"

"Aren't they always?"

"Football players?"

"Aren't they always?"

"Micah," Mom hissed.

The suits' jaws clenched. Hoon looked pained. He wrote something on his notepad without really looking at it.

Probably drawing little boats. Useless moron.

"It would be fair to say you and your friends hold a grudge," said O'Brien.

Micah laughed and shook his head. "I see what you're doing. Yeah, we don't like certain kids who've treated us like garbage all our lives. Big shock. But just because we don't like 'em doesn't mean we'd set 'em on fire."

The four men scribbled in their pads again.

"Look," Mom said, her voice trembling as she gripped the arms of the chair. "Do we need to get our lawyer in here?"

This was a bluff. They had no lawyer and couldn't afford one. Micah was surprised his mother had the guts to say something like that to a cop. She spent most of her time working and making excuses for his father's missing every school function and yelling at Micah about the messes he left in their house. If she didn't get on his nerves so much, he might have admired her in that moment.

One of the suits took a half step forward. So he wasn't just a cardboard cutout. "Ma'am, my name is Chip Mossman," he said. "I'm with Homeland Security." He flashed his identification. Then he indicated the other suit. "This is Special Agent Drew Greenwalt of the Federal Bureau of Investigation. We're here to assess the terrorist threat in Quapaw City."

"And to discover the connection, if any, between this threat and the recent murders," said Greenwalt.

"What does that have to do with us?" Mom said. "You can't believe Micah had anything to do with that. Look at him. His arms look like two strings hanging off his shirt."

"Mom!" cried Micah.

"Well, they do," she said.

"We aren't ruling anything out," said Mossman. "The unsub at the football field was described as being about your boy's size."

"What, you think I can shoot ice outta my eyeballs and fire out my butt?" Micah scoffed. "Somebody actually *pays* you guys?"

"Micah," Hoon said, dropping his notepad on his desk. The expression on his face suggested he had never considered the possibility of a student's taking on federal agents in his office and that he did not care for it one bit. "Let's keep this civil. But frankly, Mrs. Sterne's right. I don't know how a boy his age and size would have managed what allegedly happened at the field."

"Yeah," said Micah, though Hoon's assessment of his capabilities annoyed him.

"The attitude isn't helping," Hoon said.

"Sorry," said Micah, sounding anything but.

"You can go back to class now," O'Brien said, his tone flat, as he wrote in his notebook. When he looked back at Micah, his eyes were clear and piercing.

He could be trouble.

"Thanks," said Micah, standing up. "I hope you guys catch whoever did it. It's getting so it ain't safe to walk the streets. But then, for some of us, it never was."

Mom practically dragged him out the door by his ear. Once she had him outside, she grabbed him by the shoulders and shook him. "What was that all about?" she said. "You was raised with better manners than that! You *trying* to get 'em after you? You *trying* to embarrass me and your daddy?"

"No," he said. "I'm trying to get back to class. We got a test coming up."

He walked away, leaving her standing in the office and staring at him as if she had never seen him before.

＊✳＊

Responding to Gabby's text, Jamie reached the pavilion forty-five minutes or so after school let out. Christian walked with him, hands in her jacket pocket. Muted afternoon sunlight beamed through the gaps in the trees, illuminating scattered patches of leaf-covered ground. The breeze had died down, so nothing stirred except the occasional squirrel searching for food.

Gabby sat on a table, her bike leaning against a pillar. She was typing away on her phone, her brow furrowed, eyes narrowed. When Jamie and Christian stepped onto the platform, Gabby sighed and put her phone in her pocket.

"What now?" Jamie asked.

Gabby shook her head. "Freaking Micah," she said. "Apparently he showed his ass in Hoon's office."

Christian groaned. "That kid's mouth could swallow the whole damn world."

Jamie sat next to Gabby and leaned against her. "Anything else about Gavin?"

"Not that I know of," Gabby said.

"What do we do about him?" Christian asked. "Tie him up and throw him in a closet for the next fifty years or so?"

"Don't tempt me," Jamie said.

Christian sat on the bench of the table across from the others. They fell silent. Jamie watched the water through the gap in the trees. It looked as still and solid as glass. He thought about Gavin for a long time.

"Any ideas?" Gabby asked. Christian jumped at the sound of her voice. Jamie guessed she had been thinking deeply, too.

"Not really," Jamie said. "I mean, we can't make him stay quiet unless we kill him or kidnap him. But if he does talk, that's all she wrote for us. Including Kenneth."

A long pause, and then Christian said, "Well, I guess we can't really kill him. Because that would be wrong. Yeah?"

"Yeah," Jamie said. But when he thought of what would happen to him and his friends if the cops and feds knew their secret, he felt a lot less convinced.

CHAPTER TWENTY

N a'ul of the Go'kan waited in the trees hours after the daystar dipped below the horizon, his four arms and both legs wrapped around the trunk. After snapping a few branches and letting them fall, thus clearing his sight lines to the youngling's dwelling, he had chosen a position high enough to conceal himself from the lessers and their strange vehicles, which ran without any beasts to pull them. Would the target he had chosen appear before light shone on the world again? He had no idea, but the thrill of the hunt pulled at him even harder than the hunger he planned to satisfy with the youngling's lifeblood. If the boy kept to his dwelling, Na'ul would soon reconsider the use of his old tactics—burning the sanctuary to the ground, driving the lessers into the open, and ripping them to pieces. He—

Movement in one of the dwelling's windows. Na'ul gripped the trunk tighter and then stilled himself, even his breathing, so that not a single one of the dying leaves on this tree would move.

The window eased open. The odd mesh covering popped off and fell into the hedges.

Na'ul's target climbed out. Then he put the mesh covering back against the window frame. He stepped through the hedges and made his way around the house, where his two-wheeler leaned against the wall. The boy called Gavin mounted it and eased down the rock path toward the thoroughfare. A cool breeze carried the crackle of rocks under those wheels. Once on the thoroughfare proper, the youngling turned in Na'ul's direction, pumping those strange pedals with his feet.

As he had done with the first boy, the prince of the Go'kan waited until Gavin approached his tree. Then Na'ul dropped onto the street.

He rose up before the oncoming child, throwing all four arms out as if anticipating an embrace. Thrusting his head forward, he roared.

The boy's eyes widened. He cried out and yanked his vehicle sideways. It skidded out of control and dumped him on the road.

Na'ul stepped toward him as he got to his feet, bleeding from one elbow and knee. His blood stank of fear and stupid defiance.

"Get the hell away from me!" the boy shrieked.

From deep in his throat, Na'ul growled.

The boy quaked. His close-cropped hair revealed his pale scalp, glowing in the moonlight. "Help!" he shouted. "Somebody!"

"You are not the one I want," Na'ul said in his own language, sending his words to the boy on the winds of his thoughts. "But I believe your dismembered carcass will draw him out."

The boy listened, his eyes growing wider. He opened his mouth and mimicked screaming, but no sound emerged. Something wet and reeking ran down his legs and puddled at his feet. He shook his head from side to side, as if negating the night's very existence.

Na'ul of the Go'kan laughed, long and deep.

Then the boy did manage to scream, those thick and clumsy lips vibrating with the force of it, his sloping brow looking pale in the moonlight even as the rest of his face reddened with the effort.

Along the road, windows lit up.

"Help me!" the boy cried again. He turned to run.

Na'ul grabbed him and squeezed, talons puncturing the boy's body. The child screamed.

Na'ul carried him into the trees, branches and leaves striking them, the trunk shaking. In the upper reaches, Na'ul bit down on the boy's head. The blood was sour but strong.

Below, the boy's conveyance lay in the street. As Na'ul drank, lessers emerged from their dens and congregated in their courtyards. They talked and gesticulated. Soon, the weeping would begin.

One of the adult males spotted the abandoned vehicle and trotted over to it, using some kind of handheld illumination to spotlight it.

"John," the man shouted. "John Cloverleaf! Is this Gavin's bike?"

More lessers, including the one who seemed to be named John, approached. When this one saw the vehicle, sheer terror wafted from his very pores. It seasoned the blood Na'ul was still drinking. When the crowd dispersed, probably to look for the boy now dying above them, Na'ul would maim the body and leave it where even such as they could find it. And then he would wait for the opportunity to hunt his true quarry.

CHAPTER TWENTY-ONE

The next morning, Kenneth awoke to someone shaking his shoulder. He mumbled and turned over, eyes still closed, hoping whoever it was would go away. He had been dreaming something light and pleasant that had already slipped behind the veil of his consciousness, and he hoped that if he could go back to sleep, he could find that place again. But the hand on his shoulder kept shaking him. "Kenneth," said an insistent voice. "Kenneth, you have to wake up."

"Ten more minutes," he muttered.

"Now," the voice said. He had awakened enough to recognize it as his mother's. He opened his eyes. She sat on the edge of his bed. As his sleep-fog cleared, he registered her red and swollen eyes. Her hair frizzed as if she had suffered an electric shock—or as if she hadn't brushed it since she got out of bed.

When Kenneth was six years old, he had gotten a puppy for his birthday, a mixed-breed bundle of fur with big brown eyes and a crooked tail. He had loved that dog, which he had named Stitch after the cartoon character. Every day, Kenneth had thrown an old, ratty tennis ball across the backyard and howled with delight every time Stitch brought it back. They chased each other through summer's deep grass and fall's dead leaves. Stitch had been Kenneth's best friend, maybe the best friend he had ever had, including Brayden and Gavin. And one morning, someone—Kenneth had never moved past the suspicion that it had been him—left the door open, and Stitch disappeared. The next day, a neighbor found him lying dead in the street. When his mom had called Kenneth into the living room so they could tell him Stitch was dead, she had worn the same expression she was wearing now.

Kenneth sat up, his stomach rolling over. He felt as if he might vomit. "What's wrong?"

"It's bad," she said, stroking his shoulder.

A lump the size of an apple swelled in Kenneth's throat. He labored to breathe. "Who?"

Tears slipped from his mother's eyes. "Oh, honey," she said. "It's Gavin."

Later, Kenneth sat on the couch between his mother and father. Brayden slumped in Kenneth's dad's easy chair, head hanging, hands dangling between his knees. He hadn't said a word, not even when he'd first arrived and Kenneth had hugged him. They had never embraced like that in the history of their friendship. In almost any other case, either of them would punch any guy who tried to hug them, except their fathers. They didn't swing that way. But Kenneth hadn't even thought about it. He just pulled Brayden to him. Brayden had returned the hug but without strength, like his body knew what to do even though his mind had checked out.

Mr. and Mrs. Sears—Carl and Maryanne to their friends such as Kenneth's parents, Aaron and Jane—sat on the arms of the chair, each with a hand on Brayden's shoulders. Kenneth's dad and Mr. Sears had spoken only a little more than Brayden, but both Mom and Mrs. Sears had wept openly and talked about what a good boy Gavin had been, how John and Ora Cloverleaf must be dying. Funeral arrangements to be determined, visitation with the family inevitable and necessary. Who would bring what food to them, who would stay with them, who would offer to help.

Kenneth heard everything without really listening. His brain had processed the bare facts of the situation but not the emotions or how to live with them. Gavin was dead. Taken right off his own bicycle, only yards from his house. Disappeared without a trace, like they said on TV shows. And then this morning, Mr. Cloverleaf had walked out the front door and tripped on Gavin's mangled, violated body.

Oh, you bastard. You killed Jake Hoeper, probably just for the hell of it. Then you killed those two cops for trying to protect me. Now one of my best friends. I'll get you.

But, as Mrs. Sears burst into tears again and Mr. Sears tried to comfort her with their big-for-his-age, nearly catatonic son between them, Gavin's voice spoke to Kenneth. *Yeah, you go ahead and get him back. But if you had done something that night those cops died, I might still be alive. You got powers. You could probably break that monster's back with your bare hands. But you pussied out. You ran. And now I'm dead.*

I'm sorry, Kenneth thought. *I'm so damn sorry, man.*

Okay, said Gavin. *I guess I'll just come back to life, then.*

Kenneth got the message. Sorry didn't cut it. Sorry did nothing, in fact. He had spent so much of his life slapping weaker kids around, but the first time something strong stepped to him, he ran like a little bitch. He would have to live with that for the rest of his life.

Not again, he thought. *I won't run again.*

But, as his mother stood and asked Mrs. Sears to help her make some sandwiches for everyone, as they left the room leaning on each other and whispering, Kenneth wondered whether he could keep that vow.

CHAPTER TWENTY-TWO

On Monday, the student body, faculty, and staff moved through the halls and classrooms more quietly than usual, their conversations muted. No one engaged in what Mr. Hoon called "horseplay" and what Coach Graves had sometimes labeled "grabass." Teachers delivered their lectures and activities in reserved voices. Students took notes or stared at their desks in the kind of silence most teachers demanded and seldom got. In the one class Gabby had shared with Gavin, his empty desk seemed like the center of the room. The rest of them orbited it like the sun, glancing at it for a fraction of a second and then looking away. During that morning's announcements, Mr. Hoon claimed to have redoubled his efforts to bring in grief counselors. He had first made the request after Jake Hoeper's death. Would anything happen this time?

Of everyone on campus, only Micah and the two federal agents seemed unaffected. Micah had hailed Gabby with a smile on his face until she hissed at him to have some respect. He had seemed shocked, whether from the concept that Gavin deserved anyone's regard or at the way she asserted herself, Gabby couldn't say.

As for the agents, they had apparently postponed their scheduled interviews in favor of bringing back Gabby and her friends again. The four of them had well-documented problems with Gavin. Jamie had suggested that the agents probably wanted another read on their folks, too; what wouldn't a parent do to protect their child from a bully? From what Gabby could gather in her brief and whispered conversations, no one had gotten angry or defensive this time, not even Micah. In her interview, which consisted of basic *where were you at such-and-such a time* questions, everyone had seemed sad and scared. Even Mom had just stared out the window, wiping away tears, and it took a lot to silence Xiomara Davison. In the initial interview, Gabby's mom had informed the agents that they must have been crazy to think that her good girl could be involved with something like the attack on the football team. She had waved a finger at them, crossed her arms, and stared them down. This time, she was almost as quiet as Gabby's dad, who had always been bookish and reserved. The agents seemed satisfied that Gabby was telling the truth; she had been home in bed when someone took Gavin, asleep when his father had found the body.

Still, guilt and shame had wrapped themselves around her like a blanket, because when she had heard the news, she had felt relieved, like something had clenched in her chest and now had loosened, released, disappeared. Because only Gavin had thought of ratting them out, and now he couldn't. They were safe, for now.

Stop it. That's awful. Think of his family.

But if she was honest with herself, she cared a lot more about herself and her friends.

On the way out of Mr. Hoon's office, she had passed Christian and her mom, though Gabby hadn't immediately recognized her. Ms. Frey Posey, who had taken back her maiden name after her divorce, was a short, stocky woman who shared Christian's love of vintage rock-band T-shirts, blue jeans, and cool combat boots. But today, she wore an off-white dress and flats, and her hair had been professionally styled. Gabby had never seen her like that before.

It had been that kind of day—so different from most days that Gabby sometimes wondered if she had fallen through another dimensional portal and into some alternate version of her life.

Kenneth and Brayden had stayed home, and by the time school let out, the terrified student body and faculty could not leave campus fast enough.

Jamie met Gabby at her locker as she put her books and materials away. "You wanna head over to Pizza of Mind and grab a slice?" he asked, leaning against the other lockers. "I'd like to get this day out of my head."

"I'll meet you there," she said. "I've got an errand to run first."

He looked at her for a moment, eyebrows raised. When she said nothing else, he hitched up his backpack. "Okay. I'll wait for you inside."

Gabby watched him leave. Then she put her backpack over one shoulder and headed for the office. The blinds were closed, the door shut. Gabby leaned against the window and closed her eyes. She concentrated.

From the other side of the door, scratching, the thump of objects being moved around, papers shuffled. Probably Mrs. Calvert doing whatever she did in the afternoons. Regardless, it meant Gabby would have to stay on this side of the door, even if it was unlocked. She had no reason to be in the office and didn't want to answer anyone's questions.

Listen past that noise. Increase your range. Home in on the voices. The voices. The voices.

Like someone had turned up a TV in an adjacent room, a conversation revealed itself, the words gummy and slurred at first as she fine-tuned her focus, something she and the others had been practicing. Then whole sentences formed, and finally the voices, their pitches and intonations.

"None of our colleagues will be joining us anytime soon," said a deep voice with a harsh edge. It sounded like that agent, Mossman, the one with the dark hair and the clenched jaw.

"You've gotta be kidding," said someone else. A Southern accent, but not Mr. Hoon—probably Chief O'Brien. "What are y'all waiting for? Somebody to drive over half our kids with a road grader?"

"I'm here to investigate terrorism," said Mossman. "And since we have seen no evidence of a terrorist attack, you're lucky I'm still here at all."

"Yeah, I've won the lottery, I reckon."

"What about you, Agent Greenwalt?" A higher Southern voice, tinged with more fear than the others—Mr. Hoon. "Surely the FBI is interested in what appears to be an especially vicious serial killer."

"We would be, if we could confirm it *is* a serial killer. But the way these people have been mangled and bitten, the kinds of bite marks, the way that police car was crushed—it doesn't look like the work of one person."

"Well, what the devil *does* it look like?" snarled O'Brien.

"Some of my superiors think it's some sort of large animal," said Greenwalt.

"That's bullshit," said Chief O'Brien. He sounded both angry and disgusted.

"I know, Chief. I know. But no one can believe one guy ripped that kid apart or crushed that car. I don't believe it myself."

"So we're really on our own," said Hoon.

"Yes," said Mossman.

That Mossman guy—there's something about his voice. He sounds almost excited. Two kids and two cops dead, and he thinks it's some kind of opportunity.

"Great," said Mr. Hoon. "Well, if you've got more talking to do, gentlemen, you'll have to do it somewhere else. I have to go see the Cloverleafs and tell them I'm sorry their son is dead."

Gabby trotted away from the office and out the front doors, turning down her volume as she went. Outside, she ran the length of the parking lot and around the corner of the building. After a moment, all the adults exited. Mossman and Greenwalt stopped at the bottom of the steps and watched the others get into their separate cars, pull out, and leave. Once everyone else had cleared the parking lot, Mossman turned to Greenwalt, and Gabby turned up her volume again.

"So," Mossman was saying, "what else did the Engineer tell you?"

"Jeffcoat and Kragthorpe just eliminated the threat in Denver," said Greenwalt.

"Drew," sighed Mossman, "I know we're stuck here in Nowhere's Anus, but let's not compromise our colleagues by using their real names, okay?"

"Okay, *Manticore*," Greenwalt said. "The Engineer said that *Canebrake* and *Shrike* just eliminated the threat in Denver. Happy?"

Mossman frowned. Then he sighed. "Okay. Tell me about it."

"Class Ten, so the biggest problem was finding it. And it was mostly eating neighborhood pets."

"Mostly?" said Mossman.

"They're pretty sure it killed a homeless guy. Nobody who'll be missed."

"And our situation?"

"Engineer agrees it's a bogey."

"Any idea what kind?"

"No."

Mossman took something from his pocket—candy? breath mints?— and popped a piece into his mouth. "I wish we could look this shit up on Wikipedia."

"I'm sure the database is coming along nicely. Give me one of those."

Mossman handed Greenwalt the pack. Greenwalt took some and gave the roll back to Mossman, who put it back in his pocket. "I remember when you thought the whole idea of bogeys was insane."

"Yeah, until me and Doberman scragged that Class Five outside Houston," said Greenwalt. "But I still can't believe it most of the time. What do you think we're dealing with here? Three? Four?"

Mossman chewed his candy for a moment. The loud crunches made Gabby wince. "Right now, I'd say it's more like a Five. Maybe even as low as Six. It's killing people and doing damage. But it looks to be interested in one person at a time, and its powers and abilities seem limited. We got lucky."

"Tell that to the Hoeper kid, or those two cops," said Greenwalt.

"But I know what you mean. If we ever get a Class One, I'm booking passage on the next rocket to Mars."

"Anyway," said Mossman, popping more candy, "we'll proceed as planned. Any word on the weapons cache?"

"Engineer said it will be waiting at the assigned coordinates."

"If this thing's really a Class Five or Six, our Glocks may do the trick."

"Tell that to those cops," Greenwalt said again. They stood for a while longer, just watching the sky and the road. Gabby turned and skirted the side of the building, lowering her volume as she ran. When she reached the rear of the campus, she jogged across the courtyard, past the picnic tables and the trees dotting the grounds. When she met Jamie, they had a lot to talk about.

Who were the Engineer, Jeffcoat, and Kragthorpe—also known as Canebrake and Shrike? Who was Doberman? Greenwalt had called Mossman "Manticore," so they all must have had codenames. But the number of names suggested the presence of a team, and it seemed like "the Engineer" was the leader.

For what seemed like the thousandth time since their ill-fated LARP, Gabby wondered just what the hell she and her friends had gotten themselves into.

✳✷✳

The sun had been down for two hours when Jamie's cell phone buzzed with a group message.

Micah: Did u talk 2 those feds again
Christian: Like those asshats would let us off the hook

Jamie understood her frustration. They weren't playing high-school games with kids they didn't like anymore. Four people had died so far because of what they had let into the world. Now the government suspected them. Not just because Gavin had picked on all of them, but because Micah had mouthed off. The kid never knew when to stop.

Gabby: They can't really think we did this!
Jamie: We don't have the right kind of teeth
Jamie: Or the strength
Jamie: But they know we're involved
Jamie: We aren't safe
Micah: I can run them outta town
Jamie: NO
Jamie: You want them to call the National Guard?
Jamie: You want to go to jail?
Christian: Guantanamo
Micah: Like that place could hold us

It sounded like he was sulking. Jamie didn't care.

Jamie: We need to hunt this thing down
Jamie: Now
Gabby: Yes then the feds will leave
Micah: I'm down
Christian: Big of you

In replying to Christian, Micah used only the middle-finger emoji, repeated ten times.

Gabby: Where do we start?
Jamie: Kenneth's street
Jamie: Three out of four killed there

Gabby and Christian agreed. Micah said nothing for a while. Then:

Micah: I won't help him

"God, Micah," Jamie said, resisting the urge to throw his phone across the room.

Christian: Then don't come

Jamie sighed. He should make peace if he could, especially since they looked to him as the idea man, the leader, whether he wanted them to or not.

Jamie: Micah we could use you
Micah: No
Micah: I got another idea
Micah: But holler if anything happens
Micah: To you, not Kenneth

That was about the best that they could hope for under the circumstances.

Jamie: K
Jamie: L8R

Jamie took up his Earth Science textbook and tried to study igneous rocks, but his mind kept wandering back to Gavin. The guy had always been a jerk, even before they discovered the usual teenage reasons why kids hate each other. Nobody deserved to go out like that. But at the same time, Jamie kept thinking, *At least we don't have to worry about him turning us in.*

As soon as the thought had been articulated, Jamie shoved it away, his face flushing with shame. *What the hell's wrong with you? The kid's dead. There ain't no coming back from that.* And Jamie could not forget, even for an instant, how the killer had reached Earth in the first place.

They had a lot to make up for.

CHAPTER TWENTY-THREE

Approximately thirty hours later, Micah crouched beside a house on Ladd Way, across the street and three lots down from Brayden Sears's. His bike leaned against a truck parked at the curb. If anybody caught him, Micah could claim he had gotten stir-crazy and decided to get some air. He had a clear view of Brayden's place, in case anything tried to get in—or if Brayden left. He halfway hoped Brayden would be stupid enough to sneak out. Even if whatever killed Gavin wasn't hanging around, Micah might do a little damage, just for fun. He still remembered the time Brayden had atomic-wedgied him in front of Gabby. Maybe he could set Brayden's feet on fire or freeze his crotch, just to see the look on the big goof's face.

Micah still couldn't believe the others wanted to help Kenneth Del Ray, the biggest tool in the history of southeast Arkansas. The guy had thrown a grill at them, for God's sake, and they wanted to bring him into the group. What would they want to do next, form a book club? And what was with all this bullshit handwringing over Gavin? You'd think the world had actually lost somebody worth a damn.

Micah sat in the grass and waved away mosquitoes. He would be glad when the weather cooled enough to drive away the stupid bugs. The temperature usually started dropping around this time of year. Maybe zapping them from the sky one at a time would be a good way to hone his powers. He could even form some ice cubes around flies and then drop them in Kenneth's drink. Just the thought made him smile.

Which window was Brayden's? If Micah just knew for sure, he could set the bushes on fire, just for laughs, and zoom before Brayden's parents or the cops showed up.

After a while, he stood, his knees cracking. He felt no concern about what might happen if the Searses saw his shadow outside the window. He could distract them with a nice yard fire or the sight of their vehicle encased in a block of ice. Of course, any of those shenanigans might bring those two feds around, and they made Micah more nervous than he let on. They—

Something moved in the trees, the two big ones across from Brayden's house. Some of the limbs bounced, the leaves rattling like bones clacking in a coffin. Some cascaded down and formed a thin carpet around the trunk.

Maybe it's the wind.

But there was very little breeze tonight.

Squirrels?

Sure, if they weighed like eight hundred pounds.

A shape dropped from the tree. It looked like a person, only much bigger. When it rose to its full height, its head and upper torso were lost in the limbs.

Micah flattened himself against the wall, his stomach climbing into his dry throat.

The figure stepped away from the tree but not quite into the pool of light cast from the streetlamp. Its arms—holy shit, there were *four* of them—were as thick as Kenneth's waist. *Thank God I didn't go over there. That guy looks like he could pick his teeth with me, powers or not. If it is a guy. Man, screw this.* Micah eased down and pulled himself along on his belly, heading for his bike, never taking his eyes from whatever stalked the Sears house. *I'm outta here. You're on your own, Brayden, and it couldn't happen to a shittier guy.*

When he reached his bike, he walked it into the street, his heart thumping in his chest while the truck obscured his view of the stalker. Then he leaped on and started pedaling, pumping as fast as he could.

From behind him, a rhythmic *slap-slap-slap* against the pavement. He looked over his shoulder.

The thing was chasing him down the street, its four arms out-stretched as it passed under a streetlamp. Micah saw the sharp talons at the ends of its fingers, the red alien eyes, the blue skin, the impossibly wide mouth stretched open and filled with teeth at least two inches long, like the Sarlacc—*oh, God! Its mouth is like the Sarlacc.*

For all Micah's enhanced strength, the thing seemed to be gaining. Micah screamed.

The creature came on, faster and faster. What would those claws feel like when they raked across his back and plucked him off the bike, which would clatter to the street, where it would be found just like Jake Hoeper's had been—

Micah screamed again and blind-fired a blast of flame over his shoulder. The monster roared. Micah didn't dare look back.

✳

Christian, Gabby, and Jamie lay on the roof of the house across the street from Kenneth's. They had seen nothing all night except for police cars, which passed so frequently you could set your watch by them, though none of them wore a watch. No one had spoken since Jamie had deposited them, one by one, on the roof. Later, either he or Christian would have to take Gabby home, too fast or too high for the cops to see.

At the Del Rays' place, no one had so much as turned a light on or off. Except for the trees swaying in the occasional breeze, they might have been looking at a painting.

"Yo," Jamie whispered. "Something's been bothering me."

Gabby scooted closer. "What?"

"When Gavin died, I was—well, not glad. More like relieved."

Christian was propped on her elbows, eating candy from a bag. Now she raised an eyebrow. "Relieved how?"

Jamie looked away. That deep, burning shame he had felt ever since the night Gavin died began to churn inside him again. "Like, I said to myself, 'Now we don't have to worry about getting turned in.' Pretty screwed up, huh?"

Christian shrugged. "I thought the same thing."

"Really?"

She pushed the bag away and rested her chin on her palms. "Well, yeah. He just went around casually talking about sending us to some government hell? Screw that, and screw him."

"You don't feel bad at all?" Gabby asked, her voice soft, almost inaudible. She seemed tense. Maybe these thoughts had occurred to her, too.

"I feel bad for his family," Christian said. "I even feel bad for Kenneth, a little. But I didn't wish this on him. I didn't make it happen. And neither did y'all. I'm gonna save my grief for somebody who wasn't a huge dick every day of their life."

"Huh," Jamie said. Christian turned back to Kenneth's house. Gabby, who had barely joined the conversation anyway, stayed quiet. Maybe Christian had a point. The world wouldn't exactly lose much with Gavin gone, and he might have made their lives a whole lot worse, if he had lived. Still, it seemed wrong to feel anything positive about a kid getting mangled. It—

Jamie's phone buzzed in his pocket. He shifted and dug it out. "Micah," he whispered. "He wants me to call him."

Gabby frowned. "Nobody calls anybody."

"Something must be up." Jamie scrolled through his contacts. A moment later, the phone was ringing. "Come on," he whispered.

Micah answered. He sounded out of breath and scared half to death. Jamie listened for a moment. His expression must have alarmed his friends. "What is it?" Gabby asked.

Jamie held up a finger—*hang on*. "Slow down, man. Tell me again." He listened for a while longer. Somewhere in the middle of Micah's story, he broke out in goose flesh. "Jesus. Look, we need to get home. No use sitting around when we know that thing ain't here. I'll fill everybody in, and we'll talk after school tomorrow. Figure out our next move. And lock your freaking house, whatever you do. Yeah. No, that sounds good. If you can pull it off, holler at us. Okay. Bye."

He slipped the phone back into his pocket and looked at the other two. "We got trouble," he said. "And it's big. Like eight feet tall."

CHAPTER TWENTY-FOUR

The next morning, Micah's mother came into his room and shook his shoulder. "Wake up. You're gonna be late for school."

Micah rolled over and tried to put a new ability to work. Lately, bored out of his mind in science class, he had been trying to raise and lower his body temperature, measuring his success with a digital thermometer he had found in a bathroom drawer. Some of the kids looked at him like he was crazy, but he didn't care. And Mrs. Kather never saw him, so whatever.

Like his friends, he had gotten better at controlling his power. And he had been practicing for an occasion just like today.

He made his skin flush. "I don't feel like going today. I ache all over, and I think I got a fever."

Mom held a hand to his forehead, her brow knitted. "You do feel awful hot. I better call the doctor's and see if they can fit you in."

"No, no," he said. "I'll be okay. I just wanna sleep."

She looked at him for a long time, and he knew what she was thinking—what would his father say? But Dad was still on the road, and Micah doubted he would have had an opinion one way or another. School had always been Mom's purview. After a while, she nodded. "Okay. But don't leave the house, you hear? If I find out you so much as stuck one toe in the yard, I'll tan your hide, and I don't care how old you are."

"Fine, Mom. *God.*" He sounded exasperated, but he had to fight to keep from smiling. It was going to work. Every schoolkid in the world would envy him, if they only knew.

Half an hour later, after calling the school so that Hoon and the suits wouldn't send the army after him or something, his mom left for work. Micah leaped out of bed as soon as the car passed beyond the scope of his enhanced hearing. He went out the back door and across the yard to the storage building. The gaping holes where the doors and wall used to be had been covered with tarps. He pushed the door tarp aside and went in and dug out his uncle's old books. Soon, he wobbled back across the yard, barely able to see over the top of the stack in his arms. In his room, he took the top book off the pile and made several smaller stacks of the others on the floor. Then he shoved them under his bed.

Micah sat on the bed and opened the book. And he began to read.

✱

During lunch, Jamie and Gabby walked along, their arms bumping, their heads tilted together in conversation. Waiting for them at their usual table, Christian smiled. Good for them. Of course, Micah might blow a gasket; Christian had always gotten the impression that he had a crush on Gabby. But so had Jamie, and frankly, he seemed the better choice. Micah was too caught up in his own shit.

On this very table, somebody had carved a crude picture of a masked, robed figure zapping a football player with some kind of ray. A little dialogue balloon rose from the player's mouth: *AARGGHH!* The robed figure said, *Die, pretty boy scum!* Christian frowned. Had Micah been stupid enough to carve it? She would not have been surprised. If he hadn't, then somebody found the situation funny, which seemed sick. People were dead.

After he and Gabby sat down, Jamie opened his brown bag and pulled out a sandwich, some Ruffles in a Ziploc bag, and a can of Dr Pepper beaded with moisture. "I haven't heard anything from Micah yet. Y'all?"

Christian spread her lunch on the table and shook her head. "He's not here, so I guess his play-sick plan worked. But if he's made any progress, he hasn't told me."

Gabby pulled out her phone and typed away. A moment later, it dinged. "He says he's got something to tell us, but it's too long to write." She put the phone back in her pocket. Jamie handed her one of his chocolate-chip cookies. She smiled, elbowed him playfully, and took it.

Christian rolled her eyes. "God, y'all are so cute you make me sick. So what now?"

Jamie swallowed a bite of sandwich. "Well, we were gonna stop by his house after school anyway."

"I wanna see this monster for myself," Christian said. "One time Micah told me about this fish he'd caught over in the Quapaw with his dad. Made it sound like he'd hooked a whale, but it was like six inches long."

"Look," Gabby said and nodded toward the school.

Kenneth Del Ray was stomping toward them like a kaiju bearing down on Tokyo, his face pale and his eyes blood-red. He clenched and unclenched his fists. Jamie and Christian stood. Christian moved between Kenneth and the others. She had almost fought him before, and she had gotten a lot faster. If anybody had to throw down, it should be her. Whether or not Kenneth would hit a girl? Maybe they would find out.

Kenneth stopped less than a foot from Christian. He gritted his teeth and breathed shallowly, as if he might hyperventilate. "I bet y'all are real broken up about Gavin," he said, his voice toneless and flat.

"We didn't like him, but we didn't wish for this," Jamie said. "We're sorry, bro."

Kenneth's gaze was withering. "Yeah. Right."

"We *are*," said Gabby. "Nobody in their right mind wants that kind of thing to happen."

"If you wasn't a girl," Kenneth snarled, "I'd kick your teeth out."

"You could try," said Christian.

Kenneth grinned, an expression unrelated to happiness or mirth. "You wanna get outta my face."

"We're on your side, you moron," said Christian. "If you had the sense God gave a tree stump, you'd help us get the thing that killed your friend."

Kenneth's lips worked. His fists clenched, unclenched, clenched as he struggled to keep himself in check.

He's liable to try to twist our heads off, whether the cops see it or not.

Jamie must have noticed it, too. "What happened *is* our fault in a way. Including yours. You busted in on our ceremony right when things went to hell. Who knows? We might could have contained it, but you tackled Christian and got her knocked out."

"So?" Kenneth spat. "If you hadn't been—"

"Don't bullshit me," Jamie said. "You were there. You got involved. So you've got stuff to answer for, too."

Kenneth's face reddened. Veins popped out on his forehead. "I'm about two seconds from tying your guts around your neck."

Christian expected Jamie to back down, like always. She tensed, ready to punch Kenneth as many times as she could and hope she was strong enough to do damage.

But Jamie held his ground. "I'm gonna ask you one more time, and then I'll leave you and your conscience alone. Will you help us?"

When Kenneth only glared, Gabby stepped forward. "Last night, that thing was staking out Brayden's house. He may be next."

Kenneth's mouth fell open. For a moment, he seemed like a lost child looking for guidance—which he was. Then he shook his head, cleared his throat, and looked at each of them in turn. "Y'all better stay away from me if you know what's good for you." He turned and walked away.

They watched him go. Once he was out of earshot, Jamie sighed. Christian turned to him. His hands shook. The way he smacked his lips suggested his mouth had gone dry.

"You okay, dude?" she asked.

"Yeah," he said, his voice quavering. "But I was pretty sure it was on. It would have exposed us all, even if we lived through the fight."

"Well, the hell with him," Christian said. Her own hands and voice were steady, but her pulse pounded. "And what did he mean, stay away from him?" Christian said. "*He* came to *us*."

"Forget him," Gabby said. "If he's out, he's out. What do *we* do next?"

✳

After the last bell of the day, Kenneth shadowed Brayden, who walked along like a zombie, chin on his chest, hair hanging across his face. He sometimes bumped into people, knocking books out of their hands or sending them sprawling, but he seemed not to notice. The victims, when they turned to see who had steamrolled them, paled and shut their mouths and picked themselves up. Many of them even looked sympathetic. Kenneth hated them for it. Most of those kids loathed Brayden and had felt the same about Gavin. If they had come across Gavin engulfed in flames, they wouldn't have bothered to piss on him. And now they looked so *sad*, like they wanted to pat Brayden on the back and take him home for cookies and milk. Kenneth wanted to punch every one of them in the nose and send their heads flying right off their bodies like baseballs off a tee. But he didn't do that, nor did he speak to them or even look at them once they passed out of Brayden's immediate area. Instead, he followed Brayden out the door and into the semicircular driveway where parents picked up their kids.

The line was long today, like driving home would keep anybody safe from that four-armed bogeyman. None of these grown-ups seemed to have considered what that thing had done to the cops, or their car. And those guys had been *armed*.

Kenneth spotted his mother's Kia Forte in line half a dozen places behind Brayden's mom's Volkswagen Golf. Brayden got in, and they drove away. Nothing else happened. No sign of the creature. It had attacked only at night. Either it was smart enough to understand the need for cover, or it was nocturnal—*Like a vampire*, Kenneth thought again—or both. Either way, Brayden would be fine during the day. Still, Kenneth would watch. He had abandoned Gavin, and look how that had turned out.

Those freaks. They had brought that monster into the world with dark magic. Kenneth had seen it himself. Sure, he hadn't helped the situation, but if they hadn't been doing it in the first place, Gavin would still be alive. If they had only taken their beatings like geeks ought to, or if they had fought back with their fists, like anyone with guts would have done. Instead, they had screwed around with shit they couldn't control. The freaks liked to play the victims, but they were the worst perpetrators in town. Giving somebody a wedgie or a swirly was one thing. Or posting an embarrassing pic. But unleashing a vampire on steroids? That was next-level bullying.

Mom's car eased up to the curb. Kenneth walked up to it and got in, then answered her usual inane questions about his day with grunts and nods. He thought about Brayden, about the freaks, and about how to get out of the house tonight. He would watch Brayden's place, and if that thing showed up, he would prove he was not afraid. Maybe he had been scared; maybe he had deserted the cops who had tried to protect him. But now, the rage that had kept him from sleeping well, that roiled in his chest like heartburn, eroded the fear. Next time, Kenneth Del Ray would stand his ground. That thing had killed the wrong guy's friend.

✳✴✳

Micah got a quarter of the way through the first thick book before he realized it was three fifteen. His mother would be home soon. She must have stopped off at the store for something; otherwise, she would have arrived five minutes ago. He dove back into the text, still hoping to find something about portal creation or the monster that had chased him down Ladd Way. But this book seemed mostly about benign junk like glamours and prosperity spells. Just his luck—he had picked up the witchcraft equivalent of *Green Eggs and Ham*. He kept reading, though, and using his online translator to understand the Latin, which took forever. He had to type in one sentence at a time, then double-check his spelling, then get the English translation, then try to make sense of it. At that rate, getting through one book a week might be asking too much. If the other texts were written entirely in a foreign language, he might be a grandfather before he finished.

"Micah?"

Shit—she was home. He had been so caught up in the book that he hadn't heard her pull up or come in the house. He shoved the book under the bed. Then he clicked out of Translate. "Hey, Mom!" he called as he opened his list of favorite sites. When his mother appeared in the doorway, he was scrolling through a benign Reddit about anime.

"What are you up to?" she asked, eyes narrowed. Dang it, how did she *do* that? Every time he had something to hide, she just *knew*. He might as well have been wearing a sign that read *Ask Me Why I'm Guilty*.

"Nothing," he said. She crossed her arms. "*Nothing*, Mom. God."

"The last time you said that, you nearly burned down the house with my hot-glue gun. Why don't you save us both a bunch of trouble and just tell me?"

"I'm not doing anything, I said." He sounded sharper than he had intended.

She walked into his room. "Okay, I reckon I'll have to find out for myself. Give me that computer." He handed her the laptop, sighing. She took it, turned it away from him, and started clicking. A trickle of unease ran down his spine. If she was looking at his journal, he would throw a fit, and damn the consequences. She had no right. After a moment, she cocked her head and looked at him. "Why are you using a Latin-to-English program?"

Anger rose in him like vomit. She had looked at his browser history. She had taken his computer, which he had given up without an argument, and searched his history like he was some kind of criminal. He stood and reached for the computer. She held it away from him.

"Come on, give it back," he whined. "I was doing a project for history, that's all."

"What project?"

"Look, just give me the stupid computer," he hissed, and he yanked it out of her hands. But he failed to take his increased strength into account, so he jerked her across the room with it. She fell on his bed and flopped over, where she lay looking at him with wide eyes and open mouth. He was shocked, too. She got on his nerves, but he would never hurt her. Never. "Mom, I'm sorry! I—"

"*Shut up*," she barked, getting up and brushing past him. "You just wait till your father hears about this. Until he gets home, you're grounded. You'll come straight home after school. No more unsupervised computer. And if you ever get physical with me again, I'll wait until your back is turned, and then I'll hit you over the head with a chair. Do you understand me?"

She stormed out the door without waiting for a reply. He watched her go. Then he walked over and shut the door as gently as he could. He was still holding the computer. Perhaps she had been too scared to take it. He sat back down and pulled the book out from under the bed. Then he opened it, found his place, and started translating it again, knowing that no matter what his mom said, he had to keep going. His friends' lives might depend on it.

He could forget about having them over that afternoon, though. And they were probably already on their way. Well, Mom would turn them away at the door. And if she didn't, maybe they could help him make some real progress.

CHAPTER TWENTY-FIVE

By Monday, a few days after Gavin's funeral, nothing else had happened, but Kenneth could barely stay awake. He had spent the darkest hours of the previous nights watching Brayden's house and dodging police patrols. And he had to keep doing it. If that eight-foot monster showed up, Brayden would be helpless. Kenneth could not go to another friend's house and watch the parents cry like little kids. He would kill that thing or die first. His own parents had not even questioned why he had fallen asleep every afternoon. They were probably too glad he was home and allegedly safe. He wished he could tell them how he had been targeted and what he could do. Maybe they would leave town until everything blew over. But more likely they would drag him along, super-strength or not, and then Brayden would probably die.

He slogged across campus, trying to keep his eyes open. His legs felt filled with lead and covered in concrete. His feet literally dragged.

He had nearly reached the main building when he stumbled into a group of four huddled near the steps—the freaks, of course. Who else would it be? They were everywhere these days. When they saw him, they shut up and bowed their heads a little, looking all solemn and sympathetic, all except for Sterne. That freak grinned as if he had just won the lottery.

"You look like shit," Micah said. "What's the matter? It ain't like nobody died."

"*God*, Micah," said Jamie, punching him on the arm.

"Leave me alone," Kenneth muttered as he tried to walk around them.

But Micah blocked his way to the steps. Christian grabbed Micah's arm; he yanked away and sneered. "What's the matter, Kenneth? Cat got your tongue? Don't you want to bore us to death with some more of your choice insults? Jamie's still a skinny nerd. I play video games and read comic books. Gabby still LARPs. And Christian keeps right on liking girls and hanging with us, no matter what you think. So come on, tough guy. Let us have it."

"Get out of my way, or I'll move you myself." Sleep or no sleep, Kenneth knew he could break Micah Sterne in half.

Just then, Mr. Hoon strolled up and spoke to a nearby group of kids. He smiled. That was just like a grown-up—pretending everything was fine when even the dumbest kid knew better. But Micah saw Hoon, too, and let Christian pull him away. Kenneth started up the steps. Micah Sterne could go to hell.

"Your friend was as stupid as you are," Sterne called. "I'm glad he's dead."

"Micah, shut the hell *up*," Christian growled.

Kenneth stopped and turned to them. Christian looked at the ground, still holding Sterne's arm. Gabby had gone pale. Jamie looked sick.

"I'm sorry about him, man," Jamie said. "He's an idiot."

"Say that again," Kenneth said to Micah. "I freaking *dare* you to say that again."

"You heard me the first time," Micah muttered, looking away.

Kenneth glared at him for a moment. Then he turned and walked into school. Rage boiled inside him. Sooner or later, he would erupt. He no longer felt tired.

He bided his time until third period, when he asked for a pass and walked to the bathroom. There he spent a few minutes whizzing and washing his hands and looking at himself in the mirror. He had to admit that the little freak had been right; he looked like shit. His eyes were bloodshot and watery. Thanks to Sterne's mouth, he felt energized, caffeinated, but his eyes had not gotten the message. Lights still seemed too bright. Blood rushed in his ears. But at least he had woken up. And however bad Kenneth felt, Micah would feel worse pretty soon.

Leaving the bathroom, Kenneth strode through the halls until he found Micah's locker. He had memorized the freaks' locker numbers during the first week of school, figuring to have a little fun with them throughout the year. Now he planned to destroy Micah's social life. He would open the locker and rip all the textbooks in half and scour each notebook and post every scrap of embarrassing information he could find on social media. By tomorrow, everybody in school would know everything about Micah Sterne. Maybe the kid fantasized about the women in those comic books he was always reading. Maybe he drew dirty pictures of them or wrote crummy fan fiction starring himself—stuff he wouldn't dare put on his computer, which could be hacked. If so, Kenneth would spread it everywhere. No girl in town would look at him after that.

Kenneth looked around to make sure he was alone. Then he gripped Micah's combination lock in his right hand and took in a deep breath. "Ah-*CHOOOOO!*" he shouted, yanking on the lock at the same time. With a bang and a crunch, he mangled the lock and ripped the door off its hinges. Oops. He leaned the door against a recess between sets of lockers and started wiping his nose. A teacher opened her door and scowled at him. He waved his hall pass at her. "Sorry. Got a cold." She harrumphed and disappeared back into her classroom.

Kenneth expected to see the usual assortment of books and notebooks and scattered writing instruments, and sure enough, the locker held all that stuff. But on top of it sat a black duffel bag.

As far as Kenneth knew, Sterne did not take PE.

Kenneth took out the bag and opened it. He jammed his hand deep into it and felt course cloth. He bunched some up in his fist and pulled out a long, dark robe and a ski mask.

He grinned.

＊✴＊

Gabby sat in Mr. Griffin's Honors English class, listening to the man drone on about sentence fragments and comma splices. Jamie, Christian, and Micah fidgeted in their seats, occasionally looking at their phones or doodling. The class had spent the last three days on the same material, looking at sentence after sentence, doing fill-in-the-blank exercises and paragraph revisions, even though everyone had gotten the point on the *first* day. Jamie loved English, but even he looked ready to scream. He glanced at Gabby and rolled his eyes. She grinned and mimed sticking a finger down her throat. Jamie laughed.

Then the classroom door exploded inward and nearly flattened Mr. Griffin.

Gabby tried to stand so fast that she banged her upper thighs on the bottom of her desk and almost toppled over.

Kids screamed and leaped from their desks. Half of them stood where they were, while the rest ran to the back of the classroom and fought to hide behind each other. Gabby and her friends huddled together in the classroom's center. *Oh, Lord,* Gabby thought. *The monster's stopped playing around. And we're gonna have to show ourselves. It's all over.*

People were probably going to die.

Jamie leaned toward the others. "Unless it starts hurting people, try to lead it outside, somewhere nobody can see us."

Then a robed and hooded figure entered, and Jamie fell silent. He stared at the newcomer, his mouth working.

The robe was one of theirs. The guy even had a ski mask. Except for his being a little bigger than any of them, there was no discernable difference between this person and themselves when they were in costume.

It's gotta be Kenneth. Nobody else could have done that to the door. What the hell is he doing?

Mr. Griffin stood against the far wall, looking as if he wanted to claw through it and run, stopping maybe somewhere around Nevada. The robed figure gave him the finger with a meaty hand Gabby recognized. It had thumped Jamie's ear and frogged Micah's arm enough times. Definitely Kenneth.

Micah stepped forward, but Christian grabbed him and yanked him back, whispering, "Don't do anything here, you idiot!"

Kenneth watched Micah struggle with Christian. He shook his head. Then he walked over to Mr. Griffin's desk and raised a fist. He brought it down on the desk, which practically disintegrated. Fragments of metal and splinters flew everywhere. Christian cried out and pulled a thick shard of wood from her shoulder. She had let go of Micah, but he made no move for Kenneth. Maybe he had finally found some sense in that empty head of his.

A couple of kids in the back sobbed. Shonda Kamara was praying aloud.

Jamie stepped forward. "Come on, man. You don't have to do this."

"Yes. I do," Kenneth said. "And you know why."

"Let the other kids go. You can do that."

"Nah. Let 'em watch."

He came forward, reaching for Micah.

Gabby and her friends fled in separate directions, leaping over desks, running for the door, Christian dragging Micah along even as Micah stumbled behind her and tried to yank free. Kenneth ignored Jamie and Gabby. He ran right through the lines of desks, knocking them everywhere, and cut off Christian and Micah before they could reach the hallway.

Mr. Griffin, still pressed against the wall, found his voice. "Whoever you are, get out of my classroom!"

Kenneth glanced in Griffin's direction. Jamie picked up a desk and threw it at Kenneth, who punched it out of the air. It exploded, showering the class with more shrapnel. Someone screamed. Christian dashed past Kenneth, still dragging the protesting Micah along. They disappeared into the hall. Kenneth pursued.

Everybody's doing something but me. Why can't I move? Why do I always freeze? Come on, Gabriella. Move your ass.

But her traitor feet would not listen.

Jamie turned to her. "We can't let 'em out of our sight. They're liable to kill each other." He headed for the door. Gabby followed, leaving Mr. Griffin and the rest of class staring after them. Shonda was still praying.

✳✱✳

Christian wanted to turn on the jets and get as far away from Kenneth as possible, but teachers and students were already poking their heads out of classroom doors. Mrs. Calvert's unsteady voice blatted from the loudspeakers: "Attention, all faculty and staff! Initiate lockdown! We are in active-shooter protocol! This is not a drill! I repeat—" and on and on. *Jeez, lady, you're gonna bust our eardrums*, Christian thought as she spotted Mr. Hoon running down the hall, his face red and his tie flopping, yelling at everyone to get back inside their rooms and lock the doors.

"He's in Mr. Griffin's class!" Christian yelled as they passed. Hoon watched them go, his mouth hanging open. "I think he's trying to kill us!"

"Attention, all faculty and staff!" Mrs. Calvert said. "Initiate lockdown! We are in active-shooter protocol! This is not a drill!"

Mr. Hoon didn't ask why Christian was yanking Micah along like a stubborn dog on a leash, maybe because Kenneth was already on their heels, bellowing threats. She didn't blame the principal for being confused or shocked or whatever. Two minutes ago, his school had been proceeding through another orderly, boring day. Now someone had gone crazy in one of his classrooms, and to top it off, students were blatantly running in the hall.

Something crashed; Mr. Hoon squawked in surprise. Kenneth must have brushed him aside and into the lockers.

"Attention, all faculty and staff! Initiate lockdown! We are in active-shooter protocol! This is not a drill!"

As the classroom doors began to close, Christian picked up speed. She tossed a struggling Micah over her shoulder and zoomed through the halls. By the time he cried "Put me down, dammit!" she had carried them through the double doors and nearly blown them off their hinges. They raced through town, past squad cars with their lights on and concerned-looking people on sidewalks. *Man, I hope nobody's taking pictures with one of them really good cameras. Might be they could get a clear shot of who's running so fast.*

Christian did not stop until she dropped Micah on his own front yard. He landed on his ass and grunted.

"Stay here," she said, "while the rest of us try to clean up your mess."

"You can't tell me what to do," Micah said.

"Dude, really?" she said. "Tell you what. If you get in my way, I'll beat your dumb ass worse than Kenneth ever did. You got it? Can you understand that, you self-centered prick?"

Then she turned and headed back toward school, hoping Micah had sense enough to take her advice.

✳✳✳

As Christian ran away, leaves and dirt rooster-tailing in her wake, Micah stood and brushed off the seat of his pants. Of course they wanted him to stay home. How else could they protect Kenneth from him? Just more evidence of whose side they were really on. Well, he didn't take orders from anybody. There were at least a couple more robes in his uncle's trunks—if raccoons or squirrels hadn't gotten through the tarp and nested in there. Maybe he could grab one of the extras and get back to school before Kenneth left.

✳✳✳

As Gabby and Jamie ran after Kenneth, she thought, *I hope you got a plan, Jamie, because I have no idea how to get us all outta this mess in one piece with our secrets still secret.*

She nearly tripped over Mr. Hoon, who lay on the ground, wincing and holding the small of his back. Kenneth stood thirty feet up the hall, fists clenched at his sides, his back to them. She and Jamie skidded to a halt. Kenneth looked over his shoulder, spotted them, and turned, fixing them with his wild and bloodshot eyes.

"If you know what's good for you, you'll stay outta my way," he said, his voice cold. Then he ran off, shouting Micah's name at the top of his lungs.

"Attention, all faculty and staff! Initiate lockdown! We are in active-shooter protocol! This is not a drill!"

Jamie helped Mr. Hoon up. "You two get to someplace safe," the principal said, still wincing. "I don't care if you have to go home. Just don't stay here." He limped toward Mr. Griffin's room, one hand on his lower back.

"Come on," Jamie said.

"Where we going?" said Gabby.

"Attention, all faculty and staff! Initiate lockdown! We are in active-shooter protocol! This is not a drill!"

"I wish she'd quit it," Jamie muttered.

"Where?" Gabby repeated.

"I think Kenneth wants to eat Micah's liver for lunch. And it's pretty obvious he stole one of our robes to drag us through the mud. We gotta stop him."

They passed Micah's locker and its missing door. An open and empty duffel bag lay on the floor. They stood over it for a moment. "I guess we know where Kenneth got the costume," Gabby said. "I can't believe Micah brought his stuff to school. Why didn't he just call those feds and tell 'em to pick him up at home?"

"I love that kid," Jamie said through clenched teeth, "but sometimes, I could kill him."

A blur, a whoosh, a wave of dust and fragments of leaves and twigs, and Christian stood in front of them, holding their costumes. "I made a couple of stops," she said. "Is everybody still alive?"

"Yeah," said Jamie. "So far. Where's Micah?"

"If the boy has any damn sense, he's right where I put him."

Gabby looked around as she took her costume. The classrooms seemed to be locked down. Even Mrs. Calvert had finally stopped screaming at them. From outside, the still-faint sound of sirens. "Sounds like the cops are on the way."

"Yeah," said Christian. "I passed some. Come on. Hurry."

Jamie and Gabby put on their robes and masks. For the first time, Gabby felt grateful for their simple costumes—easy on, easy off.

"Kenneth knew we couldn't do shit in front of everybody when he busted in that classroom," Jamie said. "I'm getting real tired of trying to help folks who just turn around and screw us over."

From one of the other hallways, a thunderous crunch of metal. Kenneth was destroying lockers.

✳✴✳

Christian waited while Jamie and Gabby put on their robes and masks. It took them only a few seconds, but to Christian, it felt like forever. She still hadn't gotten used to how running at super-speed made everything else seem so godawful *slow*. Everything in the world moved like a snail. Hell, real snails would probably move like—what did Mrs. Kather call it in Earth Science? Geologic time.

As Gabby *finally* made her last mask adjustment, Jamie said, "We've gotta stop Kenneth before he hurts somebody or the cops show up and hurt *him*. But remember, he's in a lot of pain, and he's *really* pissed at Micah. He ain't a monster."

"Yeah, well, he ain't no angel, either," Christian said. "We're wasting time." She understood Micah's part in all this, but sometimes she wanted to smack Jamie and Gabby, who were far too sympathetic toward Kenneth. She had no desire to murder Kenneth like Micah did, but she had little interest in his state of mind, either. *Spend your life shitting on people, you're bound to stink.*

Moving slowly, so damn slowly, they trotted through the halls. Debris from smashed lockers covered the floors down one; in the others, the classroom doors remained closed, the lights off. Active shooter protocol, even though no one had a gun.

They found Kenneth in front of the main office. The admins and a couple of teachers cowered inside, some of them crying.

Kenneth faced Christian and the others, feet shoulder-width apart, hands at his sides like a gunfighter. "Where's Sterne?"

Jamie took the lead. Christian and Gabby flanked him. "This ends now," he said.

"You got that right," Kenneth said.

Christian shifted from foot to foot, the energy inside her thrumming with her heartbeat.

Then Jamie stepped forward. He walked right up to Kenneth.

Dude, what are you doing?

＊✳＊

If there's any chance he'll listen to reason, Jamie thought, *I gotta take it.*

Kenneth's damp and reddened eyes glared at him. It was like looking into an angry bull's face.

Jamie put a hand on Kenneth's shoulder, meaning to say something conciliatory. But before he could speak, pain shot through his chest, and he found himself flying across the hall and smashing through the trophy case. Lightning strobed through his back and neck. Shelves collapsed on top of him, raining trophies onto his head. Unsure whether he had been punched, kicked, or thrown, his head spinning, Jamie sat up in time to see Gabby fire a force blast into Kenneth's torso, driving him into and through Hoon's office door. Someone on the other side uttered a cry of surprise or fear or both.

Jamie raised one hand and tried to shout, "Stop!" Nothing came out but a feeble wheeze. *Note to self,* he thought. *Try floating next time, even if it's just an inch or two. Enough to engage your aura, so nobody caves your damn chest in.*

Kenneth charged back through the door, straight at Gabby, but she vanished just before he reached her. He kept barreling forward and stumbled over his own feet, splatting onto his chest and skidding. A blur near the shattered door, and Christian set Gabby down.

Kenneth rolled over and sat up, only feet away from Jamie and the broken shelves and trophies. He looked at Jamie. "One last time, scarecrow. Tell me where Sterne is, or I'm gonna turn you into hamburger."

Jamie said nothing. Even if he had wanted to, he had not caught his breath yet.

Gotta move. Gotta fly.

Kenneth stood and took a step toward Jamie, but then the air between them blurred, and Kenneth staggered backward as Christian circled him, pummeling him in the face and the stomach. Kenneth covered his face with both hands. *How does his aura work?* Jamie thought, his head still spinning. *Is it protecting him now?*

Jamie climbed out of the wreckage and motioned Gabby over.

"If I move away from this door, they'll try to run and probably get killed," Gabby said, gesturing toward the teachers huddled inside. A couple of them hid behind the office manager's desk. Three more sat against it, mouths hanging open, watching Christian and Kenneth.

"Y'all—" Jamie began, intending to order the teachers to stay put.

And then the front doors burst open, the sunlight almost blinding after the hallway's dim fluorescents. Mossman and Greenwalt entered, guns pointed at Christian and Kenneth.

"Freeze!" Mossman shouted. "Federal agents!"

"*Two* of them?" Greenwalt said.

One of the cops they had brought along cried, "Quapaw City PD! On your knees!"

Christian disappeared. Then she was standing next to Jamie, holding the four men's service weapons. The clips lay on the ground at their feet. So did the bullets that had been chambered. The slides had locked.

The feds looked at each other, eyes wide. The cops turned pale and fell back against the wall.

"What the—" Greenwalt said, spotting Jamie and Gabby.

"Scatter!" Jamie cried.

"Don't let them escape!" shouted Mossman, diving for his gun and a clip.

Gabby fired a short burst at the floor. Tile and dust and fragments of concrete erupted into the air between her friends and the adults, who roared in surprise, cursing. Kenneth appeared out of the debris cloud, skirting the wall.

Jamie turned to Gabby. "Get on my back," he said as Christian and Kenneth vanished, kicking up more gunk in the air. Jamie coughed.

Gabby jumped on, arms around his neck. He hooked his own arms under her legs and took off, flying only a few feet off the ground.

From behind them came the sound of gunshots, loud bangs that echoed through the hallways. As Jamie turned a corner and headed for the nearest exit, something crashed into two lockers behind him. Then they were outside. He flew upward and diagonally, trying to gain as much altitude as quickly as he could.

Good Lord. They shot *at us inside the school. Gabby's aura wasn't even engaged. She could have died.*

When he and Gabby arrived at the pavilion, Christian was sitting on a picnic table. She and Kenneth had both unmasked. Christian's face was pale and flushed at the cheeks, her hair soaked in sweat.

Kenneth was standing at the edge of the slab, barfing.

✳

They surrounded Kenneth while he puked up enough half-digested food and chunk-filled liquid to fill three stomachs.

"Don't worry about it, dude," Jamie said at one point. "We all yakked the first time we traveled with Christian."

Still puking, Kenneth gave him the finger.

Gabby could not stop thinking about what it had been like back there—the hallway in shambles, everyone staring at them as if they really were the freaks Kenneth had always accused them of being. Those two agents and the cops, their guns drawn—she was pretty sure she had heard shooting. They could have killed her friends. Or Kenneth. They could have killed *her.*

Jamie pulled Christian aside. Gabby stood over Kenneth, smelling the sour odor of vomit. It was all too much. Monsters, cops, guys in suits. How scared everybody was in Mr. Griffin's class. *We don't even know where to look for the monster, but we're doing a hell of a job hurting each other.*

Over by the swings, Jamie conferred with Christian. Then she took off, much slower than usual. She was actually visible this time, probably exhausted from carrying so much weight. Jamie walked back over and watched as Kenneth dry-heaved.

"She's gonna bring Micah," Jamie said. "It's time to settle this."

Kenneth wiped his mouth on his robe. "When he gets here, I'm gonna kill him, and if you get in my way, I'll kill you, too."

Jamie groaned, scowling. "No. You won't. There's four of us and one of you. Gabby can probably kick your ass by herself if it comes to that."

Kenneth got to his feet, still looking green. "If you're looking to get knocked out, keep on talking."

"You can barely stand up. And by the way, you asshole, people are dying. Including your friend. Gavin's dead because that thing's after you. You ain't gotta like us, but you got a better chance of surviving if you work with us."

"I didn't have nothing to do with that thing showing up," Kenneth said. "I—"

"Oh, shut *up*," Gabby cried. Kenneth's eyes widened, and he took a step back. Gabby was pretty surprised herself, but she had had enough of Kenneth's bullshit. "We've already been through this. We screwed up, but so did you. You just had to pick on us for the fifteen hundredth time. Besides, like Jamie said—it's your ass on the line. You really want it hanging out there alone?"

A vein pulsed in Kenneth's forehead. His mouth worked, as if he were chewing his words before he spat them in Gabby's face. She tensed, ready to blast him as hard as she could if he made a move. She took off her ski mask. Jamie did the same. A breeze blew through the treetops, dislodging leaves and pine needles that rained around them intermittently. A bird and a squirrel chattered at each other. Sunlight filtered through the foliage and bathed the three teenagers. *The world will go on*, Gabby thought, *even if we kill each other*.

Then Kenneth flapped his hand and turned away. "Fine. Whatever. But keep Sterne away from me. And when that vampire-cannibal thing is dead, all bets are off. You got me?"

Gabby unclenched her fists. The tension drained from her muscles. The energy that had been thrumming and thrumming, cycling up until it charged every cell in her body, eased up. Jamie exhaled. Then a wind stirred, and Christian, still masked, halted ten feet away, a bucket of Popeyes chicken in one arm. Micah stood beside her.

Christian pulled off her mask, tucked it under one arm, and pulled out a drumstick, ripping meat from the bone. Her hand trembled.

"What'd I miss?" she asked, her mouth full. She was still holding the back of Micah's shirt. She had held him that way so often lately that it was like somebody had sewn them together. Gabby imagined Christian was probably getting sick of it.

"Let me go," he said.

"Listen first," Christian said.

"I know you won't like this," Jamie said, "but we're gonna work with Kenneth. We've already talked to him. He's gonna cool out. Now it's your turn."

Micah yanked away from Christian. "Dammit to hell, y'all. That assclown hates you. Why are you always on his side?"

"It ain't about sides. You think I *like* Kenneth after everything he's done to me, and to you guys?"

"Kenneth has powers," Gabby said. "That means he can help. You don't gotta invite him over to video game night."

Kenneth sneered. "Like I'd come."

Micah's face burned. Rage baked off him. Gabby found herself backing away and, again, hating herself for it. *He wants to fight us all. He'd do it if he thought he could win. God, would he kill us if he had the chance? What happened to the kid I've hung out with ever since I could remember?*

Micah glared at Kenneth. He went to the pavilion and sat on a table, turning away from them all. They stood there, hands on their hips or in their pockets. Gabby couldn't speak for the others, but she had no idea what to do next.

CHAPTER TWENTY-SIX

After they'd joined forces with the asshole, Christian had taken Micah home so he would be there when his mother arrived. No sense in getting him grounded even longer. At least they still cared about him *that* much. The next day, though, Micah's mom had picked up an extra shift and planned to be gone until eleven fifteen or so that night. Now the whole group, including Kenneth, sat in a loose circle in Micah's room—Micah and Christian on the edge of the bed, Gabby in his broken-down faux-leather desk chair, Jamie and Kenneth on the floor. Kenneth looked uncomfortable.

Good. I wish I could have figured out a way to make him sit on a bunch of Legos. Or butcher knives.

Still, Micah felt much calmer than he had yesterday. He could bide his time, plan, make whatever he did look like an accident. After all, Kenneth would be driving soon enough. Teenagers crashed their cars all the time.

He pulled the books out from under the bed and laid them in front of Jamie. Everyone leaned back, as if proximity might give them some terrible disease.

"Micah, maybe you can start by telling us what you've been up to with these things," Jamie said.

Micah poked one book with his toe. "I've only looked at this one so far. I've been trying to translate it. It's mostly spells—ingredient lists, chants, that kind of thing. Small stuff."

"That ain't the one we used in the shed," Christian observed.

"I know," Micah said. "I figured I'd start with something else, since things went so bad that night."

211

Gabby picked at a piece of fluff sticking out of the armrest. "It seems like if we're gonna undo what we did, we should start with the book we actually used."

Micah frowned. "Well, maybe you wanna take it home and work on it by yourself. Me, I'd rather not."

"I agree with Gabby," said Jamie. He picked up the book in question and held it out to Micah. "Let's translate our spell."

Of course you agree with her. Your brains fell into your dick. Still, Micah stood and took the book.

Kenneth was sitting between Micah and the desk, so he scooted across the floor and made an exaggerated *after you* gesture. "Ladies first," he said, grinning.

Bite my ass, moron.

But Micah said nothing. Like a good little geek.

Gabby got out of the desk chair. Micah sat in it and laid the book on the desk; then he opened his laptop. "Somebody read this to me," he said. "It takes forever to type in all this shit when I gotta keep checking my spelling."

"Not a good idea," said Christian. "Remember what happened last time we said that stuff out loud?"

Jamie shivered.

Micah took a deep breath and opened the book. He flipped through it until he found the chant they had used. The pages felt dirty, so he wiped his hands on his pants. Then he bent over the keyboard and got to work.

✳✳✳

The sun had nearly set when Micah pushed away from the desk. Eventually, he had begrudgingly admitted that Christian was right, so he and Jamie had been hunched over the computer the whole time,

Jamie spelling out the chant letter by letter, Micah typing it in, Jamie writing down the translation in Micah's Earth Science notebook. That had taken only twenty minutes or so, but while they were working, Gabby and Christian had flipped through the other books and found some kind of supernatural catalog. It was called *Daemonēs, Mōnstra, et Bēstiae Obscūritātis*—roughly, *Demons, Monsters, and Creatures of Darkness*. Christian had pored over it, Gabby sitting next to her on the bed, while Micah and Jamie finished the translation.

Kenneth had walked aimlessly about the room, seeming lost. Christian did not sympathize. She had no desire to share a room with the guy, either. She had spent too much of her life ready to fist-fight him. That kind of shit tended to stress you out. Kids like Kenneth were major reasons why teen suicide rates had risen, why this one fourteen-year-old she had read about got a bleeding ulcer, why high school seemed like hell to so many people. No, Christian had no desire to hurt Kenneth herself, or let him be hurt, but if it happened despite their best efforts, she would shed no tears. And if Micah needed to vent, she would listen, because she understood, even if she didn't condone.

Kenneth passed by, glanced at the pages she and Gabby were examining, and cried out. Everyone turned to look at him. The color drained from his face so quickly that Christian wondered if he would faint. Instead, he snatched the book out of their hands.

"Hey!" Gabby cried. "Rude much?"

"I saw it," Kenneth muttered, rifling through the pages. "It's in here. The *thing.*"

Jamie started. "Wait a minute. You've seen it?"

Kenneth turned pages, not looking up. "Yeah. The night it killed those cops on my street. It was after me."

Christian reached out and pulled Kenneth's hand away from the book. "Dude," she said. "Why didn't you tell us?"

Kenneth frowned, glancing from her to the book and back again, clearly impatient. "I'm telling you now. I mean, it ain't like we're friends.

You don't tell me shit. Or do you think I hadn't noticed you've been practicing your powers?"

Christian opened her mouth to protest, then closed it again. He was right about that much. They had invited him to join their group, and he had refused. After that, no one had kept him updated, not really.

"That's not the same thing, though," Gabby said. "It don't take a lot to imagine we'd practice, so we don't kill ourselves or somebody else. But how were we supposed to guess you knew something about the monster? Something that might be the key to staying alive?"

Kenneth threw his hands in the air and scoffed. "Look, do you want me to find the thing in this book or not?"

Micah sneered. "He ain't gonna apologize, y'all. Because he don't care if we get killed. I told you."

Kenneth's eyes narrowed. His face reddened, and he started to put down the book.

"Chill, all of you," Jamie said, standing up. "What's done is done."

Kenneth settled back, still scowling. Micah looked disgusted but kept quiet, a minor miracle. Gabby's face was blank, but she gripped the edge of the bed as if afraid she might float away.

"Now," Jamie continued. "Kenneth. Tell us what happened."

Still staring Micah down, Kenneth took them through his evening bike ride, his encounter with officers Thielan and Reiff, how the three of them had started toward Kenneth's house.

"Then this huge shape dropped outta the tree. When it stood up, it had to be eight or nine feet tall. Its skin looked weird—blue, or dark green, maybe really dark gray. Four arms, really ripped. I mean, muscles on top of its muscles. Mouth like an open garbage can with a zillion teeth."

Christian glanced at Micah. He still looked like he wanted to use Kenneth's head as a basketball, but some other expression flickered, too—recognition?

"And then?" Jamie asked.

Kenneth explained how the cops tried to fight the monster, how badly that went for them. "It all happened so fast. I couldn't save 'em."

"And then it came after you?" Gabby asked.

Kenneth sat up a little straighter. His expression hardened, as if daring anyone to contradict him. "It tried. And I wanted to stand my ground. Beat its ass. I told it, I said, 'You son of a bitch, I'm gonna kill you.' And I started to run at it. But then I looked again. Saw them cops' bodies, what it did to their car. And I just—went inside."

Micah snorted. "You left it on the street, where it could have killed your whole neighborhood. And then you led it to your house. To your parents. You chickenshit."

"Screw you, Sterne," Kenneth spat. "You weren't there. And remember: I know your story. When you saw it, you ran like a bitch, so don't play tough guy with me."

Micah started to say something else, but Jamie interrupted. "Was that the end? When you went inside?"

Kenneth said nothing for a moment as he and Micah had a staring contest. He finally answered when Jamie stepped between them. "No. I went to my room. When I opened my window, it was squatting down and looking inside. And then it talked to me."

Now even Micah looked shocked. "What?" Gabby said.

Kenneth turned to her, his expression softer. "Yeah. I mean, whatever it said out loud just sounded like a bunch of clicks and gurgles. But in my mind, I heard English."

"What did it say?" Gabby asked.

Kenneth swallowed hard and stared at the floor for a moment. When he looked up again, his eyes were wet, his voice unsteady. "It said, 'You think you're safe, but I'm patient. And I'm hungry. Sooner or later, I'll feed, and you'll die. You and all your friends.'"

Christian and Jamie locked eyes; Jamie's jaw tensed. He looked as scared as Christian felt. *Come on, dude,* she thought. *You're the leader around here. If you're scared, I'm liable to pee my pants.*

"Go ahead," Jamie said to Kenneth. "Find it."

Kenneth went back to the book. Everyone else looked at each other, eyes wide. Micah had turned pale.

Kenneth stopped flipping and stared at the page, hands trembling. Christian had never seen Kenneth afraid, and now the kid looked like he might soil his underwear. She felt a twinge of sympathy and tried to squash it, but it took hold stubbornly in her heart. After a moment, Kenneth handed her the book. She spread it on her lap. Gabby leaned in so quickly she almost knocked it off again. Jamie and Micah crowded around, too. Together they looked at a reproduction of a painting that showed an almost cartoonishly muscular creature with a mouth so full of teeth it might have swallowed half a dozen buzzsaws. Its skin was bluish. All four of its arms ended in powerful hands with talons as long and sharp as shark's teeth.

"That's it, all right," said Micah. "The thing that chased me away from Brayden's."

"God," Jamie whispered. Gabby moved closer to him.

"More Latin," Christian said.

Micah groaned. "Great. Give it over."

Christian passed him the book, and he and Jamie got back to work.

As evening descended outside, they finally finished. Jamie looked at the papers he held in his hands and licked his lips. Even Micah looked daunted.

"That bad?" asked Gabby.

"Worse," said Jamie. "We gotta think about this. Here." He handed the paper to Christian. "You three read it quick. We all gotta get home before it gets dark. We'll meet tomorrow at lunch. I got a feeling this is something we need to talk about face to face."

"Screw waiting," said Kenneth. "Let's get it done now."

"No," said Jamie. "If that thing catches us in the dark and we ain't ready, we're all dead. I'm not sure we got a chance as it is. Just hurry up and read this."

Christian began to read. Gabby crowded her. Even Kenneth leaned in and blocked most of the light. In Jamie's scrawl, the paper read

> *Chant:*
> *Eldritch energies from the other realms, hearken now*
> *Spread wide the gates between worlds*
> *Bend the fabric of universes*
> *Call forth the denizens of the ravaged lands*
> *Bring them nigh to us*

They had repeated this chant several times. Christian swallowed again, feeling as if an ostrich egg had stuck in her throat. Without asking Gabby and Kenneth whether they were done, she switched to the other sheet of paper and read this one aloud.

> *The Go'kan (no translation)*
> *This bipedal demon race dwells in a world of all but perpetual darkness. Their strength is much greater than humans'. They rule by force and use the blood and flesh of an indigenous race very similar to human beings as food. Go'kan are monarchical warriors and fear almost nothing. Battle them at your peril, for they will rip the life from your body and devour your bones. Those foolhardy enough to engage them in combat have discovered they fear fire. They can be killed by impaling their hearts, which reside in the center of their chests. Living in darkness as they do, they cannot abide sunlight. Their skin will suppurate and burn.*

Christian turned to Jamie. "Who wrote these books? How do they know this stuff?"

"No idea," said Jamie. "It could be bullshit. But what else do we have?"

The shadows outside had gotten longer, deeper. "We should go," Christian said.

Kenneth snorted. "If dark's gonna bring that thing to us, I say we let it. After what happened to Gavin, I owe it."

Micah looked giddy at the prospect. He probably hoped Kenneth would wind up so much blood and gristle on the asphalt.

Gabby crossed her arms over her chest. "The whole point of what we're doing here is to make a plan. I don't think 'wait for it in the street' qualifies."

"The hell with that," Kenneth said. "I'm done running."

Jamie shook his head. "Nobody's asking you to run. Just to wait till we can make a strategy. This ain't a schoolyard fight, Kenneth. No teacher's gonna jump in and save us if we're getting our asses kicked. Just be patient."

Kenneth looked at Jamie a long time. Then he gritted his teeth and shrugged. "Whatever. But I ain't waiting long." He turned and walked out the door.

"We should go, too," Jamie said. "Micah, can you translate that last paragraph? We need all the intel we can get."

"Yeah," Micah said. "Earth Science ain't exactly tempting me to be responsible tonight."

✳✳✳

Jamie hadn't been home ten minutes when his phone rang. Micah again—man, it felt weird to get an actual phone call from a kid his age. When he answered, Micah read him the last paragraph without even saying hello. "'The Go'kan are bound by ancient custom never to enter a dwelling uninvited, whether it belongs to a friend or an enemy. Thus it is that their enemies' children are never allowed outside their abodes until they reach the warrior's age of sixteen winters. Any being ensconced within its own lodge remains safe from every Go'kan's tooth and fang.'"

"God," said Jamie. "They're just like vampires. You kill 'em the same ways. They can't come in uninvited, which explains why it didn't bust through Kenneth's window and take him. They drink your blood like you're a milkshake."

"You think crosses would work on 'em?"

"I doubt it. That thing ain't got nothing to do with religion. It ain't even from Earth. That crucifix deal sounds more like something writers would dream up because their parents made 'em go to church."

Micah took a deep breath. "So what do we do now?"

"We use this information," Jamie said. Ideas were already forming, possible strategies, potential objections, counterarguments. His pulse raced as if he had physically exerted himself. "And we play Van Helsing. Tomorrow and Thursday, we'll make a plan and work out any kinks. On Friday, tell your mom you're sleeping over at my house. We've got to make some stakes. On Saturday, we go hunting."

CHAPTER TWENTY-SEVEN

At lunch on Wednesday, Jamie met with the others. They were already munching sandwiches and chips when Jamie sat next to Kenneth, the only seat left at the small picnic table. The other three had crowded in on the other side and were watching Kenneth mow through a stack of three sandwiches stuffed with bologna, cheese, onions, and pickles. Jamie could barely stand to sit in the stink cloud those sandwiches emitted, but he had to make do. Everyone who passed stared in surprise at the four freaks and the jock bully breaking bread together.

"Thanks for coming, y'all," Jamie said. No one answered. Kenneth continued to shovel food into his mouth. If he kept it up at that rate, he would weigh four hundred pounds by the time he reached his mid-forties. Of course, given everything that was happening, who knew if they would even reach twenty? "Let's talk about the plan. I think we should use Kenneth as bait to lure the monster into the open. Then the rest of us will attack it from all sides."

Kenneth snorted and swallowed a hunk of sandwich. "Figures."

"I say we draw it to the football practice field," Jamie said, shooting Kenneth a *Dude, come on* look. "No trees there for it to hide in. Micah and Gabby, you got the long-distance powers, so we'll put you on opposite sides of the field, and when the vampire-thing gets there, y'all blast away. Micah, you can make fire, so you got the best chance to hurt it. Maybe you can even kill it."

"How am I supposed to get it to the practice field?" Kenneth asked through a mouthful of Doritos. "It's not like I can text it and dare it to show up."

"That's where I come in," said Christian. "Right? If Kenneth can draw it out, I'm supposed to snatch him up and carry him to the field."

"Right," said Jamie. "Only don't go *too* fast. You don't want to lose it. Maybe it can track us some other way, but since we don't know for sure, we gotta depend on visual bait."

"And what about you?" asked Kenneth. "You gonna stay home and watch YouTube while we're getting killed?"

"I'll be in the sky," said Jamie. "That way, I can direct everybody. Now, once we get it to the field, here's what I think we should do."

He talked until the lunch hour was almost over, and when he finished, he wolfed his sandwich while the others fired questions at him. He waved most of them off.

"Don't shake your head at us, man," said Christian. "This is kind of important."

"We can work out the logistics later. Right now, just concentrate on step one. Me and Micah will tell our parents we're spending the night at each other's houses on Friday. Gabby and Christian can do the same. Kenneth, can you find somebody to cover for you this weekend?"

"Brayden," Kenneth said. "Especially if I tell him I'm doing something for Gavin."

"Good," said Jamie. "We'll all meet at Micah's. Your mom's working a split shift this week, right?"

"Yeah," said Micah. "She's working eleven to three, and then seven to eleven. She'll come home and go to bed a little after midnight."

The bell rang, and they gathered their trash and headed back inside. Jamie smiled. It felt good to be on the offensive for a change.

✷

The Entmanns dropped Christian off at her empty house. Mom had left the thermostat too high, so the place felt stuffy and claustrophobic.

Christian would not be staying long, but she wanted Mom to think she had hung out at home after school, so she lowered the temperature a couple of degrees. Then she went to her room, dug deep in her closet, and pulled out her robe and mask. She didn't intend to be seen while running this errand, but no sense taking chances.

She pulled on her costume and sped out the door, along the side-walks, and into the park, where she dashed around in search of fallen limbs. She avoided all the mothers and children, though some cast curious glances at the whirlwinds of dust and dead flora that seemed to spring up from nowhere. An hour later, Christian had transported ten loads of fallen branches to Micah's house and piled them behind the storage building. Half of the limbs would probably be too flimsy or too brittle to use as stakes, but they had to start somewhere. When she had dumped the last load, she ran home and stripped off the robe and mask. Then she headed for the kitchen, where she planned to eat everything in sight. It was always like this after a run. She grabbed a bag of Cool Ranch Doritos, a loaf of bread, and jar of peanut butter. If she had to, she'd make a few frozen pizzas.

CHAPTER TWENTY-EIGHT

The sun was setting on Friday evening when Kenneth arrived at Micah's. He carried only the Louisville Slugger he had gotten for Christmas when he was twelve, a thirty-two incher that had been too heavy for most of the other players on his team. Watching them struggle to swing it, the way it dipped as they followed through, had made him proud. He had always been stronger than most of his classmates, even Brayden; only Gavin, being big and almost a year older, had had no problems with the bat. Now it was all Kenneth could find around the house that might be useful. God, he hated to see it carved up, like it was just another piece of forest trash Christian had found in the park. But Kenneth had decided that if he could help get rid of that monster, he owed it to Gavin, even if the freaks still got on his nerves every time they spoke, or moved, or breathed.

His mom had insisted on driving him to Brayden's, so he had been forced to borrow his friend's bike to get to Micah's. The stupid freaks would probably laugh at him—*awww, lookit the big man who couldn't get away from his mommy*—but screw them. They didn't live at ground zero for everything that was happening.

Kenneth stored the bike behind Micah's busted, precariously leaning shed, right next to a pile of tree limbs almost as tall as the building itself. Christian had been busy. Jamie had mentioned how Sterne's mom had blown a gasket when she saw the shed and had believed her son's protestations of innocence and ignorance only because the damage seemed beyond his capabilities. Kenneth couldn't think of a good explanation that he would have given his own parents, if this had been their shed. He would have felt sorry for most anybody else, but he couldn't bring himself to care about Sterne's troubles.

He craned his head around the corner of the shed. Jamie, Christian, and Gabby were huddled against the house's back wall, talking in whispers. Big shock—they still didn't trust him enough to speak without planning every word first. He trotted across the yard. They looked up as he approached. He nodded at Jamie, who nodded back. Christian and Gabby only stared. He squatted against the wall five or six feet away from the others—part of the group but still alone.

"Hey," Jamie said.

"Sup?" Kenneth said.

"I was just telling them that there's a black SUV parked on the street a few houses down."

"So?"

"I've never seen that kind of car at any of these houses."

Kenneth shrugged. "So somebody got a new ride."

Gabby elbowed Jamie. "That's what *I* said."

"And maybe you're right," Jamie said. "But it's the same kind those feds drove. I think one of us should check it out."

"I'll go," Christian said. "It's not dark enough yet for you to fly without 'em seeing you."

"Okay," Jamie said. "But be careful."

A *whoosh*, and she was gone. Kenneth sat on the cooling grass and waited for the signal that they could go inside.

✳✴✳

Christian zipped over Micah's fence, through his yard, down the street, and under the SUV Jamie had seen. She lay on her back, staring at the undercarriage, the pavement still warm. A rock dug into her hip. She eased her right hand underneath her and dug out the stone. The car's engine ticked; it emanated heat, so that Christian felt like she was in a tanning bed, warmed from above and below. The vehicle rocked a bit, probably from the agents' movements. Christian closed her eyes and tried to picture the interior of the SUV—Mossman, the dark-haired one with his expressionless face and his air of suspicion; Greenwalt, the redhead, a little taller and more human. Maybe they drank Coke or coffee or Red Bull, something to keep them alert.

Listen to them. Only them. *Not the wind, or the bugs in the grass, or the tires' creaking. Just them. Listen. Listen.*

That turn-up-the-volume sensation again, and then their voices coalesced and clarified, as if they were lying on either side of her.

"… might be some kind of mutant, but he's definitely no spy," one of them said. A deepish voice, a cold tone—Mossman.

"I thought for a while he might just be out for a ride," said the other one—Greenwalt. "Until he came here."

"Maybe they're planning their next move."

"Or playing video games."

"Either way, it shows they're a lot chummier than they claim. That means they've been lying to a lot of people, including us. We could arrest them just for that."

"But if they aren't the killers, we'd look incompetent. Maybe they'll do something stupid tonight."

"We can always hope."

Some kind of crinkling noise, as if they were opening a plastic bag, then a series of crunches.

"Hand me those M&M's," Greenwalt said. More crunching.

"God, I'm sick of this hick town and its hick people," said Mossman. It sounded like his mouth was full.

Yeah, well, we ain't exactly fond of you, either.

Christian decided she had heard enough. Jamie had been right; the feds were staking out the house. They had followed Kenneth here, and they wanted to catch somebody so badly they practically drooled.

She rolled out from under the car, stood, and zipped back to the others.

✳✳✳

As soon as his mother's black Ford Escort backed out of the driveway and headed up the street, Micah opened the patio doors. He did not look at Kenneth. More than he wanted to set things right regarding whatever they had brought into the world, he ached to smash Kenneth's face in. But everybody had made their positions clear, even Christian, who seemed more sympathetic to Micah: Kenneth was not to be touched, at least not while the town was being menaced. So, like a scolded puppy, Micah kept his mouth shut and followed everybody to the living room, where everyone but Kenneth took a seat. That was fine. It wasn't like he was about to tell the shithead to make himself at home.

Micah sat on the floor in front of his guests, Kenneth hovering somewhere to his left, and cleared his throat. "Okay. We're here, and we got enough wood to whittle a few dozen stakes. The problem is, it's almost dark. Out there, we're fair game, and we can't exactly dump all that junk on my mom's carpet."

"Christian can bring the wood in," Jamie said. "We can carve in here if you got the drop cloth."

"Yep," Micah said.

"Or I could just do all the carving," Christian said. "I can go a hell of a lot faster than y'all."

"Good idea," Micah said. "Except I'm not sure we got enough food in the house to keep you going."

"Christian, make as many stakes as you can," Jamie said. "But yeah, you can't empty the fridge. Combine that with the holes in the shed, and Mrs. Sterne's liable to think something weird's going on."

"Something weird *is* going on," Gabby muttered.

"Anyway," said Jamie, "we'll get as much done as we can and finish the rest before dark tomorrow."

"And then?" Christian asked.

"Then we hunt. In costume. If the cops come after us or our parents throw a fit, well, we'll just have to deal with it. Anybody got any ideas where we should put Kenneth once we're ready?"

"We could just stand him on the practice field and ring a dinner bell," said Christian.

Micah cackled, but no one else laughed.

"What about you?" Gabby asked Christian. "You can cover the whole town in, like, three seconds. We could find it that way, and then just take Kenneth there."

"Well, I already gotta lug Kenneth to the practice field once we find the monster," Christian said. "If we go that route, I'm going to need a lot of fuel."

"Why don't we just knock over the Korner Mart, steal all their food, and stuff Christian's face every time she needs it?" Micah asked. "Then the rest of us can just put our feet up and applaud."

Christian grunted. "Dude. I'm fast. I'm not a professional monster hunter."

"We won't need to find the monster," Kenneth said. "It's hunting us. It's hunting *me*. If I just walk outside after dark, it'll come. It's probably out there right now."

They sat in silence for a while, not looking at each other. *Jesus*, Micah thought. *Del Ray really knows how to ruin a mood. I ain't no baby, but thinking about that giant standing right outside, ready to squash us—I'm about to piss my pants.* But why shouldn't he be scared? They were planning to hunt, fight, and destroy an otherworldly creature that had killed grown-ups and smashed cars with its bare hands—and teeth.

Even from a distance, Micah had felt that thing's fearlessness, its drive, its utter lack of mercy. If they gave it an opening, it would slaughter them all. Kenneth must have known it, too. *Of the five of us, only me and him know what the monster's really like. That's another reason to hate that thing: it's connected me to Kenneth Del Ray.*

Somebody had to break this silence, or they would get nowhere all night. "Look," Micah said, "I—"

Then a car approached, its engine thrumming. Tires hummed on asphalt. The car turned into Micah's driveway. Headlights splashed against the living room curtains. Everyone froze.

"Is that your mom?" Jamie asked. "What's she doing back? She just left!"

Micah turned to his friends—and Kenneth—and yelled, "Hide!"

They scrambled for Micah's bedroom, muttering to each other and bickering. It sounded like they were fighting over who could fit under the bed and who got the closet. Micah went to the front window and pulled the curtain back. *It's gotta be one of her migraines. God, it's like parents plan ways to ruin whatever you wanna do.* Mom's migraines seemed to be getting worse lately. The last one had forced her into bed for two solid days, during which she could not eat or stand the slightest light.

Now Mom's old Escort sat in the driveway, headlights on. Micah cursed under his breath. She killed the engine and got out, shutting the door behind her. She hiked her purse onto her shoulder and walked toward the front door.

Micah was starting to back away when something caught his eye— movement in the trees across the street. Then the creature that had chased him that night outside Brayden's burst from the trees and leaped for his mother.

Micah grabbed the door and threw it open without thinking, running out and pinwheeling his arm like a third-base coach sending the runner on home. "Mom! Get in the house! Come on! Run! RUN!" But she didn't run. She stopped in her tracks, looking at him as if he had just grown an extra head. *Oh God, is her headache so bad she can't even hear that thing pounding on the pavement?* The creature arced through the air toward her, and some part of Micah wanted to raise his hands and blast it, to use the weapons he now carried with him everywhere, but he had lived his whole life without those abilities, and in his panic, he did nothing except wave her on, ignoring what the rational part of his mind told him to do. And then, as Micah watched in horror, the abomination from some horrible world picked up his mother, grasping her around the torso with two hands and by the thighs with the other two, and tore her in half at the waist.

"MOM!" Micah shrieked as the monster tossed away Doreen Sterne's legs and held her torso over its head, dropping blood and organs into its mouth. Micah cried out again miserably.

Down the street, the SUV parked beside the road turned on its headlights and started up, its motor revving.

The others boiled out of the front door and ran up beside him.

"Oh my God!" Jamie said, and then he threw up all over the driveway.

Christian retched.

Gabby gasped. Then she screamed.

Kenneth turned pale and took three steps back toward the house.

The creature threw Mrs. Sterne's body aside and stepped toward them.

The car down the street squealed away from the curb and zoomed forward, bouncing over the gutter and into Micah's front yard, where it smashed into the creature's leg. The vampire roared in pain, or perhaps surprise.

Micah stared at it, his eyes wide, his mouth hanging open, tears running down both cheeks.

CHAPTER TWENTY-NINE

"**G**et him inside!" Jamie shouted, and Christian grabbed Micah by the shoulders and pulled him toward the house. Gabby followed them, Jamie behind her with one hand on the small of her back.

Kenneth brought up the rear. He slammed the door so hard the frame buckled and warped. "It can't come in, right?" he cried, his voice too high-pitched, as if he were on the verge of utter panic. "That's what the book said! It can't get us in here!"

"We *can't* stay inside," Christian said. "It'll kill whoever's in that car, if they're still alive now."

"That's *their* problem!" shouted Kenneth. "We didn't ask 'em to come here!"

"God, shut *up*," Gabby snapped.

"I thought you were a tough guy," Christian said. "Talking all that shit about facing down the monster on your own. Turns out you're a bigger chicken than Foghorn Leghorn."

Kenneth stared at her for a moment and then rushed her, but Christian zipped out of the way and clobbered Kenneth on the back of the head. He splayed across the carpet on his face.

"Stop it!" Jamie shouted. "We got enough problems! Here!" He threw Christian's bag; she caught it. Then Jamie tossed Kenneth's bag onto the floor beside him and dropped Gabby's by her feet. "Everybody get your asses dressed."

"Are you nuts?" said Kenneth from the floor. "If we go out there, that monster will—"

"We were gonna fight it anyway," Jamie said. "Might as well be now. Suit up."

"You're crazy, man. We'll *die*."

Jamie glared at Kenneth. "*Some* of us have been fighting bigger guys our whole lives. You can do it this once. Or don't. Just don't get in the way." He opened his own bag and took out his mask and robe.

"I think Micah's in shock," Gabby said. "Should one of us stay in here with him?"

"We need all hands on deck," said Jamie. "Especially you, if Micah's outta commission. Christian and me will distract it. You hit it hard." He turned back to Kenneth. "You too, if you're up for it."

From outside, screams and crashes and the shrieking of twisted metal.

"Come on," Jamie said.

Everyone but Micah threw on their costumes and ran back outside.

Gabby stood between Jamie and Christian. Her stomach kept trying to crawl into her throat. She trembled so badly that she worried she might skitter down the walk and right into that monster's arms. It had fallen on top of the SUV, the hood of which had crumpled nearly halfway to the windshield. The creature's weight had crushed the roof and shattered all the windows. Now it pushed itself off the car and rolled back toward the street, growling low in its throat.

Micah and Kenneth were right. It's huge! What are we supposed to do against something like that? What am I supposed to do? I'm nothing! Everybody says so! I'm just a half-breed freak. I should run. Run. Run.

Gabby started crying. Gratitude for the mask overwhelmed her like a sickness. She wanted to fall to her knees and give thanks and puke at the same time. At least no one could see.

The monster stood, stumbled back toward the other side of the street, flexed its leg over and over, growled.

In the SUV, the feds kicked at the inside of the passenger door. With a metallic squeal, it opened enough for them to crawl out. Blood gushed from Greenwalt's nose as if someone had turned on a tap.

"You okay?" Mossman asked.

"Yeah," said Greenwalt. "I thig I broge by node, though."

Then that blue horror rushed forward and drove one massive fist down on what remained of the hood, flattening it. With a swipe of another hand, it knocked the roof off the car. The feds screamed.

Mossman pulled his service weapon.

The creature leaned down and looked at them, its eyes burning, thick ropes of blood dripping from its mouth.

Mossman fired into its face.

It roared again and staggered away.

"Jamie," Gabby said, her voice shaking. "What do we do?"

"Our best," he said. "Before it kills them, too." He pointed down the street. People had come out onto their porches and driveways to see what was happening. Some toted hunting rifles and shotguns and pistols. If all those people started shooting, somebody would die, and probably not the giant mother-killing vampire thing. Would their protective auras stop a bullet? Deep in Gabby's stomach, fear coiled like a snake. Jamie's power of flight and Christian's speed would only do so much good against their adversary. Only Gabby and Kenneth had a real chance of hurting it. Micah, too, but he had not spoken a word since they dragged him into the house.

Unfortunately, Kenneth seemed even more frightened than Gabby. "Oh, shit. Oh, shit," he said, over and over.

If they don't snap out of it, it's gonna be up to me. I'm not ready for this shit. I shouldn't even be here. I'm no superhero. Right?

"You ready?" Jamie asked.

"No," Gabby said. "Not even a little."

Jamie turned to Kenneth. "Are *you* ready?"

Gabby could not see most of his features under the ski mask, but when he turned, his eyes were as wide as half-dollars, and his voice shook. "No. It's gonna kill us. It kills everybody it touches. Can't we just call in the National Guard or, I dunno, move?"

No one replied.

The vampire-thing stood and threw its arms wide, its chest thrust out as it bellowed into the night. The feds crawled to Mrs. Sterne's Escort and ducked behind it. They looked like the cops in movies and TV shows, the kind who shot killers and bank robbers from long range, behind open car doors, with .38s.

"Christian, Kenneth. Y'all hit it," Jamie said.

Christian looked at Kenneth, whose wide eyes threatened to pop right out of his mask. "Piggy-back, dude. We can't just watch this. Think of Gavin."

Kenneth stood still for a moment longer. Then he sighed. "Screw it," he muttered. "Let's go get murdered." He jumped on Christian's back, and they zoomed toward the creature. Christian set Kenneth down in front of it and disappeared. Kenneth planted his feet and threw a punch at the thing's midsection, pivoting his hips, all his weight behind the blow. The creature doubled over and flew backward, its guttural roar transforming to a high-pitched scream that might have been fear or outrage.

"Back 'em up," Jamie said, grabbing Gabby's hand. "And be careful." He took her in his arms and kissed her.

When he let her go and flew away, Gabby ran forward. A wild voice in her mind kept repeating *first real kiss first real kiss*. She willed the voice away as she reached the cars. Just then, a strong breeze blew past the feds. They were looking around, confused, having suddenly found themselves unarmed. Christian had zoomed past and took their guns. Smart—the last thing they needed was for someone to get shot. Besides, Mossman and Greenwalt might as well have been shooting pop guns, for all the damage they were doing.

As if her thought had summoned it, a shot rang out from somewhere behind the creature. It staggered forward, roaring, and then turned toward the populace.

Lordy mercy, Gabby thought. *Which grown-up ain't got no better sense* than to run out here and shoot at something like that when they could be safe in their houses? And folks say kids don't think before they act.

Greenwalt ran down the street, waving his arms. "Hold your fire, you morons! Federal agent! Get back in your houses!"

The vampire-thing turned toward Greenwalt, but it spotted Kenneth, who had been falling back toward the cars. It roared again, and Kenneth gave it the finger. Gabby doubted the gesture would mean anything to a monster from another dimension, but excitement and pride burst through her.

That's right, Kenneth. Show it we ain't scared, even if we're freaking terrified.

The vampire-thing tensed and ran at Kenneth, pounding the ground so that the trees shook with the force. Thick muscles flexed in its legs and all four arms. It opened its terrible jaws and roared again.

From somewhere above, Jamie shouted, "Blast it, Gabby! Now!"

Nononono!

It reached for Kenneth, its long fingers flexing.

"NOW!" Jamie screamed.

Half-breed freak.

Loser.

No. NO. HELL NO.

Gabby braced herself, held out both hands, and fired, energy welling from her toes and the top of her head, mixing and swelling in her chest, flowing through her arms. Two sizzling white beams burst forth, her legs straining to hold ground.

The twin beams struck the monster in the side, driving it through the air and into an oak tree across the street, splitting the trunk in half. The thing rolled through the yard and landed near the neighbors' house.

The feds ran past her, away from the carnage.

Good. Get outta our way.

The monster started to rise.

Oh no you don't.

Gabby fired again, feeling herself now, giddy with the way the energy pulsed and raced and then released. Her force beams struck her enemy in the chest and drove it into the brick house, knocking a hole in the wall, shattering a window, and caving in part of the roof.

"Oops," Gabby said, laughing despite the fear and the horror. "Hope nobody was sleeping in there."

Kenneth ran toward the creature as it pushed itself out of the hole, brick and mortar and shingles falling around its head. Jamie floated over Kenneth and hollered, "Don't knock it into any more houses! There's people in there!"

"Huh?" said Kenneth, looking up at Jamie.

As he did, the monster backhanded him, knocking him across the street, where he skidded into Micah's yard, tumbling over and over until he finally lay still in a heap. Then the creature leaped and tried to grab Jamie, who shot straight up out of its reach. It came back to earth with a crash and roared as Jamie buzzed back and forth like a mosquito.

A blur passed Gabby, the wind billowing her robes, and Christian stopped in front of the monster, waving her hands in the air.

"Hey, ugly!" she yelled. "Here! Here! Come get me!"

"Get outta there!" Jamie shouted as the Go'kan brought two enormous fists down, smashing the place where Christian had been standing, dirt and grass flying into the air as if the yard had been mortared.

But Christian was sitting on the back of the feds' ruined car, swinging her legs like a little kid on a big chair. "You missed," she called.

The creature roared and lumbered toward her. As it passed the tree, it picked up the shattered trunk and threw it at Christian, who vanished. The trunk smashed into the car, further crumpling the chassis.

Gabby raised her hands again and prepared to fire, but Kenneth was struggling to his feet behind the monster.

Jamie flew figure eights around the creature's head as it swatted at him with all its arms. Holding out her hands like a sleepwalker, Gabby waited for an opportunity to shoot without hitting her friends. *I bet I look really stupid.*

Christian zoomed in, actually ran up the creature's leg and chest, and kicked it in the face. She seemed to hang in the air for a second as it bellowed and swiped at her, but then she was gone again, too fast for Gabby to follow.

"Get outta the way!" Gabby yelled. Now that she had joined the fight, the fear, that awful voice that always spoke in her ear and told her she was a useless half-breed freak, had faded to a mere whisper. She wanted more of that feeling she got as the energy pulsed and throbbed and then released. She wanted to blast that blue demon through the ground and into the earth's core.

But Jamie dove in, and the vampire swatted at the air, clipping his legs. He spun out of control and crashed into Micah's yard, kicking up grass and soil and dead leaves.

Gabby ran to him. He had carved a ten-foot trench in the yard and lay at its terminus, wincing. She thanked God for Jamie's aura. Without it, he would have broken into a dozen pieces. He tried to sit up but fell back, moaning. She knelt beside him and held his head in her lap, stroking his hair. "You okay?" she asked.

"I'll live," he croaked. "Shoot that thing before it kills us."

Gabby hesitated as a shadow passed across the moon, leaving them in deeper darkness.

"Run," Jamie whispered, his eyes goggling. Gabby swallowed hard and looked over her shoulder.

The creature stood above them, glowering. It had blocked out the moonlight like an eclipse. It bared its bloody teeth.

And then it opened its mouth and spoke, its voice like rocks scraping together at the bottom of a deep well. Gabby could not understand the language, but somehow, in her mind, the garbled sounds translated into a series of words and sensory images that conveyed the creature's meaning perfectly.

"Now that I finally have you all together, I will feast. Thank whatever gods you worship that your pathetic lives will sustain the Go'kan's one true prince."

It sounded happy. And hungry.

"Shoot it," Jamie whispered. "For God's sake, shoot it."

Gabby raised her shaking hands.

The vampire lifted one huge leg, ready to stomp them into hamburger.

Then it fell back and hovered in the air a few feet above the ground, roaring in outrage and surprise, limbs flailing like an overturned turtle's. It rose higher, revealing two human legs, a torso, a face. Kenneth was hoisting the monster over his head. "I'm gonna kill you," Kenneth said through clenched teeth.

"Get us outta here," Gabby said.

Jamie scooped her up and flew away, circled around, and headed back to earth as Kenneth bent his knees and elbows and shoved, throwing the Go'kan back across the road, where it smashed the front of the same house it had already wrecked. The rest of the roof collapsed on it, the outer walls folding inward.

Jamie and Gabby walked up and stood beside Kenneth, who gave the monster the finger again. Then he sat down, hard, shaking his head.

"You okay?" Jamie asked.

"Freaking peachy," Kenneth said. They each took one of his hands and pulled him to his feet. "How about you two?"

"Scared half to death," Gabby said.

"My ears are ringing like crazy," Jamie said. "It knocked a knot on my head, I think."

Christian appeared next to them, holding two bags of Doritos and shoveling them into her mouth. "Sorry," she said, crumbs flying. "I was about outta juice. Did I miss anything?"

Everyone looked at her like she was crazy. She shrugged.

Across the street, the rubble shifted, fell, exploded outward. The creature stood, debris falling from its body and piling around its feet.

"Aw, man," Jamie muttered.

"Anybody think we should just go back in the house?" Christian said. "Like somebody with good sense?"

"That's what I said in the first place," Kenneth said.

In the distance, the high-pitched whine of police sirens and what sounded like an ambulance rose and fell. They all looked toward the sound.

Jamie sighed. "We can't," he said. "The cops won't have a chance."

"All right," said Kenneth. "I'm sick of this. Let's kill that thing so I can go to the hospital for a month."

The four of them stood shoulder to shoulder, their robes whipping against their bodies as a strong wind passed. Gabby's ski mask itched. She resisted the urge to scratch her nose. She could not afford to take her eyes off their enemy for even one second. Doing so once had nearly gotten her and Jamie killed.

"Ready?" she said and felt all of them tense. She raised both hands again.

Then someone stepped up behind her and Jamie and pushed them both aside.

"Get outta the way," Micah said tonelessly. "It's mine."

He sent a thick tongue of flame across the road. It engulfed the creature and the ruined house and the tree in the yard. The monster's shriek exploded in their ears and in their minds. Everyone but Micah slapped their hands over their ears and fell back. Micah pumped out flame, the conflagration growing higher and higher, and with a babbling mixture of English and images and that odd guttural language, the monster shared its pain with them, driving them to their knees. It leaped high into the sky and bounded away, now running, now jumping long distances.

Everyone got to their feet. Across the street, the fire already threatened the other houses.

"Jeez, man," said Jamie.

"I bet it's heading for the pond," Micah said, sounding distant. "Let's go."

He gestured at the fire to put it out. Then he started toward the park without looking to see if they were following. After a moment, they were.

CHAPTER THIRTY

Jamie had left the sirens, the fire, and the others behind in order to follow the creature's running, leaping trail through the streets and the park. The town seemed deserted. He guessed the combination of the curfew and plain old terror had driven most folks inside. *Well, all the better for us. If they don't see us, or that thing I'm chasing, then they won't have anything to say when the feds come calling.*

When he saw his quarry dive into the pond, Jamie dug his phone out of his jeans pocket and texted Christian, and by the time he settled on the ground near the water's edge, she had deposited Gabby and zoomed away. The monster's head popped up in the middle of the pond, though Jamie could barely make it out from that distance, even in the bright moonlight.

"Is that it?" said Gabby, squinting.

"That or the biggest turtle anybody's ever seen," said Jamie. "You better blast it. We can't let it get away."

Gabby raised her hands and fired. Her force blast illuminated the night, the water sparkling on either side of it. The bolt struck the Go'kan and drove it back underwater. Jamie whooped and clapped Gabby on the back. She grinned and pumped her fist.

✳✳✳

Na'ul dove to the bottom of the pond. The waters soothed his skin, yet the pain still ripped through him like swords were being shoved into him from all directions at once. The younglings had done the unthinkable. They had fought him, hurt him, driven him away. The adult female had slaked his hunger somewhat, but he needed more, a larger meal, if he were to heal. Even then, his skin would be scarred, disfigured. Far worse than what they had done on that thoroughfare, the younglings had tracked him here. They had the temerity to *hunt* him. No one hunted a prince of the Go'kan. He would rip those children to pieces. Especially the strong one, and the one with the fiery hands. They would pay.

He swam for shore, his lungs burning for air. Humiliation and rage burned in his chest, his mind, like the fires that cursed child had unleashed. He would take to the trees and hide, recoup his strength, and then lay waste to this world. He would make it a desert of bodies and blood and burnt dwellings. He would kill every lesser being he saw. No more games. Only glorious slaughter and blood.

✸

Christian set Kenneth down beside Jamie and Gabby and then took off again, their robes billowing in the wake of her departure. "What's going on?" Kenneth asked.

"It's in the pond," Jamie said. "Gabby shot it. Did the fire department get to that house?"

"Naw, but the fire's already out. Sterne's walking this way. Kid's gone off the deep end. He's leaving a trail of fire and ice on the road."

Damn it, Jamie thought. Micah might as well have held up a sign that said *Superpowered teenager here. Please send government.*

"You saw what happened to his mom," Gabby was saying. "You can't blame him."

"I didn't say I blamed him," Kenneth said. "I wouldn't wish that on anybody, not even him. I'm just warning you. He ain't in the mood to worry about collateral damage."

Before anyone could reply, Christian and Micah appeared. Christian was scarfing a Big Mac.

"You stopped for food *again*?" Jamie said.

"It's that or pass out," Christian said.

"Where is it?" Micah said, his voice even and toneless.

"In the pond," Jamie said.

"Okay," said Micah. He started for the water. Christian and Jamie grabbed him. He shoved them away.

"Stop it!" Christian yelled. "You can't breathe underwater, and you probably can't *see* either! You *want* to get killed?"

"It tore my mom in half," Micah said. "It ate her insides. Her blood's all over the street. I'm going after it."

"Not underwater, you're not," said Jamie. "Committing suicide ain't gonna bring anybody back."

"Hey," Kenneth said. "Look over there."

They followed his gaze. On the far side of the pond, the monster had risen from the water and was trudging to shore. It was moving much slower than it had before, though Jamie had no idea whether it was really hurt. It was intelligent, strategic, cunning. For all they knew, it might be trying to lure them in. Jamie was about to suggest they circle the pond and flank it when Micah raised his right hand and fired a jet of flame across the water. The fire ripped through the air, sizzling and crackling and raising a thin steam cloud. The monster heard it or felt it and dodged. The flame hit a tree, which burst into flame from trunk to tip.

"Be careful!" Jamie yelled. "Don't set the park on fire!"

Micah turned and looked into Jamie's eyes. His face seemed somehow unreal, like he was a wax figure instead of a living, breathing boy. When he spoke, his voice sounded drained, emotionless. "If I have to burn down these woods to kill it, then I'll burn 'em down. If I have to turn the whole town into a parking lot, I'll do that, too. Stay outta my way."

Jamie gaped at Micah. The kid was obviously still in shock, but he seemed serious. He would sacrifice anything for revenge.

Well, Jamie couldn't let that happen. He stepped in front of Micah. "We do this together, and we do it the right way. There are four of us. You can't get us all."

Micah sneered. "Maybe we ought to let it kill your momma and then see how you feel."

"*Dude!*"

"Come on, y'all," Christian said. "Remember who the real enemy is."

Micah glared at Jamie. For a moment, Jamie was pretty sure Micah was going to throw down. *I hope I can fly outta the way in time. Or maybe Christian can move me fast enough.*

Across the pond, the monster was getting to its feet.

"Micah," Gabby said. "Look at that blue piece of shit over there. Do you wanna argue, or do you wanna kill it? You can't do both."

Micah glanced at her. Then he looked back at Jamie. The sneer disappeared; the blankness returned. "So what's the plan—*boss?*"

Jamie winced, but they had no time to deal with Micah's attitude now. "Christian," said Jamie. "Get Kenneth and Micah over there. Me and Gabby will fly across. Y'all try to drive it back into the water and keep it there. If you can't, at least don't let it reach the woods." He turned to Gabby. "Do you think you can shoot straight if I'm holding you in the air?"

"No idea," Gabby said. "But we gotta try something."

"When you get done with them," he said to Christian, "we'll need a stake." He stepped behind Gabby, grasped her under the arms, picked her up, and flew away as fast as he could.

He pushed harder than he ever had, the same way he would try to force his body to run faster in a race. Power surged through him, energizing every cell in his body. *If you could get electrocuted and not get hurt, this is what it would probably feel like.* Down on the shore to his right, something moved, a blur, a dust-and-grass-and-dirt cloud—Christian on the move. Jamie turned up his effort again. He wanted to get Gabby on the ground before Micah started throwing balls of fire and ice.

But Christian was too fast. As Jamie and Gabby reached the middle of the pond, a tree-trunk-thick column of flame shot from a silhouetted figure on shore and barely missed the hulking creature, which dodged again. The flame dissipated after thirty yards or so as Micah turned his concentration elsewhere, but it set the grass on fire where it had passed. A blur zoomed over the flame, which disappeared, smoke rising in a long line. Christian must have stomped out the fire on her way back to Kenneth.

Jamie and Gabby reached the battle site. He set her down a few yards into the woods.

"Stay out of Micah's line of fire," he said, panting. Flying that fast and carrying another person really took it out of him. "Don't let that thing reach the woods."

He flew away before she could reply. He hoped it wasn't the last time he'd see her.

✳✸✳

As Kenneth came to rest near the tree line and Christian ran off, three or four trees were on fire nearby. He wondered if Sterne would remember to put them out. Probably not, knowing that little shit. Gabby blasted away, clipping the monster with those weird force beams of hers, knocking it away from the woods. Sterne shot balls of fire and miniature icebergs, which consumed or splintered the trees, evaporated the pond or splashed down into it like chunks falling off a glacier into the sea. Kenneth watched for an opening, a way to help, but he also studied the creature's pattern. Gabby was hitting it with some of her shots because most of its attention was focused on Sterne. That geek was the key. The monster was scared of him—or, more accurately, of his fire. As much as Kenneth hated to admit it, they needed Micah.

Up ahead, Gabby's beam hit the vampire in the chest and knocked it back into the water, but as it landed, it gripped one of the ice boulders

Sterne had thrown, rolled through the shallows, and scrambled to its feet. It threw the block into the woods, backtracking Gabby's beam. The ice smashed between two trees, rattling them and knocking hunks out of the trunks and dislodging leaves and limbs. Gabby cried out. Micah shot more fire and ice. Entmann buzzed around the vampire's head. It swiped at him, growling. One of Micah's firebursts hit it in the right upper arm. It screamed and dropped into the shallows, dousing the flames as it rolled to avoid Micah's follow-up blasts.

Kenneth turned and ran through the woods, leaping over branches. He found Gabby lying under the trunk of a skinny tree, flat on her face. Beyond her lay the remains of the ice boulder. It must have knocked over the tree, and the tree must have fallen on her head at the exact moment between blasts, when the "protective aura" Entmann wouldn't shut up about hadn't engaged. Kenneth slipped off her ski mask. Her eyes were closed. A trickle of blood ran from her left temple. But she was breathing evenly. Hopefully their handy new fast-healing power would fix her up. Kenneth carried her back to his spot and propped her against a thick trunk. Out on the beach, that blue-armed bastard was throwing fastballs at Sterne, scooping up debris with all four arms. Sterne dodged some of it and blasted the rest out of the sky. Entmann tried to distract the monster, swooping above its head. Then he pointed something at it. A pop and a flash—had Entmann *shot* it? With, like, a *gun*? Where had he gotten a pistol, anyway? The giant roared and pawed at its face as Christian rushed in. She stopped beside Sterne, holding what appeared to be Kenneth's Louisville Slugger. Sterne balanced himself and prepared to fire again. In water up to its ankles, the giant tensed.

Kenneth spotted a decent-sized tree nearby. He could probably fit his arms all the way around its trunk. Maybe he could use it like a baseball bat or a javelin. He ran for it, but as he got there, the woods on the far side of the pond lit up with flashing red and blue lights. People swarmed onto the banks. Cops and God only knew who else. *Great*, thought Kenneth. *Just what this night needs.*

✳

Minutes earlier, Jamie, flying high in order to see the whole battle-ground, had spotted police cars and fire trucks and ambulances pulling into the parking area. He watched the battle for a moment, torn. Should he stay with the others, or should he check out all this activity?

Hell. I bet those feds are down there, too.

Micah and Kenneth had their hands full. Gabby had disappeared, and Christian had run off to get a stake. He couldn't just leave his friends. But what would happen if the cops crept up and shot somebody? Or if that thing just murked them?

Damn it to hell.

He flew low over the pond, zoomed out through the park, and rose into the treetops over the cops and feds and firemen as they all disembarked. Then he turned up his hearing and his vision, focusing on the feds and the police chief.

"You know what's going on in this town," Chief O'Brien said as he and his officers put on their vests and loaded up.

"Classified," said Mossman, checking his service weapon.

"Right," said O'Brien, shaking his head. "Well, if you think one of those teenagers could have torn that woman in half, you're an idiot."

Mossman laughed. "You'd be surprised what some people are capable of. I could tell you some stories. But then I'd have to kill you."

O'Brien did not laugh. "If any of my civilians get hurt because you're keeping secrets, you'll answer to me. Fed or not."

"Okay, tough guy," Mossman said. Then he called Greenwalt over and whispered. "So all our weapons were crushed?"

"Yeah," Greenwalt said. "I tried to tell you at the scene, but these rubes kept interrupting. I pried the trunk open—everything's toast."

Mossman ground his teeth. "Well, shit. If things get out of hand out there, we'll retreat. No sense dying with these hillbillies."

Greenwalt grunted. Mossman walked away. Greenwalt stared at him, mouth slightly open.

Dude's cold, Jamie thought. *Even too cold for the other one, it looks like.*

The parking area was separated from the grounds by steel cables strung through concrete posts. Two deputies got out with wrenches in hand and started taking down the cable in front of the cars. Jamie flitted from treetop to treetop, keeping one eye on the vehicles and one on the fight with the monster. Once the cable was down, the other vehicles followed O'Brien in, lights pulsing, sirens blasting. The chief parked on top of a little hill. The other cars fanned out. Everyone got out and followed the hill's slope to the water's edge.

Concealed in the tree directly above them, Jamie looked across the pond to see what these adults were seeing. Shadowy but visible in the bright moonlight, several small figures buzzed around a much larger shape that kept falling into the pond and getting up again, throwing objects that caused the others to scatter. A handful of trees were on fire. Irregular flame bursts emanated from one of the small figures—Micah. Weird white beams shot from another and struck the larger being several times—Gabby.

"God Almighty," said O'Brien. "What *is* that?"

"I'd say it's a Go'kan fighting a bunch of mutated kids," Mossman said.

"What?"

"Believe me. You don't want to know."

"I count three small ones," Greenwalt said.

"Yeah," said Mossman. "But there may be others."

That's my cue, Jamie thought. *Might as well get some good out of them being here.*

He dropped out of the tree and picked up one of the deputies. The cop screamed and kicked, but Jamie had gotten a lot stronger. He pulled the cop's gun from its holster, carried the man ten or twelve yards over the water, and dropped him in. As the officer splashed down, Jamie flew perhaps five feet above the water as fast as he could go, holding the gun in one hand.

"He took my service weapon!" cried the cop he had grabbed, sounding waterlogged.

Jamie turned his hearing and vision back to normal and flew straight at the Go'kan, gaining just enough altitude so that he could look down on it.

When it turned, Jamie shot it twice in the face.

It bellowed. The bullets had made it even madder.

Kinda figured that wouldn't work. Maybe if the cops saw, they'll stay away. What are they gonna use on it? Pepper spray?

Micah was walking the monster down again when Christian arrived with the Louisville Slugger, its grip carved into a sharp point. Jamie was about to soar back into the air and direct everybody when the giant reached up and grabbed him by the head.

✶✳✶

Gabby stumbled out of the trees, still rubbing the back of her head. What had hit her, anyway? Her skull felt stuffed, tight, as if someone had pumped a bunch of air into it. Every little bit of light hurt her eyes, every sound, though she already felt better than she had when she first woke up. Her healing power might have saved her from a concussion or something worse. It might have even saved her life.

Along the shoreline, Micah faced the Go'kan while Jamie came in hot from across the pond. When Jamie shot their adversary in the face, Gabby pumped her fists and shouted. Even Micah grinned.

But then the creature snatched Jamie out of the air, one massive fist covering his whole head, and slammed him to the ground. Jamie's grunt was muffled under that huge hand. The giant leaned into him, grinding his head into the dirt. Jamie's fists beat against the fingers as he kicked and bucked.

Please let his aura save him. Please.

Micah and Gabby braced themselves, prepared to fire, but then Christian zipped up next to them.

"No!" she shouted. "It could yank Jamie up and use him as a shield! If his aura ain't on, you could kill him!"

Micah cursed and lowered his arms. "Well?" he said to Gabby. "You gonna take a shot or what? *You* can't set him on fire."

"Christian?" Gabby asked.

"Do it," she said. "Don't go full-force. Aim for its head."

Gabby nodded. Her mouth had gone dry. "Can't you get Jamie out of there first?"

"I doubt it," Christian said. "It's got him good. Now shoot, before it crushes his skull."

Gabby braced herself, spreading her feet shoulder-width apart. She concentrated on the thing's head as it hunched over Jamie's struggling body, its mouth open, dark drool spilling out.

You can do this. All those people who made you feel worthless? They were full of shit. You can prove it right now. Take the shot. Save him.

✴✳✴

When the Go'kan grabbed Jamie and smashed him to the ground, the impact jarred every bone in his body and drove the breath from him. He grabbed the monster's enormous fingers as the pressure began to crush him.

As soon as his bare skin touched the vampire's, images exploded in his mind, not just pictures but scenes so real they could have been cast on a 3-D movie screen in a surround-sound theater.

A dark, alien world, the sky darker and deeper than any Jamie had ever seen. The stars winked like jewels on crushed black velvet. Two moons hung in the sky at ten and two o'clock. Some monstrous skeletal bird passed across one moon, its wingspan like a pterodactyl's. The sharp, acrid odor of burning flesh stung Jamie's eyes and nostrils.

Nearby stood a grass-and-log hut, on fire. People dressed in skins ran from the flames, dragging what looked to be a crudely carved table, more skin-clothes, primitive weapons like spears and knives of sharpened bone. And now shadows descended on them, leaping from nearby trees, rising from the darkness itself, huge and many-limbed, powerful, muscular, bellowing like an alpha lion marking its territory. These new arrivals fell on the humanoids, ripping the puny weapons from their hands and tossing them aside like weeds. One creature sank its long fangs into the neck of a woman and held her off the ground with one hand. She went limp. Another beast herded a group of two or three children into shadows from which hideous noises arose, the coppery scent of blood in the air. And two other hulking assailants carried a male lesser forward, his knees dragging the raw ground, rocks digging rivulets in his flesh. This man looked at his captors, frightened yet defiant, hatred flashing in his eyes like the fire behind him.

Jamie chuckled, deep and guttural. The creatures tossed the male forward. He landed on his face in front of Jamie, who stepped on the back of the man's neck with one overlarge and bluish hoof. The other two creatures knelt in front of Jamie and saluted, two fists to the centers of their chests, their other palms flat on the ground. Jamie laughed again, and then he reached down and yanked up the male by his neck. A pulse thumped just under the skin, and Jamie used his four hands to draw the male closer, closer, closer—

✳

Na'ul's mind swam through murk that laid low any conscious thought. Unbridled hunger roared in his gullet. Every part of his body strained. He quaked and writhed, colder and weaker than he had ever felt. When he forced his eyes open, his arms flailed in front of his face—but only two! Thin and frail! Not even blue!

A giant lesser, female and gentle, picked him up. She wore some sort of uniform, a strange thin covering over both hands, a piece of cloth strapped over her lower face, another circular piece engulfing the top of her head. She cooed at Na'ul, and he was filled with an odd mixture of terror and peace.

Everything blurred.

When his vision cleared, he faced down the youngling he had been hunting for weeks, the biggest of those he had fought only moments ago, the strongest. The bestial child roared something Na'ul could not understand, balled his fist, and threw a looping punch that struck Na'ul in the face. Bright, hot pain flared in the prince's nose and radiated through his jaw, his neck. Then a stew of emotions—anger, fear, humiliation. Na'ul wanted nothing more than to rip off the larger boy's head.

Another odd fog drifting in—then the world coalesced into one face—hair the color of charred wood, eyes that caught the daystar light. Warmth flooded Na'ul's chest and spread throughout his body. He wanted to flee, to find some deep hole to hide in, to take her hand, to pull her close—

Something struck Na'ul between the eyes, breaking the link. A heavy blow, as if his father had bashed him with the royal scepter made from the thigh bone of some champion of the lessers. The prince of the realm lost his grip on the youngling he had driven into the ground. He stumbled to the pond and sat hard in the water.

"Great shot, Gabby," one of the younglings cried.

Na'ul went prone and let himself sink just below the surface, the cool water clearing the last of the youngling's horrible, alien thoughts from his head. What had just happened between him and that child? Na'ul had never experienced anything like it before. He had never heard of it in the stories his tutors had told. When that youngling had touched him, skin on skin, Na'ul had ceased to be himself, a violation so deep and profound he could not find a name for it. Those emotions he had felt, the ones that lay at the heart of the child's history, hurt more than the fire, more than the strange forces the female wielded, more than the projectile weapon this youngling had used against him.

He opened his eyes and sat up. The water reached his waist and lapped against his charred skin. He was Na'ul, son of the mightiest monarch his race had ever seen. And he would visit his wrath upon these children and their world, until this whole dimension lay empty save for their bones and rotting flesh.

CHAPTER THIRTY-ONE

Jamie lay on the ground, his robe and mask covered in dust and dead leaves and pine straw, his head in Gabby's lap. Christian had dragged him away from the shallow crater where the Go'kan had tried to mash him like a potato. Now she stood, along with Kenneth and Micah, over Jamie's limp body. Kenneth, seemingly filled with adrenaline and momentary courage, wanted to pursue the vampire, but Christian had stopped him. "Let it come to us or drown," she said. So they had waited—only a couple of minutes so far, though it felt like an hour.

When Jamie's eyes finally fluttered open, Christian realized she'd been holding her breath. Jamie tried to sit up and threw punches at the air. Gabby pulled him back and cradled his head and whispered to him. Christian knelt and grabbed at his fists, trying to calm him down.

Finally, Jamie's struggles weakened, and some awareness returned to his eyes. He held his hands palms up to them and then rose, shaking his head. "Whoa," he whispered.

"You okay?" asked Christian. Micah and Kenneth crowded around.

"I know what it is," Jamie said. "That thing."

"Me too," said Kenneth. "It's an ugly sandwich with extra ugly sauce."

"No," said Jamie. "It's a prince."

For a moment, everyone fell silent. Then Gabby said, "Um, *what?*"

And so Jamie told them about what he had seen—the world of the Go'kan, a kingdom ruled by Na'ul's family, the dark land with its twin moons and sprawling nightscapes and inhabitants that served as the rulers' food.

"The Go'kan don't come into your house, just like the book said,"

Jamie croaked, his voice hoarse. "But if they catch you outside, you're lunch. They mostly need blood, though they'll eat the rest of you, too. They love to hunt. It's been having *fun*. At least until Micah set it on fire."

"God," Christian said. Just looking at the creature Jamie called Na'ul provoked a spinning sensation in her head, a sense of unreality. But knowing that it was intelligent, strategic, part of a whole society that thrived on murder—Christian's entire conception of the universe had changed. Who knew what lay out there in the deep woods, the darkest waters, the stars and planets over their heads?

"A prince, huh?" asked Kenneth.

"Yeah," Jamie said. "I don't know how I know that, but I do. And he plans to kill every living thing on this planet. We've *really* pissed him off."

So now everything had been laid bare. Unless the feds called in the National Guard, Christian and her friends were all that stood between Na'ul and the slow death of everything they loved. Well, fine. She had never minded a fair fight, and five kids against a giant blue vampire from some other dimension or world seemed like—

The bushes around them rustled. Twigs and branches cracked.

Aw, shit.

✳✳✳

Mossman, Greenwalt, O'Brien, and two QCPD deputies had surrounded Micah and the others. Now they burst from cover, weapons drawn.

"Federal agents!" Mossman shouted. "Everybody *freeze*!"

"Quapaw City PD!" cried O'Brien. "Do what he says!"

Micah looked around wildly. Jamie and Gabby had leaped to their feet. Now all five of them stood in a circle, back to back. Micah faced Mossman, who smiled. His trigger finger twitched.

This asshole wants *to shoot us*. That pissed Micah off. "You think those guns can stop us? I could cook you where you stand, and you couldn't do nothing about it."

"*Shut up!*" Gabby hissed. God, she was such a girl.

"Miss Davison," Mossman said, still smiling. "Does your mother know you like to hang around with this terrorist boy band?"

"We ain't no terrorists," growled Kenneth. "We're trying to keep you idiots alive. Now get outta here before—"

"Before what?" Greenwalt asked. "Make a move, boy. I'll put a round right between your eyes. All of you are under arrest."

From the dark waters, something enormous splashed, as if a safe had fallen into the pond.

"Incoming!" Mossman shouted.

A huge form fell among them, all muscular arms and tree-trunk legs, swinging its four fists back and forth. One of the cops—Micah thought his name might be Snead, the one the kids with cars hated so much because he set up speed traps on main roads—took a glancing blow to the chest and flew through the air. He disappeared into the woods.

Micah and the others darted in all directions as Na'ul roared. Chief O'Brien and the other local cop fell back. Mossman and Greenwalt both dropped to one knee and fired, the bullets thunking into Na'ul's calves and thighs. The Go'kan bellowed and smashed his upper right fist into the other deputy, who arced through the air and splashed down in the pond, his shoes still on the ground where he had stood. O'Brien was firing now, but he hadn't bothered to aim. Bullets cut the air near Micah's head.

"Stop shooting at *me*, you dick!" Micah shouted as he hit the ground and rolled away from Na'ul and O'Brien's line of fire.

Micah came up zapping Na'ul with both hands. Gabby's bright force beams sliced the air. The whole world turned to fire, ice, and screaming lines of pure white energy. The ground churned. And in all the carnage, Micah lost sight of the creature, of the feds, of the sky itself.

✳

When Na'ul leaped out of the water and swung his massive arms, nearly obliterating one of Chief O'Brien's deputies, Jamie flew straight up and out of the monster's reach. Gabby and the others scattered, she and Micah firing as they retreated. Micah's fire and ice sailed over and into the pond. Gabby's bolts splintered trees or zipped across the water and fizzled out as her concentration turned elsewhere. Christian and Kenneth had disappeared.

Where's the Slugger? Gabby thought. *Does Christian still have it?*

She popped out from behind a tree and unleashed a double force blast. Na'ul leaped over it and snarled at her. The feds and Chief O'Brien were emptying their weapons at Na'ul, who roared and ran at them, still swinging those massive arms. The humans fled into the woods, shouting at each other about reloading. Micah stood his ground on shore, firing shot after shot of flame. Na'ul turned toward him, dodged, ran at him, dodged again, Micah circling away from the creature, keeping distance between them.

As Gabby set her feet and shot her beams, striking Na'ul in the back, the feds and the chief emerged from the woods. They stood on the beach twenty yards away, yelling at each other and gesticulating.

For God's sake, will y'all just get outta here?

Christian appeared near Gabby, but Kenneth was not with her. Jamie flew down to them. "You two keep the cops away," he said, panting. "They're gonna get their fool selves killed!"

"I can't leave," Gabby said. "You said me and Micah have the best chance of stopping the vampire."

"No time to argue," said Jamie. "Save the people. Then stop Na'ul."

"Here," Christian said, handing Jamie the baseball bat. "When we get Na'ul down, bring this to us."

Jamie nodded and flew away as Christian grabbed Gabby and zipped off. A split second later, she stood in front of the cops and agents and fired little bursts of energy at their feet. "Get outta here before you get smooshed!" Gabby yelled.

The adults danced and dove about. She kept making them dodge until they had nearly reached the trees again. Then they started disappearing one by one—Christian again. Hopefully, she would carry them at least to the center of town. Stopping Na'ul would take time, and distractions could get them all killed. Gabby turned back to the battle.

Na'ul stomped hard with one foot, creating a deep boom like thunder. The ground shook. Trees shivered, raining leaves and small branches. Micah, who had been pressing the Go'kan prince hard with his flame, lost his balance and fell.

Na'ul leaped high into the air, arcing, ready to stomp Micah into paste.

Kenneth intercepted Na'ul with a flying tackle, shoulder lowered into the creature's midsection, driving him into the pond. They splashed down in the shallows. For a moment, their shadowed figures wrestled, kicking up spray. Then Kenneth was sitting on Na'ul's chest and punching the creature in its face over and over, the meaty thwacks of fist on flesh like someone slapping the water with an open palm. Na'ul's arms flailed at his side, as if he were too injured or shocked to defend himself. The water around them churned white.

"This is for Gavin, you piece of shit," Kenneth said.

Gabby ran over and helped Micah up. Jamie flew down to the water with the stake.

"It was gonna squash me," Micah said, his voice hollow and distant.

"Well, it didn't," Gabby said. She patted Micah on the shoulder. "Jamie! Give Kenneth the stake!"

But Na'ul plucked Kenneth off with one hand and tossed him away,

Kenneth's arms and legs pinwheeling in the air until he splashed down near the center of the pond.

Then, before Jamie could fly away, another of Na'ul's arms back-handed him. He cartwheeled through the air and vanished into the woods, dropping the stake into the shallows.

"NO!" Gabby screamed.

"Find the stake," Micah said, his voice colorless. He raised his right hand and shot a five-foot-thick column of flame straight at Na'ul, who rolled away. The flame hit the pond, hissing. Boiling steam rose in a thick cloud. Micah poured it on, chasing Na'ul along the shoreline with fire. The steam decreased their visibility even more.

Gabby looked at the forest, focusing on the point where Jamie had disappeared. She looked back at the pond, marking the place where the bat had fallen.

If Na'ul gets by us, God knows who'll die next. Maybe nobody. Maybe everybody.

I love you, Jamie.

Gabby set her jaw, took a deep breath—*don't you dare cry*—and ran to the water.

Making sure to keep himself between the monster and the woods, Micah drove forward, blasting fire and ice as Na'ul splashed through the shallows. The water around Na'ul was starting to boil. *I'm gonna cook you like a lobster, you son of a bitch. This is for Mom.* Micah dropped his left and concentrated, channeling all his energy through his right arm. The red flame turned orange, then yellow, then blue. Thick steam clouds obscured almost everything, but still Micah poured it on. Na'ul's roars grew higher in pitch, louder, constant. *Burn, you sack of shit. Burn.*

Then a dark cylindrical object sailed out of the steam, heading straight for Micah.

Is that a log? he thought, diving sideways. The object struck his leg, windmilled him through the air. He hit the ground hard, pain and light shooting through his head.

Na'ul came out of the steam clouds, roaring, teeth bared.

Jamie stumbled out of the woods down the beach a ways. "Shoot him!"

Na'ul had gotten close enough for Micah to see his suppurating skin, some of which sloughed off his body. Other parts of him had charred like a piece of meat left too long on a griddle. He spotted Micah and roared.

"Shoot, you dumbass!" Jamie screamed, hobbling toward them, favoring his left arm and leg.

Yeah, yeah, Micah thought, his head thudding. Without getting off the ground, he shifted and gestured, and a thick rope of ice zoomed over and encased Na'ul's legs from ankles to thighs. The Go'kan crashed to the ground and lay there, pounding at the ice with his lower arms.

That's right, shithead. I got you.

Struggling to stay conscious, his limbs weighing a hundred pounds each, Micah hauled himself to his feet.

✶✸✶

Gabby splashed into the pond at the place where she believed the bat-stake had fallen. She fell to her hands and knees, using Micah's flame bursts as illumination. The battle had splintered some of the trees along the shoreline, casting limbs and fragments into the shallows, and Na'ul had churned the mud and gunk at the bottom into thick clouds. Now, in the dark, she had to find a whittled piece of wood in all that mess. *Where the hell is Christian? She could do this a lot faster.* Gabby flailed through the water for a few moments before stopping, forcing herself to breathe, to think. *Do a grid search, like we use to find the guerilla patrols in* Jungle Raider. She turned toward the shore and crawled, examining every piece of wood, tossing the rejects onto the shore.

Yards away, Jamie took to the sky as Micah stood his ground, spreading his feet shoulder-width apart and raising both hands.

"Get outta there, you idiot!" Jamie cried.

Micah blasted away, fire spreading over Na'ul's head and torso, ice still encasing his legs. The Go'kan screamed in agony. Even with all the other noise, the sound of his flesh spitting and crackling carried clearly on the breeze. The smoke that drifted over the water burned Gabby's nostrils and throat. Na'ul rolled and beat at the fire with his palms. He bashed his ice-encased legs against the ground.

Hurry up. Find the stake.

Micah walked toward the thrashing creature. His hands weren't even raised.

"Don't!" Jamie yelled from somewhere above, but Micah either ignored him or didn't hear. He now stood no more than fifteen feet from Na'ul, watching as the creature beat out the last of the fire. The flesh of Na'ul's chest had melted, like a candle left burning overnight. The giant trumpeted in misery.

Micah set Na'ul on fire again. The flames lit the night, casting long and spindly shadows across the beach and water.

Na'ul screamed and thrashed, knocking off the last of the ice, swinging his arms blindly, trying to crush Micah, who simply stepped out of range. Micah watched a moment longer and then turned, heading for the woods. He leaned against a tree, watching expressionlessly as if he were at a Little League game. Na'ul rose and staggered back toward the water, his shelter throughout the battle.

Gabby looked incredulously at Micah, who did not move. *Is he trying to stretch this out? Hurt Na'ul as much as possible? And if he is, what does that say about him?*

The vampire reached the shallows. Still on her knees, Gabby fired a double blast that struck Na'ul in the side. He staggered, nearly fell, managed to keep his balance, turned toward her. His face was a charred mass of unrecognizable mush. Could he even see?

Then the Go'kan stumbled, went to one knee, bellowed. He tried to stand and only sat down, hard.

Kenneth slogged out of the pond twenty yards away. He gained the bank, looking exhausted, and stumbled toward Na'ul. When he reached the giant, Kenneth kicked him in his horrid face, knocking him onto his back.

Forget them. Find the stake. Hurry the hell up.

But as she waded, Gabby could not stop watching. Kenneth pulled himself onto Na'ul's chest, took a seat, and pounded the monster in the face, the smacks echoing across the pond. One of Na'ul's shuddering arms reached up and tried to push Kenneth away again, but Kenneth brushed it aside.

Gabby sloshed through the water, her robes and mask soaked and heavy.

Her left hand closed on something round and solid and smooth. She grabbed it and yanked it out of the mud. Na'ul must have rolled on it, driving it into the bottom. She wrapped both hands around it and yanked it free, then waded out of the water and ran as fast as she could along the shore.

As she reached the figures struggling in the shallows, Na'ul managed to backhand Kenneth with two fists at once. The vampire's strength had waned, so Kenneth only fell off the monster's chest, but it was enough. Na'ul sat up, groaning in his deep, guttural voice.

Gabby dropped the bat-stake on the beach and double-blasted Na'ul in the face.

The Go'kan fell back again, squealing in pain. From somewhere above, Jamie screamed, "Yeah! Get some!"

Gabby poured on the force, driving Na'ul into the foot-deep water over and over. Beside the mess of ruined flesh that had once been a giant blue vampire, Kenneth pushed himself to his feet and swayed. A

whoosh, and Christian appeared at Kenneth's side, holding a sledgehammer. Jamie landed nearby, trotted over, and picked up the bat. He
handed it to Kenneth. "You wanna do the honors?"

Kenneth took the bat. Gabby stopped firing and backed away,
exhausted. Her legs felt rubbery. Spots played in front of her eyes. She
dropped to her ass on the beach, pain shooting up from her tailbone.
She didn't have enough energy to groan.

Na'ul braced on his elbows, raising himself just above the water.
His breath tore in and out in short, shallow exhalations.

Kenneth raised the bat high over his head in both hands, sharpened
end pointed down. "You like eating stuff from our world?" he said. "Eat
this shit."

Na'ul, blind and agonized, shrieked.

Kenneth brought the bat down, driving it deep into Na'ul's chest.

The Go'kan howled, the sound low in his throat, then rising from
that deep baritone to a glass-shattering alto, his ruined lips pulling away
from his fangs, his limbs thrashing, his head snapping from side to side.

Kenneth was jostled off again. He fell, turned over, crawled out of
the water as Na'ul grasped the bat in one huge, taloned hand.

No, Gabby thought.

Christian climbed onto Na'ul, holding the sledgehammer. "Don't
worry," she said to Kenneth as she passed him. "I got you."

The hammer fell, struck the end of the bat, drove it deeper. Na'ul
roared.

The hammer rose and fell, faster and faster, until nothing was visible but a vibrating, arcing motion. The *rat-a-tat-tat* sounded like a giant
woodpecker on a petrified tree as Christian worked the stake through
Na'ul's meat and gristle and bone. The Go'kan's wails rose into the night
sky like the call of a nightmare bird.

Kenneth had clawed his way up the beach. He collapsed on his belly
to Gabby's right. She sat with her knees drawn up. Jamie squatted to

her left, one hand on her knee. Micah walked over and stood a few feet from Jamie, arms dangling at his sides.

Christian slowed, dropped the hammer onto Na'ul's belly, and tumbled into the water. The bat's barrel protruded only an inch out of the Go'kan's body. He opened his mouth impossibly wide and vomited a column of black blood high into the air, showering everyone, the ground, the shallows with gore.

"Oh, God," Christian said, gagging. She had gotten the worst of it.

Na'ul's head fell back. He lay still.

Micah waded out and helped Christian up. Together, they walked out of the gory pond and joined the others.

✳✳✳

Christian stood before her friends, hands on her knees, head hanging. She felt like she could eat a herd of horses. Kenneth pushed himself to his feet. He took off his mask and wrung it out, alien blood dripping from his fingers. Jamie helped Gabby up. They looked down on the thing that had killed so many people in so short a time. It lay with its head and upper torso in the water, its feet on dry land. Jamie patted Micah on the shoulder. Micah did not look up, so Jamie put his arm around Gabby.

After a moment, Jamie and Gabby turned and walked to the tree line. Christian and Kenneth followed, leaving Micah alone with the body of his mother's killer. The four of them bunched up, slumping under their wet robes, breathing hard.

"We did it," Gabby whispered.

"Yeah," Jamie said. "I can hardly believe it."

"I wish we could have done it sooner," said Kenneth. "I should have listened to y'all. About teaming up and finding that thing. Before it killed Gavin and—and the others."

"I wish that too," Christian said, and it was true. She had loathed

Gavin Cloverleaf, but no one deserved what had happened to him. His parents didn't deserve to lose their only child. And the two police officers, Jake Hoeper and his family, Mrs. Sterne—one monster had ripped apart so many lives.

"This ain't over," said Jamie. "There'll be others."

"Huh?" said Kenneth.

"You saw all those shapes spill outta the door we opened. If they're all like Na'ul, this is just the beginning. We've gotta find 'em all. Stop 'em. Kill 'em."

"Great," Kenneth muttered.

"We could use your help," Gabby said. "I don't know if we could have killed Na'ul without you."

For a while, Kenneth didn't answer. Finally, he wiped more of the Go'kan's blood from his face and nodded. "Yeah. I don't know if we can ever be friends. Too much shit has happened. But if something else comes for us—for this town—then I'll stand with you. For Gavin."

They watched Micah standing over the vampire's body for a while. He didn't move or make a sound.

"How long do you think he'll stand there?" Christian asked. She shivered. That stillness, the quiet—creepy. *What if Micah never comes back to us?*

"Not long," Jamie said. "We gotta go. The cops and them will be back any minute now."

"Micah," Gabby called.

Without looking at them, Micah raised his right hand—*wait*. Then flame emanated from that hand, and Na'ul's body caught fire. Micah swept the flame up and down, increasing the intensity until the heat raged so much they all had to fall back into the woods or get scorched. More steam rose off the water. Micah and the body disappeared into it.

"Why ain't Sterne's clothes on fire?" Kenneth asked. "Why don't that steam burn him up?"

"Probably the same reason Christian's costume don't shred off when she runs," Jamie said. "Whatever magic we got extends at least that far."

Gabby turned to Kenneth. "For whatever it's worth, I'm glad you're with us."

Kenneth looked sad and weary. "Well, we're all freaks here, I guess. Nobody else can do what we do."

Jamie put a hand on his shoulder. "Being a freak ain't so bad. In fact, if we're a team, comic-book-hero protocol says we need a name. Might as well go with the Freaks, right?"

Kenneth laughed without humor. Gabby and Christian smiled. No one argued.

Micah walked out of the steam and joined them. They watched for a moment. When the clouds cleared, only the water remained. Micah must have burned the body to ash.

God, Christian thought. *He just cremated something covered in water. How much hotter can he get? How cold? How powerful are the rest of us?*

Micah took off his mask and looked at the rest of the Freaks, his face serene. "Let's get outta here," he said. "That thing stinks."

They turned and made their way through the woods, swinging toward the streets of Quapaw City, where they could rejoin their families, their friends, all the citizens living their lives as if giant vampires didn't exist. As if no one flew or ran at super speeds. The Freaks took off their makeshift costumes and pawed through downed limbs and briars, listening for sounds of pursuit. They would stop by the pavilion and store the robes in the cobweb-strewn rafters until they could come back with their duffels. Perhaps they would even rest for a little while.

What about the authorities, though? They would be making their way back to the battleground, where they would find nothing but, maybe, a scattering of charred and wrecked foliage. Christian doubted there would be anything to incriminate the Freaks definitively, but still, those feds had come to arrest them, even after seeing that worse things were loose in Quapaw City. What could a bunch of teenagers do against the government?

Christian had no idea. Her mind felt full of fog. She was exhausted and starving and still scared half to death. And there was still so far to go. Tomorrow would be just as complicated as today.

CHAPTER THIRTY-TWO

Two days later, Micah sat on his couch, staring at the blank TV. The place felt cold and cavernous, like a tomb, but temperature no longer affected him. Perhaps it was a side effect of his abilities. The authorities had managed to track down his father, who had driven through the night and most of yesterday. He had picked up Micah at Jamie's house, and they had come home, but Micah still felt alone. He had never seen his father cry before, not even at family funerals. The man had always seemed to be made of steel. Now he was barely holding himself together, had sobbed in his bedroom all night.

Today, a late Sunday afternoon, Dad reclined in his easy chair, a beer in one hand, half a dozen empty bottles on the side table, his eyes red and haunted. And he had not even seen his wife ripped in two like a sheet of paper. Whenever Micah thought about that moment, despair and nausea and dark rage filled him from head to toe, as if the universe had opened him up and funneled everything bad that had ever happened straight into his soul.

Ever since Micah had realized that Jamie and Gabby were together, his gut had twisted whenever they sat together or held hands. *It's cool*, he would think. *They should get to be happy*. But then the questions would start: Would Micah be alone for the rest of his life? Who would love him, if not her, the only girl who had ever shown him any kindness? And what would he do if his friends chose Kenneth Del Ray over him?

Neighbors and friends' parents and his parents' coworkers had brought over enough food to feed half a continent. Micah and Dad had stored as much as they could in the fridge, casseroles and side dishes and desserts. So far, Dad had eaten nothing. Micah had tried, paying little attention to what he put on his plate, barely tasting it. He had thrown up much of it later, and then he had eaten again. He had to keep his body fit, the machine fed, because he would need all his energy for what was coming. He had seen the creatures boiling out of that dimensional rift as clearly as anyone. Much work lay ahead, work that made Algebra I homework and practice ACT tests seem pointless.

He and Dad would bury his mother, and Micah would mourn, and then he would go back to school, hang out with his friends, get back to his life—at least on the surface of things. Deep down, though, he felt the clarity and purity of his mission in his bones, his glands, his blood. He would kill anything that did not belong on Earth. And he would enjoy it. When he had set Na'ul on fire that last time, he had felt a Christmas-morning glee. It was the happiest he had ever been in his life.

Yes, he would find them all, and he would kill them. Every last one.

Then he would deal with Kenneth Del Ray.

Micah lay his head against the couch's arm. He closed his eyes and fell into a dreamless, shallow sleep in which every creak of the house, every whistle of the wind, made him twitch and groan, as if dark things were pursuing him even then.

CHAPTER THIRTY-THREE

On Monday, Jamie came out of the school building five minutes after three, saw Gabby waiting at their favorite picnic table, and walked toward her with his head down, his hands in his pockets. The bruises on his face, throat, and back had mostly healed—another perk of his new souped-up metabolism, he supposed—but it still hurt to walk, even to breathe. He hoped no one had noticed his slow gait, because everyone knew something terrible had happened on Micah's street, that something titanic had occurred at the pond. Of course, nobody could agree on exactly what they had seen. Rumors of a giant scuttered among the kids at school, but most of them seemed to think "giant" meant a seven-foot-tall man. Others had heard that cops and terrorists were duking it out. Of course, the biggest group had seen nothing at all. They seemed to discredit all the rumors. But Jamie was afraid that would change in time.

Kids gossiped. Text messages flew. Social media updates zipped along faster than Christian could run. In the restroom near the science labs, someone had even drawn a crude picture of five people in masks and robes setting fire to the school. This picture had been labeled *THE FREAKS ARE COMING!*

Huh, Jamie had thought. *We didn't even need to name ourselves. To the kids at this school, we've always been freaks.* No Justice League or Avengers in Quapaw City. Just those who fit in and those who didn't.

When Jamie reached the table, Gabby smiled and stood. She took his hands in hers. He kissed her on the cheek. They were official now, he supposed, though they had not gone anywhere together without the others. They had kissed only once. He would never have told anyone, but he was terrified he had screwed it up, that she wouldn't want to do it again. Then again, they had time to figure it all out.

They took their seats and waited. Christian and Kenneth walked together, angling for the table. That showed how much things had changed. Kenneth hadn't bullied anyone since agreeing to help Jamie and the others. He hadn't even called anyone names. Christian had liked teaming up with him only marginally more than Micah had, but there they were, together, in public. Some of the passing kids cast sidelong glances at Kenneth and Christian, recognizing that a shift had occurred in the high-school universe. The two of them passed Brayden, who waved hesitantly. After a moment, Kenneth waved back.

That's good, Jamie thought. *They've always been a couple of assholes, but even assholes deserve a real friend.*

When they reached the table, Kenneth sat next to Gabby. Christian chose to stand, hands in her hoodie pocket, the hood pulled low over her eyes. "So," she said. "Anybody heard from Micah?"

"I DMed him last night," Gabby said. "He didn't say much."

"We should swing by and check on him today," Jamie said.

"I'll pass," said Kenneth. "I doubt I'd be welcome."

"Probably not," said Christian. "But he'll come around. Micah's not dumb. Wouldn't hurt if you apologized, though."

"For what?" Kenneth asked. "It ain't my fault he's such a geek."

Jamie shook his head. Some things, apparently, would never change. The rest of them had tried to leave the past behind, for the sake of their own survival, if nothing else. But Micah and Kenneth seemed ready to drag each other into the muck for the rest of their lives. Something would have to be done about them.

But that was a problem for another day. "Anybody got any ideas what we should do next?" he asked.

"You're the brains of this outfit," said Christian. "You tell us."

There it was again. Jamie had not asked to be their leader and didn't want the job. He did not want to think about fighting monsters from another universe, and he did not want to be responsible for his friends' lives. But it seemed that he would have to bear those burdens anyway, at least for now. "Well, the feds are still in town," he said, "so we should lie low for as long as we can. If you gotta practice your powers, keep it small. Do it somewhere they likely can't watch. In the meantime, we look for the other monsters."

"What are we looking *for*?" Kenneth asked.

"How should I know?" Jamie said. "I ain't never done this before."

For a while, they sat in silence. Gabby cleared her throat. Christian kicked at a rock buried in the dirt. Kenneth picked a loose splinter from the picnic table. All around them, kids headed home. The wind kissed the trees, dislodging dying leaves as the season marched forward toward the colder months. Jamie could see nothing but dark days full of strife in their futures. But if he had to face something like that, at least he was doing it with his best friends.

And also with Kenneth Del Ray.

"Come on," he said. "Let's go see Micah."

"See you later," said Kenneth as he walked away.

"Bye," Gabby said. "Hey, did y'all hear what they're calling us?"

"Yeah," said Christian. "Kind of weird. Like we put the idea in their heads."

Gabby blinked. "Can we do that?"

They looked at each other, at a loss. Then they laughed.

"Well, anyway," said Christian, "it don't bother me. Who the hell wants to be normal?"

Jamie grinned and slapped her on the shoulder. Then he, Christian, and Gabby headed for the bike rack. He and Gabby unlocked their rides. Christian, still bikeless, trotted alongside them toward Micah's house, where they would do what they could to help him get through the day. They would do it again tomorrow, and the next day, as long as it took.

EPILOGUE

Chief O'Brien sat behind his desk, looking over the reports he had written, as well as those of his deputies. Ralph Snead lay in a hospital bed over at Drew Memorial in Monticello. He had suffered several broken ribs, a bruised spleen, a broken coccyx, and two cracked vertebrae. It would be months before he could return to duty, if he ever did. The other officers' reports read like something out of a Stephen King novel. O'Brien had no idea what to do with the information. He couldn't very well file it. Everyone would think he and all his men had lost their minds.

Mossman and Greenwalt walked in, Mossman carrying an envelope. The agent had sustained a couple of second-degree burns on his right forearm during the brouhaha and now wore a thick bandage that puffed up his coat sleeve into a football shape. Greenwalt had suffered only minor scratches on his face.

They took the chairs across from O'Brien without being asked. Greenwalt removed his sunglasses; Mossman did not. O'Brien couldn't remember ever seeing the man without them.

"I expected you fellas to be halfway back to wherever you came from by now," said O'Brien, though that wasn't true.

"No," said Mossman, handing him the envelope. O'Brien took it and lay it on his desk. "Aren't you going to read it?"

"Lemme guess. You boys are sticking around for a spell. And you're taking over the investigation into all the weird stuff going on around here."

Greenwalt nodded. "We going to have any trouble with you or your men?"

O'Brien opened a drawer, swept the envelope into it, and closed it again. Then he stood. "That office you been using still good enough for y'all?"

"That will be fine," Mossman said. "Though when the rest of our team gets here, we'll probably find our own HQ."

"All right. If you gents will excuse me, I'm gonna go see my officer at the hospital."

O'Brien walked past them and out the door. Outside, he put on his own pair of sunglasses and got into his car. He looked through the dirty windshield at his little town, the quaint residential streets and the local businesses and the simple folk living relatively simple lives. What would happen next?

I hope them young'uns got enough sense to lay low, he thought as he lowered the sun visor and started the car. Then he put the vehicle in gear and pulled away, headed toward Monticello.

✻❋✻

Mossman and Greenwalt returned to their office, a tiny room barely big enough for two desks. Mossman sat in his chair and groaned, rubbing his lower back.

Greenwalt sat and brushed some dust from the desk's surface. "So when *will* the rest of the team get here?"

"Engineer doesn't want to destabilize a place like Chicago or LA for the sake of this one-horse town," Mossman said. "But if I had to guess, I'd imagine they'll be here within a couple of weeks."

"What do we do in the meantime?"

"Same as always," said Mossman. "We watch."

"Hard to believe a bunch of kids got the drop on us," Greenwalt said. He took a pack of Life Savers out of his desk drawer, opened it, and popped two into his mouth. "And we don't even have any evidence that they're the bogeys."

Mossman smiled, but there was no humor or warmth in the expression. He held out his hand. Greenwalt passed him the pack. He took three candies and handed the roll back. "That's on us," he said. "We assumed we were looking for one perp, and not a human. Next time, we'll be ready. We know who they are. We know what they can do. And when the others get here? Then we'll outnumber them."

Mossman turned, banging his knees against the desk, and opened the blinds on the office's only window. Outside, the sun was setting. Soon, darkness would reclaim Quapaw City, where anything at all might rise from that gloom and rip the fabric of reality to shreds. When that happened, he and his team would stand against it, crush it, save the world. And if those kids got in the way, not even God could help them.

ACKNOWLEDGMENTS

Thanks to Kalene Westmoreland, my life partner, my first reader, my love.

Thanks to my family—especially Shauna, John, Brendan, Maya, Nova, and Luna.

Animals keep me grounded and steady when people can't. Thanks to all of them, but especially those who live in my house—Nilla, Cookie, and Tora. Y'all sure are fun.

My deepest appreciation to Mark Sedenquist, Megan Edwards, and everyone involved with Imbrifex Books. Every one of you does a fantastic job. I'm honored to work with you.

Maya Myers, my editor, made this book better by miles. Thanks for all your hard work, your honesty, and your support.

Much gratitude to Amanda Reeves, who translated some English phrasing into Latin.

Thanks to God, for everything.

And thanks to you, reader. It's always my honor.

ABOUT THE AUTHOR

BRETT RILEY is a professor of English at the College of Southern Nevada. He grew up in southeastern Arkansas and earned his Ph.D. in contemporary American fiction and film at Louisiana State University. His short fiction has appeared in numerous publications including *Folio, The Wisconsin Review*, and *The Baltimore Review*. Riley's debut novel, *Comanche*, was released in September 2020, and *Lord of Order* was published in April 2021. He has also won numerous awards for screenwriting. Riley lives in Henderson, Nevada.

Connect with the author online:

OfficialBrettRiley.com

@brettwrites

@brettRileyAuthor

Sneak preview of **Travelers**, the second book in the **Freaks** superhero series, which will be in bookstores and wherever fine books are sold on August 2, 2022.

CHAPTER ONE

I was the last to travel through the hole between worlds, and when I arrived, I filled it in behind me. The children who opened the aperture believe they undid their night's work by closing their book of magic, as if something begun with an ancient dance and a song could be stopped so easily. They were wrong.

On that night, I had been sitting on my green hill by the river of time, feasting on the meat of a deer older than white man's language. A ripping sound, like some shredded heavy cloth, and then the hole burst into being, glowing like a star. I shielded my eyes. The children's song floated through, faint at first, then louder, like the approach of war parties. Shadows danced in circles, spirits perhaps, and then the starlight flared, and the opening churned and swirled—a nexus. Beasts from other worlds appeared and vanished, leaping or being sucked into the land where the children sang. I had encountered these creatures or their kin on my journeys across the omniverse. Some were gentle, some dangerous. Some could devour a civilization, a world, a whole plane. Many, many more were drawn to the light as fire lures certain insects. I knew that, in moments, those beings would reach the nexus and cross over. But still I sat, for this event concerned me not at all. Hardly the first time some brash fool had doomed its fellows.

Then the song's words grew louder, and I recognized the language. Not mine or that of the humans I once walked among, but the tongue of that people's great enemy. The singers came from my native land, or one very like it on the sidereal chain. A pup from an infinite litter that was itself only one of a limitless species. The omniverse was deep and wide and always growing. Even such as I could never see it all.

But *that* world. Its people. Maybe even *my* world and not one of its reflections.

I would not let them die in the mouths of monsters and mad gods. Some other way, yes, as all things must die. But not that way.

And so I hurled myself through, knocking aside the horrors that had not yet passed over. I landed in a tiny lodge filled with trinkets and tools—bladed weapons white people used to tame the land, boxes full of memories. On the ground lay children dressed in long, coarse garments. Two slept. The rest stared into the starlight they had summoned, shielding their eyes. Their terror struck me like a demon wind. In the middle of the lodge, their book lay open, a line of sheer power connecting its pages to the bottomless gap in the fabric of being.

I opened my mouth and spat out half my heart. As the children struggled, I threw it into their aperture, where it grew and grew until it squeezed the killing light out of this reality, diverting that world-crushing power to the end of the sky.

Then, darkness.

One of the lodge's walls had been destroyed from the inside. Splinters and dust lay everywhere. A great force had burst through. One of my fellow travelers.

The children still lay at my feet, dazzled and sluggish. Their raiment was strange, as if they had cut holes in blankets and wore them like skins. Even then, the smallest coals of power glowed inside them. They had taken their first steps down a hard trail from which they would likely not return. Though their book had closed when I destroyed the nexus, it emanated dark power in gusts both intermittent and rank. Where had children found such a tome? And how had no one taught them the sly ways written language can steal your life and send your tribe west into the sunset?

I stepped outside, each movement a war with myself. I had walked the paths between universes, but now, if I had brought a horse, I would have ridden even those few steps. Vomiting out your heart leaves you weary, diminished.

The night air kissed my fur. The grass was cool under my feet. On the wind, an odor like burning hair, the scent of anger mixed with confusion—my fellow travelers.

I needed to see them. I became a falcon and soared high above the trees.

Riding the winds, I found another scent, like that of the kill a bear leaves half-buried to season itself with decay. But where was the corpse? Those winds spoke of smoke-choked skies and melting ice, of herds and flocks hunted and butchered until not even the ghosts of their footprints remained, of fouled rivers and misshapen fish and thick forests cut down to the roots.

This was my homeland, where I had walked for centuries, tricking the First Peoples and fattening myself on the forest's plenty. But it was not the world as I had left it.

I flew higher, watching those that did not belong here. Each had already gone its own way, as if the presence of the others repelled it.

My eyes grew heavy. Sleep would come soon.

As the travelers moved beyond the borders of the village, I marked them. Down in the stone waterway beneath the city fled a Go'kan, a four-armed blood-drinker bigger than any bear. I knew him. A prince of his people, his name was Na'ul, which, in the Go'kan tongue, means Breaker of Bones. I once spent a few winters in his world, watching his race feed. He even tried to eat *me*, to his sorrow. Now I wished I had killed him instead of driving him away and moving on. Unchecked, he would purge his humiliation through inflicting destruction on my home world.

I could have tracked him and, even in my weakened state, killed him. But if I did that, I would have lost the other travelers. Who knew if I could find them again?

So weary. Perhaps I had given more than half my heart. Even for me, such matters leave much to chance.

Six trails led far away. Two rode the air, two the water, two the forest paths. As long as they did not threaten the land I once loved, I cared nothing for them.

Besides Na'ul's, two other sets of tracks ended nearby. One being had scurried through the human village and splashed into the river beyond its borders, nestling somewhere deep in the muddy bottom, its lifeforce strong and steady like sleeper's breath. Perhaps it felt as I did. Or maybe this was its way. I had not seen its form, so I could not be sure, but evil dripped along the path it traveled like blood from a wounded deer. Hopefully, it would sleep forever. But I marked it anyway—its scent, its dread energy.

The other creature had risen from the children's lodge, growing as it flew. It came to rest deep in the woods between villages. I knew its form, its tribe. Once they roamed this world, this sky, like scaled hawks. Their breath laid waste to whole forests. Their claws could rend a horse or a bear to pieces with one slash. A more dangerous creature had seldom walked the earth. Still, she would likely keep to herself, if allowed. And, like me, she would soon need a long sleep. Her kind dreamed away the colder months.

Three travelers who seemed intent on dwelling here, at least for now. One certain threat, two more possibilities. Na'ul would wake first. His force seemed most vital that night, though he was by far the least of us.

I hoped he would keep. Sleep called to me, gentle but insistent.

I landed in the woods, far from every human village I could sense, and changed back to myself. Then I dug my burrow, crawled inside, and curled up, dreaming of the old days, of scampering amid trees and thickets and fields of sweet clover. Perhaps, before I left this world again, I might play tricks, as I was born to do, as I did for ages here in the place where people still told my stories.

They called me Rabbit. It was not the name I was born with, but it had always seemed as good as any.

The author is currently writing the third book in the *Freaks* superhero series, which is scheduled to be published in Summer 2023.